selected short stories of
Premchand

maple press

SELECTED SHORT STORIES OF PREMCHAND

ALL RIGHTS RESERVED. No part of this book may be reproduced in a retrieval system or transmitted in any form or by any means electronic, mechanical, photocopying, recording and or without permission of the publisher.

Published by

MAPLE PRESS PRIVATE LIMITED
office: A-63, Sector 58, Noida 201301, U.P., India
phone: +91 120 455 3581, 455 3583
email: info@maplepress.co.in
website: www.maplepress.co.in

Reprint 2021 in India

ISBN: 978-93-50333-06-8

Contents

A Gift of Holi

I

Maikulal had come to play chess with Amarkant, but when he found him packing his luggage, he asked, "Are you going somewhere, brother? If you have time, let's play chess."

Amarkant replied while putting his belongings in the box, "No brother, I am extremely busy today. I need to leave for my in-law's house tomorrow. And I need to make the preparations right now."

Maikulal asked, "Why are you making all the preparations today? Their house is so near. Perhaps you are going there for the first time."

Amarkant replied, "Yes, I am going there for the first time. I did not wish to go but my father-in-law has been requesting me to visit them for a long time."

Maiku said, "Then you must leave by tomorrow evening. You will reach there in half an hour."

Amar said, "My heart is already skipping beats in anticipation. Until now, I had met my wife only in my dreams but tomorrow that dream will turn into reality. Dreams are always beautiful, but who knows what reality will unfold?"

Maiku asked, "Have you bought any gift for her? Do not go empty-handed. She must have been expecting a gift from you."

Amarkant had not bought any gift. He was still a novice and was not aware of the delicate nature of a conjugal relationship.

Maiku suggested, "You must purchase something for her today, my friend. You are going there for the first time; you must make a good first impression."

Amarkant asked, "What should I buy for her? I had not even thought about it. Tell me about something that would be attractive but not very costly, since I need to send some money home. Father has asked for some money."

Maiku lived away from his parents. He replied ironically, "When your father has asked for money, then how can you ignore his demand? It is not a very usual thing for him to ask for money from you."

Amarkant could not understand the irony in his words and said, "Yes that is why I have not got any new clothes stitched for Holi. But if it is necessary to take a gift, then I will have to buy something. Tell me something that would be cheap but beautiful."

Both of them started thinking about the gift. It was an important decision, as that gift would decide the success of his married life. They kept discussing the perfect gift but could not arrive at any firm decision.

At that moment, a *Parsi*[1] lady passed by in a car. She was wearing a very beautiful and fashionable *sari*[2]. Maikulal said, "If you will buy such a beautiful *sari* for her, then she will be very happy. The color was so attractive and the work was so beautiful. You can buy it at Hashim's shop. I don't think it will cost you more than twenty-five rupees."

Amarkant also liked the *sari*. He was thinking that his wife will be very happy seeing the *sari* and it would enhance her beauty as well. He said, "Yes, even I like the *sari* but some demonstration is going on outside Hashim's shop."

Maikulal said, "Don't worry! People are still buying goods from him. It is a matter of choice, after all!"

Amarkant was hesitant. He said, "But I cannot cross the group of volunteers who are standing outside the shop."

Maiku pitied his cowardice and said, "You can go there by the back door. There will be no one there."

"Can't we get it from some Indian shop?"

"You won't get that *sari* at any other shop."

1. *Parsi* : A Zoroastrian community who migrated to the Indian subcontinent from Persia during the Arab conquest of Persia of 636–651 AD.
2. *Sari* : A garment consisting of a length of cotton or silk elaborately draped around the body, traditionally worn by women from South Asia.

II

The sun had set on the horizon. With the twinkling of fairy lights lit in the shops, Aminabad looked very attractive and beautiful at dusk.

Amarkant stealthily reached Hashim's shop. Volunteers were still holding demonstrations and many people had gathered outside the shop. He had tried thrice but was unable to muster the courage to go inside the shop. But he wanted to buy the beautiful *sari* for his wife.

Finally, he decided to enter by the back door. He saw that there was no volunteer there. He went inside quickly and came out after twenty minutes with the *sari*, but now the situation had changed. Three volunteers were now guarding the door. Amarkant stood transfixed for a moment and then started running at full speed. Unfortunately, he collided with an old woman who was coming in that direction. She fell down and started shouting at him, "Are you blind? You will also get old someday."

Amarkant could not escape. While he was apologizing to the old woman, the three volunteers came there and surrounded him. One of them put his hand on the packet of the *sari* and said, "You cannot take this foreign cloth with you. We were calling you and you ran away."

The second volunteer said, "You ran like a thief."

The third volunteer said, "People are going to jail and the country is on fire, and you are still purchasing these foreign goods."

Amarkant held the packet tightly with both his hands and said, "Will you let me go or not?"

The first volunteer put his hand forward to take the packet and said, "How can we let you go? You cannot leave with that foreign cloth."

Amarkant held the packet outside his reach and said, "You cannot stop me."

He took a step forward but two volunteers lay down in front of him. Now he was in trouble. Many people gathered around and comment started pouring in from all directions.

"He looks like a gentleman."

"These people call themselves educated. What a shame! Every day, five to ten people get arrested from this shop but why would you bother about it?"

"Snatch that packet from him and tell him to go and report to the police."

Amarkant found himself in a difficult situation. He was unable to think of any idea to escape. He was angry at Maikulal and was now regretted taking his advice.

People kept commenting about him and then suddenly somebody snatched his cap. When Amarkant tried to take it back, then someone took away the packet from his hand and it disappeared quickly amidst the crowd.

Amarkant became angry and said, "I will report to the police."

A man said, "Yes, yes! Please go, report and get all of us hanged."

Suddenly a young woman arrived at the scene. She was wearing a *Khaddar*[3] *sari* and was carrying a bag. When she saw this ruckus, she asked, "What is the matter? Why are you creating a commotion here and troubling this man?"

Amarkant was now relieved. He appealed to her, "These people have snatched away my packet and hid it. I call this theft and dacoity. This is neither *satyagraha*[4] nor patriotism."

The young lady consoled him, "Don't worry! You will get your packet back. It must be with these people. What was there in the packet?"

A volunteer said, "Sister, he had bought a *sari* from Hashim's shop."

The young lady said, "He can buy clothes from anywhere. You have no right to snatch away his clothes. Give it back. Who has the *sari*?"

Within a minute Amarkant's packet was returned to him and the crowd started dispersing. The volunteers also left the place. Amarkant

---

3. *Khaddar* : An Indian homespun cotton cloth.

4. *Satyagraha* : A policy of passive political resistance, especially that advocated by Mahatma Gandhi against British rule in India.

thanked the young lady and said, "If you had not arrived on time they would have never returned my packet. They were also planning to beat me."

The lady replied politely, "Everyone should protect their belongings. But why did you buy a *sari* from that shop? When you know that British are torturing us to a great extent, then why did you buy their cloth? How can we make you understand this grave situation?"

Amarkant felt ashamed that he had forgotten all about the patriotism that he used to discuss with his friends. He said, "I have not bought it for myself. A lady had asked for it, so I had no other option but to buy it."

"Why didn't you explain the situation to her?"

"I tried, but she was not ready to understand. I think you can convince her better."

"If I get an opportunity, I will definitely explain it to her. After all, women rule over men in these matters. Where do you live?"

"I live in Saadganj."

"What is your name?"

"Amarkant"

The young lady quickly hid her face behind a veil and bowed her head. Then she said in an affectionate tone, "Your wife does not live with you. Then how could she demand the *sari*?"

Amarkant was surprised at this question and asked her, "Where do you live?"

"Ghasiyari Mandi."

"Are you Sukhda Devi?"

"It could be possible. There are so many ladies with that name."

"Your father's name is Jwala Dutt?"

"There can be many men with that name as well."

Amarkant took out the matchbox from his pocket and burnt the *sari* in front of Sukhda Devi.

Sukhda asked, "Will you come tomorrow?"

Amarkant replied in a strained voice, "No Sukhda until I do not complete my penance for this mistake, I shall not come to visit you."

Sukhda wanted to say something but Amarkant left the place quickly.

III

It was the occasion of Holi but for the freedom fighters, there was no festival. They were still picketing in front of Hashim's shop. Amarkant had also joined the group. He was wearing a *Khaddar kurta* and *dhoti* and had a tricolor flag in his hand.

A volunteer said to Amarkant, "You have changed. You were against us a few days back but now you have joined our group. You must have been in great trouble if Sukhda Devi had not come to your rescue that day."

Amar said, "I thank you all for that, otherwise, I would not have been here today."

"You should not have come today. Sukhda was saying that she won't let you come today."

"After yesterday's insult, I do not have the courage to face her. When she, being a woman, is capable to do all these things, then we men are made to endure all kinds of pain, especially when we are bachelors and have no dependents to support."

At that time, the police arrived with a truck and an inspector came out. He went to the volunteers and said, "I arrest you all."

All the volunteers got into the truck while shouting the slogan of '*Vande Mataram*.' Amarkant was sitting in the first row. The truck was about to move when suddenly Sukhda came with a garland in her hand. The door of the truck was still open. She stepped onto it and put the garland around Amarkant's neck. Her eyes were filled with tears. And then the truck moved on. It was a blissful Holi.

Later on, Sukhda went in front of the shop and started shouting at the top of his voice, "Do not buy or wear foreign clothes. It is treason against our country!"

The Holy Panchayat

I

Once there were two close friends, Jumman Sheikh and Algu Chaudhary. They used to invest in business dealings together. They had unfaltering trust in each other. When Jumman went for the *Hajj*[1], he left his house under the care of Algu and whenever Algu went somewhere, he would leave his house under the custody of Jumman. They never ate together nor were they from the same religion; all they shared in common was their opinions and ideas. After all, that was the real basis of true friendship.

This friendship started at an early age when they were just children. Jumman's reverential father, Jumeraati Sheikh, used to teach them. Algu had served his teacher with extreme dedication. He used to wash his plates, fill his hookah and do all kinds of work. Algu's father was an old-fashioned man who believed that serving the teacher has higher importance than gaining knowledge. He used to say that knowledge is not acquired by studying but rather with the blessings and kindness of the teacher. Thus, if serving Jumeraati Sheikh did not yield any results, then Algu should be content with the thought that he tried his best and it was not in his destiny to become an educated man.

But Jumeraati Sheikh did not believe in this concept of education. He had immense faith in his stick and it was due to this stick that Jumman was respected in all the nearby villages. Even the clerks of the court could not question the documents prepared by him. The postman, the constable and the peon, all were desirous of his blessings. Algu's reputation was based on the money he had while Jumman Sheikh was respected for his invaluable knowledge.

---

1. *Hajj*: The greater Muslim pilgrimage to Mecca, which takes place in the last month of the year and which all Muslims are expected to make at least once during their lifetime if they can afford to do so. It is one of the Five Pillars of Islam.

II

Jumman Sheikh had an old aunt (*Khaala*[2]) who had some property in her name but she did not have any children or close relatives. Jumman had made false promises to her and transferred her property in his name. The aunt was welcomed in his house and was highly pampered, until the transfer. A number of delicacies were made for her to relish. But as soon as the transfer deed was stamped, all this hospitality came to an abrupt end. Jumman's wife, Kariman, now served the *rotis* along with her bitter and sharp words. Jumman Sheikh also turned obdurate. Every day, the poor aunt listened to these harsh words: "God knows for how long this old woman will live! She thinks that by transferring some land in our name she has bought us. She cannot eat *rotis* without *dal*[3] fried in *ghee*[4]. We could have bought a whole village with the money that we spent on her!"

For some days, the *Khaala* patiently listened to all this. But when she was unable to tolerate it any longer, she complained to Jumman. But Jumman did not consider it right to interfere in this domain. The problem dragged on for a few more days. At last, when *Khaala* could stand it any longer, she said, "Son! It is no longer possible for me to stay at your house. Just pay me a regular allowance and I shall cook my own food."

Jumman answered scornfully, "Do you think that money grows here?"

Khaala courteously replied, "But I do need some money for my sustenance."

Jumman said in a serious tone, "We didn't know that you will remain alive for so long."

Khaala was offended. She threatened to call for a *panchayat*[5]. Jumman laughed it off, the way a hunter laughs at the deer who is

---

2. *Khaala*: Urdu equivalent for aunt.
3. *Dal*: (in Indian cooking) split pulses, in particular lentils.
4. *Ghee*: Butter made from the milk of a buffalo or cow, used in South Asian cooking.
5. *Panchayat*: A village council.

about to be entrapped. He said, "Yes, yes, you must definitely call for a *panchayat*. Let us come to a firm decision. Even I am fed up of these daily quarrels."

Jumman had no doubt that the decision of the *panchayat* would be on his side. Who was there in the nearby villages who did not owe him a debt of gratitude? Who would dare to become his enemy? Who had the courage to face him in combat? After all, angels will not descend from heaven to conduct the *panchayat*.

III

After this incident, the old woman leaned on her stick and kept wandering from one village to another. Her back was now bent like a bow. It was difficult for her to walk but it was necessary to settle the issue at hand.

There wasn't anyone left in front of whom she had not shed tears of woe. Some people dismissed her story by showing false sympathy, while others condemned the world for this injustice. Some said, "You have your one foot in the grave, you may die tomorrow but your greed cannot be satisfied. What do you want now? Just eat your meal and remember Allah! Why do you bother about land and tilling?" There were also some gentlemen who got a humorous opportunity to jest and make fun of her. Very few kind and compassionate people actually heard her tale and consoled her. Finally, she came at the door of Algu Chaudhary. She threw away the stick and said, "Son! You should also come for the *panchayat* for a few minutes."

Algu said, "What will you get by calling me? Many people from nearby villages will be there."

Khaala replied, "I have cried my heart out to everyone. But it depends on them to come or not."

Algu said, "If you say then I will come, but do not expect me to say anything there."

Khaala asked, "Why son?"

Algu replied, "How can I answer that? Jumman is an old friend of mine. How can I go against him?"

"Son, will you go against honesty and truth just for the sake of losing your friendship?" asked *Khaala*.

Even if all the treasury of our sleeping conscience is stolen, it remains unconscious. But when it is challenged, it suddenly comes alive. Algu was unable to answer this question but the words kept reverberating in his mind, 'Will you go against honesty and truth just for the sake of losing your friendship?'

IV

One evening, the *panchayat* finally gathered under a tree. Sheikh Jumman had made all the preparations in advance. He had spread his sheet and arranged for *paan*[6], cardamom, hookah and tobacco. However, he was sitting at some distance with his friend Algu Chaudhary. Whenever someone came to attend the *panchayat*, he would greet him with salaam and welcome him. When the sun was set, and the birds had started tweeting on the trees, the *panchayat* began. Every inch of the ground was now occupied, but there were mainly spectators who had come to watch the *panchayat*. Of all the people who were invited, only those who had to settle something with Jumman had come to attend the *Panchayat*. A fire was smoldering in one corner and the barber was continuously filling up the *chillums*. It was impossible to decide if the smoke rising from the burning cow-dung cakes was denser or that from the puffs exhaled by the hookah smokers. Young boys were running here and there. Some would indulge in abusive arguments while others would cry. There was uproar from all directions. Seeing the assemblage, the dogs had gathered around in large numbers, thinking that a big feast is being held.

When the *panchayat* had settled down, the old woman put forward her case:

---

6. *Paan*: Betel leaves prepared and used as a stimulant.

"Members of the *panchayat*, it has been three years since I transferred all my property in the name of my nephew, Jumman. You all must be aware of this fact. Jumman had accepted to provide food and clothes for me until my death. I somehow spent a year with him after all the sufferings imposed upon me. But now it has become intolerable and I am no longer able to cope with it. Neither do I get proper food to eat nor any clothes to wear. I am a helpless widow. I cannot go to court and file a case. To whom can I tell my woeful tale except for you people? I shall heartily accept the solution that you provide. If you think that I am wrong, feel free to slap me in front of everyone. If you find any fault with Jumman, advise him not to earn the curses of a destitute woman. I shall obey your decision without any questioning."

Ramdhan Mishra asked, "Jumman Mian, whom do you choose for the *panchayat*? Decide it right now. Afterwards, you will have to accept the decision of the *panchayat*."

Jumman looked around and observed that most of the people were the ones who disliked him for some or the other reason. He said, "The word of the *panchayat* is the word of Allah. *Khaala jaan*[7] may choose anyone she likes. I have no objection."

Khaala shouted loudly, "O son of God, why don't you choose the *panchayat*? Even I must know something."

Jumman retorted with anger, "Do not force me to open my mouth in public. You may choose whomsoever you like."

Khaala understood Jumman's insinuation and said, "Son, you must fear Allah! The *panch*[8] is neither anyone's friend nor anyone's enemy. What all do you say! If you do not trust anyone, then let it go. You must have faith in Algu Chaudhary. Therefore, I choose him as the *sarpanch*[9] from my side."

Jumman Sheikh was overjoyed at her decision, but hiding his true feelings, he said, "Let it be Algu. For me, Ramdhan or Algu makes no difference."

---

7. *Khaala jaan*: An Urdu term of affection, used for loved ones.
8. *Panch*: A member of the panchayat.
9. *Sarpanch*: Head of the panchayat.

Algu did not wish to get involved in this dispute. He tried to avoid it and said, "*Khaala*, you know that Jumman is a close friend of mine."

Khaala said in a serious tone, "Son, nobody sells his honesty and faith for the sake of friendship. God resides in the heart of the *panch*. The words uttered by the mouth of a *panch* are actually the words of God."

Thus, Algu Chaudhary was made the *sarpanch*. Ramdhan and other opponents of Jumman silently cursed the old woman.

Algu Chaudhary said, "Sheikh Jumman! We are old friends. Whenever I needed help, you were there for me and whenever you were in trouble, I tried my best to serve you. But right now, *Khaala* and you are equal in our eyes. You may now put forward your defense case to the *panchayat*."

Jumman was extremely confident that the ball would be in his court now. He thought Algu said such things just to show people that he was unbiased. Thus, he said calmly, "Members of the *panchayat*! Three years ago, *Khaala jaan* had transferred her property in my name. I had accepted that I would provide for her food and clothes until her death. God is witness, that I have never ill-treated her. I consider her equivalent to my mother. It is my duty to look after her; but if there is some rift between the women of the house, then what can I do in that? *Khaala jaan* asks for a separate monthly allowance from me. All the members know about the property that I own. The profit is not enough to provide a monthly allowance to her. Moreover, no such allowance was mentioned in the transfer deed. Otherwise, I would never have transferred the property in my name. That is all that I wanted to say. Rest is up to the *panchayat* to decide."

Algu Chaudhary had to regularly visit the court. Therefore, he was a completely rational person. He started cross-examining Jumman. Every question he asked seemed to be a hammer stroke on Jumman's heart. Ramdhan Mishra was mesmerized by these questions. Jumman was surprised to see Algu's behavior, 'Just a few minutes ago, Algu was sitting with me and we were talking gladly. And now he has completely changed and is bent upon rooting me. Is he trying to settle an old score? Will the long friendship of ours be of no use?'

While Jumman Sheikh was lost in this mental struggle, Algu announced the final judgment, "Jumman Sheikh! The members of the *panchayat* have thought about this matter. They find that it would be morally correct to give a monthly allowance to *Khaala jaan*. We think that there is enough profit from *Khaala's* property to provide a monthly allowance. This is our final decision. And if you do not agree with us then the transfer deed of the property would stand annulled."

Jumman was stupefied to hear this decision. When your own friend behaves like an enemy and stabs at your neck, then what do you call it other than the vagaries of time? The one whom you completely trust, cheated you at the time when you needed him the most. The real friendship is tested during such times of need. This was the friendship of *kalyug*[10]. Such crooked and deceitful people are responsible for bringing so many calamities in the country. Diseases like cholera and plague are the result of the punishment inflicted upon us due to these misdeeds.

But Ramdhan Mishra and the other members of the *panchayat* were heartily praising Algu Chaudhary's sense of justice. They said, "This is what we call a *panchayat*. This is how true justice is done. Friendship has its own place but it is extremely important to follow one's *dharma*[11]. The earth is still intact due to such veracious people; otherwise, it would have sunk into the abyss of the underworld by now."

This decision shook the very foundation of the friendship of Algu and Jumman. Their relationship had turned very formal, and their interactions were not at all affectionate. They used to meet but in a manner in which a sword meets a shield. The old tree of friendship was unable to sustain even a single stroke of truth. It must have surely stood upon the sandy ground.

10. *Kalyug*: According to Hindu mythology, the fourth and present age of the world; the foremost era that is characterized by total decadence.

11. *Dharma*: The eternal and inherent nature of reality, regarded in Hinduism as a cosmic law underlying right behavior and social order.

In Jumman's mind, the treachery of his friend had spread its roots. He was obsessed with it and always looked for an opportunity to take revenge.

V

It takes time to accomplish good deeds, but it is not the same for bad deeds. Jumman soon got the opportunity to avenge his loss. Last year, Algu Chaudhary had bought a nice pair of oxen from Batesar. The oxen belonged to the Pachchain breed and were extremely beautiful and had long horns. For months, people of the nearby villages came to look at the oxen. Coincidentally, after a month of Jumman's *panchayat*, one of the oxen died. Jumman told his friends, "This is the punishment for his treachery. One may not think about it, but God keeps an eye on everyone." Algu suspected that Jumman had poisoned the ox. Even his wife had put all the blame on Jumman and said, "Jumman must have done something to the ox."

One day, Algu's wife had an argument with Kariman regarding this and both the ladies were indulged in a war of words. Streams of verbosity flowed from their mouths. All the figures of speech such as ironies, allegories, metaphors and similes were exhausted but the argument did not end. Jumman somehow pacified them. He scolded his wife and took her away. Meanwhile, Algu used his stick to make his wife understand.

What was the use of a single ox? Algu searched for a match but was unable to find it. In the end, he decided that he should sell it. There was a trader named Samjhu Sahu who drove a single-ox cart in the village. He used to carry *gur* and *ghee* from the village to the market and brought salt and oil from the market to sell it in the village. The strong build of Algu's ox impressed him. He thought that if he got hold of this ox, then he would easily make three tips in a day. These days it was difficult to make even one trip. He examined the ox, made him run for a trial, discussed the prospects with Algu, bargained for the ox, and brought the ox to his house. He had promised to pay the price of the ox within a month. Algu was also in need to sell the ox, so he agreed without thinking about any loss.

As soon as Samjhu Sahu got a new ox, he started driving him hard. He started making three to four trips every day. He was not at all bothered to feed the ox with fodder or give him any water; he was only concerned with his business trips. He took him to the market and put some dry fodder in front of him. The ox hardly got any rest and was again yoked to the cart. When he was at Algu's place, he used to have an easy existence. It was yoked to a chariot rarely and then he would go at a constant speed for miles together. It used to enjoy a scrumptious meal that included clean water, grounded *arhar dal*, fodder mixed with seedcake and sometimes he even had a taste of *ghee*. An attendant was appointed to look after him, brush his hair and clean and pat his body. It enjoyed a life of peace and enjoyment but here he was grinded for twenty-four hours. Within a month, he was emaciated. The moment he saw the yoke, his blood dried up. It was difficult to even move a step. His bones had become visible. But he had immense self-respect. Thrashing was intolerable for him.

One day during the fourth trip, he was burdened with a double load. Exhausted by the day's work, the ox was unable to move. But Sahuji started whipping him. Thus, the ox ran with all his strength but after covering a short distance, he came to a halt in order to rest for a while. But Sahuji wanted to reach his destination as soon as possible and therefore, he brutally lashed the ox. The poor animal once again made an effort to run but his feet wobbled and he fell down, never to rise again. Sahuji whipped him mercilessly, pulled his legs, pushed up a stick into his nostrils but he fell dead. Sahuji suspected some trouble. He intently looked at the ox, and then unyoked him, and started wondering how he would drive the cart home. He screamed and shouted but the lanes of the villages grew empty after sunset. There was no one in sight. In his anger, he again whipped the ox and cursed him, "You wretched animal, if you wanted to die, you should have at least reached home. Why did you die midway? Now, who will pull the cart?" Sahuji was fuming with anger. He had sold many tins of *ghee* and sacks of *gur*[12] today and an amount of two hundred and fifty rupees was tucked at his waist in a pouch. Also, a few sacks of salt and some tins of oil were still left in the cart. It was not possible for him to leave all these things here, so he decided to spend the night there and guard the cart. He had planned to remain awake all through the night. So he smoked a *chillum* and sang a song to pass the time. But he was only able to stay awake till midnight. He thought that he had been awake all through the night, but when he opened his eyes at daybreak, he found that the pouch with the money was missing. A few tins of oil were also missing. In his anguish, the poor man started beating his head and fell flat on the ground. He reached his home early in the morning, weeping and wailing loudly. When his wife heard the whole story, she started crying and then cursed Algu Chaudhary for having sold them such a baleful ox that led to the loss of their life-long earning.

Several months passed on. Whenever Algu asked for the price of the ox, Sahuji and his wife would yap at him like dogs and started abusing him, "Just look at him. We have lost our life's earning. Everything is lost but he is bothered only about his money. You had given us an emaciated ox and now you are demanding a price. You have deceived us and made us buy a ruinous animal. Do you think we are fools? We belong to the family of *banias*[13]. You won't be able to cheat us so easily. You must first go and wash your face in a ditch and then come and ask for the money. If that is unacceptable to you, then take our ox and use it for two months in exchange for one. What else do you want?"

There were many ill-wishers of Chaudhary. On such occasions, they came together and supported Sahuji. Thus, Algu was forced to return home empty-handed. But it was not that easy to give up an amount of one hundred and fifty rupees. One day he lost his temper and Sahuji went inside his home in search of a *lathi*[14] . His wife entered

---

12. *Gur*: (in South Asia) a type of unrefined, solid brown sugar made from boiling sugar cane juice until dry.

13. *Banias*: A trader or merchant.

14. *Lathi*: (in South Asia) a long, heavy iron-bound bamboo stick used as a weapon, especially by police.

the battlefield and raged on a war of words that led to a hand-to-hand tussle. She ran inside her home and closed all the doors. The villagers heard the hullabaloo and gathered around. They advised both the parties not to be involved in such tussles and suggested that they must call for a *panchayat* to settle this issue. Both Sahuji and Algu agreed to the proposal.

VI

Preparations for the *panchayat* began and both the sides started forming their groups. And after three days, the *panchayat* assembled under the same tree during the evening. It seemed like the crows were having their own *panchayat* and the controversial topic was that whether they had any rights over the pea pods or not; and until the settlement of this issue, they considered it right to protest against the security guard. A flock of parrots were sitting in the tree and discussing that human beings had no right to call them crooked when they themselves never hesitate to riot against their own friends.

When the *panchayat* had settled down, Ramdhan Mishra said, "Why should we waste any more time? Let us elect the five members. Tell us Chaudhary, who do you elect?"

Algu said in a humble voice, "Let Samjhu Sahu choose."

Samjhu stood up and arrogantly replied, "Jumman Sheikh from my side."

As soon as he heard Jumman's name, Algu's heart began to beat fast. It seemed that someone had slapped him hard. Ramdhan was Algu's friend and was able to sense the situation. He asked, "Chaudhary, do you have any issues?"

Algu replied half-heartedly, "No, why would I have any issue?"

The knowledge about our responsibilities often corrects our narrow outlook. When we lose our way and wander away from our designated path, then awareness and knowledge become our guiding light.

For example, a newspaper editor, while sitting peacefully in his simple hut, uses his audacity and freedom to create powerful writing to attack the council. But there comes the time when he himself joins the ministry, and at that time his writing changes towards the ministry and becomes so thoughtful and righteous. The reason for this is the realization of one's responsibility.

Citing another example, a young adult's wild, tactless and clumsy behavior during his youth remains a reason of concern for his parents. They remain afraid that he may bring a bad name to the family. But as soon as the burden of a family falls upon him, the undisciplined young man develops a patient and persevering personality. This is a result of the awareness of responsibility.

As soon as Jumman Sheikh took the position of the head of the *panchayat*, even he became conscious of his responsibility. He thought, "Right now, I am sitting on the highest throne of justice and righteousness. Whatever I would say would be taken as the word of God and no personal bias should contaminate this divine voice. I must not deviate even an inch away from the truth."

The *panchayat* began to question both parties. Both parties tried to justify their cases. Everyone agreed on the point that Samjhu must pay the price of the ox. But out of the lot, two people wanted to give him some concession, since he was the one who suffered maximum loss due to the death of the ox. On the contrary, two other villagers wanted to punish Samjhu in addition to the payment, so that no one would dare to mistreat any animal in future. In the end, Jumman announced his judgment:

"Algu Chaudhary and Samjhu Sahu! The *panchayat* has carefully deliberated on your dispute and has arrived at the decision that Samjhu must pay the full price of the ox to Algu. The ox was not suffering from any disease when he bought it. If he would have paid the price then and there, this dispute would never have occurred. The ox died because it was driven too hard and was not fed properly."

Ramdhan said, "Samjhu has killed the ox for his own benefits, therefore, he must be punished for this."

Jumman said, "That is a totally different issue. We cannot do anything about it."

Jhagdu Sahu said, "Samjhu must be given some concession."

Jumman said, "It depends on Algu Chaudhary. It is up to him to decide if he should give any concession or not."

Algu's happiness knew no bounds. He stood up and shouted, "Victory to Panch-Parmeshwar!"

The slogan echoed from all sides, "Victory to Panch-Parmeshwar! This is justice. This not the work of man. God resides in the heart of the panch, this is His grace. Who can prove wrong as right in front of the *panchayat*?"

After some time, Jumman came to Algu, hugged him and said, "Ever since you had passed the judgment against me, I had become your sworn enemy but when I was given the same power today, I realized that one cannot see anything but justice from that position. Brother, please forgive me. Today I am convinced that the *panchayat* is nothing but God's mouthpiece."

Algu started crying and his tears washed off the bitterness of their hearts. The withered plant of friendship became green again.

Eidgah

I

After thirty days of fasting during *Ramadan*[1], *Eid*[2] finally arrived. What a delightful and pleasant effect it had! The trees were extraordinarily green, the fields were unusually lush and the sky was exceptionally red. So sweet was the sunshine today that it felt as if it was greeting the whole world on *Eid*. The whole village was bustling with activity and everyone in the village was getting ready to go to the *Eidgah*[3]. Everyone was busy in the preparations, people were running around getting their outfit ready. You see someone running towards the neighbour's house to borrow needle and thread to sew the button on his kurta, someone's shoes got stiff, so he was running towards the *teli*[4] to buy some oil. Others are busy providing fodder and water for the oxen, as it would be noon before they returned from the *Eidgah*.

A three-mile walk and then meeting and greeting thousands of people, made it impossible to return before noon. The young boys observed fasting until afternoon and some did not fast at all, but the joy of going to *Eidgah* is something that belongs to all. *Rozas*[5] generally made the elders happy, while *Eid* made the young happiest. Young boys used to chatter about *Eid* all day long and now it is here. All they want is to go to the *Eidgah*. People were not yet moving towards it. The young boys don't care if there is *ghee* and sugar in the house; they just need to eat their *sewaiyan*[6]. They do not know the

1. *Ramadan:* The ninth month of the Muslim year, during which strict fasting is observed from dawn to sunset.
2. *Eid:* A Muslim festival.
3. *Eidgah:* The open-air enclosure usually outside the city (or at the outskirts) reserved for Eid prayers.
4. *Teli:* A member of a low Hindu caste of characteristically oil makers and merchants.
5. *Rozas:* A day of fasting in the month of Ramadan.
6. *Sewaiyan:* A sweet dish prepared with milk, vermicelli, *ghee*, sugar and dry fruits, especially on the occasion of Eid.

reason why their fathers are running towards Choudhary Qaim Ali's house. How are they supposed to know that if Choudhary backed out, then the occasion of *Eid* would turn into Moharram within no time. Their own pockets are right now filled with the treasure of *Kuber*[7]. Again and again, they would take out the treasure from their pockets, count it delightfully and keep it back. Mehmood counts, one, two... ten, twelve! He has twelve paise[8]. Mohsin has one, two, three... eight, nine... fifteen paise. They wish to buy uncountable things with their countless money, toys, sweets, bugles, balls and what not.

One of the young boys is Hamid. A four or five years old, innocent-looking, lean and thin boy. His father died last year because of cholera and his mother grew paler and paler and one day she passed away. No one knew about her disease. She never told anyone, even if she had, who would have heard her plea? She buried it deep in her heart and when the pain became unbearable, she bade goodbye to the world. Now Hamid sleeps in the lap of his old grandmother, Ameena and is as happy as ever. His grandmother told him that his father has gone away to earn some money and would return with bagfuls of money. Moreover, his mother has gone to the house of Allah to bring him many goodies. This is the reason behind Hamid's happiness. Hope is a big thing and that too hope of the children! Their imagination can make mountains out of molehills. Hamid has no shoes to cover his feet; his head is covered with a worn-out cap that has a ribbon that has turned black, and he is still happy. When his father will bring bagfuls of money and his mother will return with loads of gifts, he would fulfill all his heart's desires. Then he will see from where his friends - Mehmood, Mohsin, Noorey and Sammi will ever bring so much money.

The unfortunate Ameena is sitting in her small room and crying profusely. It is the auspicious occasion of *Eid*, and there is not a single grain in her house. Had Abid been alive, *Eid* would have never come and gone like this? She was sinking into this hopelessness and

7. *Kuber*: Lord of wealth.

8. *Paise*: A monetary unit of India and Nepal (and formerly of Pakistan), equal to one hundredth of a rupee.

darkness. Why did this useless *Eid* come at all? *Eid* was not welcome in this house. But what about Hamid? He knows nothing about the matters of life and death. He has the light inside him and hopes outside. Misfortune may hit him with all its force, but Hamid's joyful heart will destroy it and turn out triumphant.

Hamid went inside the house and told his grandmother, "Do not be afraid *Amma*. I shall be the first one to return. Do not worry at all."

Ameena is unhappy. The other children in the village are going with their fathers. But who is Hamid's father other than Ameena herself? How can she let him go alone? He might get lost in the crowd. No, she will not let him go. He is a little kid. How would he walk for three miles? He would get blisters in his feet, as he does not even have shoes to cover his feet. She could take him up in her arms for short distances. But who would cook the sewaiyan then? If she had some money, she would have bought all the ingredients on her way back and instantly cooked the dish after returning. But now it would take time to collect all the ingredients. There was only the option of borrowing the ingredients. She had stitched the clothes of Fahiman the other day and got eight *annas*[9] in return. She had tried to save the money for *Eid* but yesterday the milkmaid had strongly demanded her payment. She has nothing for Hamid, but she needed to give Hamid milk daily. The milk cost two paise, and she is now left with only two *annas*. Three paise are in Hamid's pocket and five paise in her purse. This is all she has, even though it's *Eid*. Allah alone would help her now! The washerwoman, the barber and the sweeper would come and ask for sewaiyan as well. And nobody likes to have it in small quantities. How could she avoid them all? And why would she do that? After all, this festival only comes once in a year. Everyone wishes to spend life peacefully and their destiny is linked to hers as well. May God protect the boy! These days will also pass.

The villagers started walking together towards the *Eidgah*. Hamid was also going along with the other children. Sometimes, all of them would run and take a lead, and then rest under a tree while waiting

---

9. *Annas*: A former monetary unit of India and Pakistan, equal to one sixteenth of a rupee.

for others to join them. Why are these people walking so slowly? It seems that Hamid's feet have grown wings. Can he ever get tired? They reached the edge of the city. On both sides of the roads are the orchards of the rich, with a boundary of *pucca*[10] walls. The trees are laden with mangoes and litchis. Occasionally, a boy would aim a stone at the mangoes. The gardener would come out of the orchard cursing the boy, but as they were already at a safe distance from him, they would laugh out loud. They have made a fool of the gardener.

Huge buildings have become visible. One of the buildings was a court, one was the college and one was the club-house. The young boys started wondering how many students must be studying in this college. Not all of them are boys. Some are grown-up men with big moustaches. They just go on studying! God only knows until when they shall keep studying, and what will they achieve after studying so much! Hamid's *madrasa*[11] has only two-three grown-up boys who are worth three cowries. They are beaten up every day as they shrink away from doing any work. Even here, there must be such people, thought Hamid. The club-house is known to have magic shows. Hamid has heard that the skulls of the dead run here. There are many grand shows that are held here but no one is allowed to go inside. And the *Sahibs*[12] play there in the evenings. Even the *mems*[13] play here as well. The boys thought that if we give these things to our mother what do they call it; 'bat,' then our mothers won't be able to even hold it. When she would try to swing it, she would fall down.

Mehmood said, "By God! My mother's hands would shake at this!"

Mohsin said, "But your mother is able to grind *maunds*[14] of wheat. Why would her hands shake if she caught this 'bat'? She brings hundreds of pitchers of water daily from the well. Your buffalo alone drinks five pitchers. However, if a *mem* was asked to draw just one pitcher she would definitely blackout."

10. *Pucca*: Solid and permanent walls made of brick and mortar.
11. *Madrasa*: A college for Islamic instruction.
12. *Sahibs*: The English Gentlemen.
13. *Mems*: The English Ladies.
14. *Maunds*: A traditional unit of mass used in British India.

Mehmood said, "But she can't run, or jump around like this."

Mohsin replied, "Yes, she can't jump around, but the other day when my cow entered the field of Choudhary, she ran so fast that even I was unable to catch up with her."

They went forward. The sweets shops came into sight. The shops were beautifully decorated today. Who eats so many sweets? "Just look at them," thought the boys, "every shop must have *maunds* of sweets stacked into them. It is said that the *Jinns*[15] come at night and bought them all. Father used to say that at midnight, a man went to every shop, and bought all the remaining sweets by paying real rupees, similar to the ones that we see."

Hamid was unable to believe it, "How will the *Jinns* get rupees like these?"

Mohsin said, "There is no dearth of rupees for the *Jinns*. They can pick them up from any treasury that they like. Even the doors of iron cannot stop them, dear. What do you know about it? They even possess jewels and diamonds. If someone pleases them, they give him a basketful of jewels. They are here this moment but within five minutes, they shall reach Calcutta."

Hamid asked again, "Are they very huge in size?"

Mohsin said, "Their heads are as large as the sky. If they stand upon the earth, their heads would touch the sky. But if they wish they can reduce their size to such an extent that they may enter a *lota*[16] as well."

Hamid said, "How do people please them? If I get to know this technique, I would please at least one *Jinn*."

Mohsin said, "I don't know about that. But I know that Choudhary Sahib has many *Jinns* under his control. If anything is stolen, Choudhary Sahib will find it out and even tell you the name of the thief. Jumrati's calf was lost. They searched for it for three days, but in vain. They ultimately went to Choudhary Sahib and he immediately

15. *Jinns*: An intelligent spirit in Arabian and Muslim mythology that is able to appear in human and animal forms.
16. *Lota*: A round water pot, typically of polished brass.

told them that it was locked up in the kine house and they actually found him there. The *Jinns* go to him and inform him about the workings of the entire world."

Now he understood why Choudhary was so rich and why everyone respected him.

They moved on. This was the police line. All the constables had their drilling exercises here. At night, the poor fellows patrolled and guarded the whole city to prevent thefts.

But Mohsin objected, "These constables guard the city? You don't know dear, but these people are the ones who steal and commit thefts. All the robbers and dacoits of the city have a deal with these constables. That is how these people have so much money. My uncle is a constable in a police station. His salary is only twenty rupees but he sends fifty rupees to his home. By God! I had once asked him, 'Uncle, from where do you get all this money?' He smiled and said, 'Son, Allah gives me all.' And then he himself added, 'We can earn lakhs of rupees in a day if we wished. But we only take the amount that won't give us a bad name or get us dismissed from our job.'"

Hamid asked, "If these people assist in the theft, why does nobody catches them?"

Mohsin took pity on his innocence and said, "You idiot, who will catch these people? They themselves are supposed to catch the thieves. But they are severely punished by the almighty for their ill-deeds. Just a few days ago, my uncle's house caught fire and everything was burnt to ashes. Not even a single pot or pan could be saved. For so many days, they had no other option but to sleep under a tree. Can you believe it? They slept under a tree. Then they finally borrowed a hundred rupees from someone and bought some utensils."

Hamid asked, "One hundred is more than fifty, right?"

"Fifty and one hundred is way apart! There can be no comparison. Fifty can be somehow put into one bag but it is impossible to put a hundred even in two bags."

Now the city started getting denser. They confronted groups of people going towards the *Eidgah*. All of them were wearing bright-colored dresses. Some people were coming in an *ekka*[17], others in a motor car, all of them were drenched in perfume and their hearts were filled with joy. This small group of villagers was moving along patiently, unaware of its precarious existence. For the children, everything in the city was strange and unique. They looked at one thing and kept staring at it, unmindful of the repeated horns of the motors. Hamid was nearly run over by a motor car.

Suddenly they were able to see the *Eidgah*. The thick *imli* trees shaded it. Underneath was a *pucca* floor covered by a printed sheet. *Rozadars*[18] had come to say their *namaz*[19]. Rows were filled with them, but even then they extended over to the place where there was no *pucca* platform covered with the printed sheet. The latecomers came and stood in the back rows, as there was no place in the front. There was no distinction of wealth or status here. Everyone was equal in the eyes of God. Hamid, his friends and other villagers also came, performed the *wuzu*[20], and stood in the last row. It was a beautiful sight, well arranged and completely organized. Lakhs of heads bow together in obeisance and then everybody stands up at once. Then they bend forward and sit down on their knees. This sequence is repeated again and again as if numerous electric bulbs light up and then go off in unison. This was an extraordinary sight that filled one's heart with pride, devotion and bliss. This timeless and collective act depicted the spirit of brotherhood that seemed to have strung all these souls in a single thread.

II

The *namaz* was over. People hugged each other and then rushed to the sweets and toy shops. Everyone including the elders was astonished looking at so many rides. The swinging cradle- Pay one

---

17. *Ekka*: A small vehicle with two wheels that is pulled by a horse.
18. *Rozadars*: The person who fasts during the holy month of Ramadan.
19. *Namaz*: The ritual prayers prescribed by Islam to be observed five times a day.
20. *Wuzu*: The Islamic practice of ritual washing before daily prayer.

paisa and have a ride. One moment you shall feel that you are flying in the air, and the next moment you will feel that you are falling to the ground. The merry-go-round, wooden horses, elephants and camels are hanging from iron rods. Pay one paisa, and enjoy twenty-five rounds. Mehmood, Mohsin, Noorey and Sammi went and sat on these horses and camels and took a ride. Hamid was standing far away. He has only three paise. He cannot waste one-third of his treasure just for these rounds.

All descend from the merry-go-round. Now they will buy toys. There are rows of toyshops on this side. There are many types of toys, sepoys and milkmaids, kings and lawyers, water-carriers, washerwomen and *sadhus*. They are extremely beautiful and looked as if they will come alive at any moment. Mehmood bought a sepoy, the one with a khaki dress and a red turban, carrying a rifle on his shoulder. It seems that the sepoy was going for a march. Mohsin developed a liking for the water-carrier. The water-carrier back was bent and carried a goatskin water bag. It held the mouth of the bag with one hand and happiness was reflected on his face as if it was singing a song. It seemed as if it was about to splash the water from the bag. Noorey was in love with the lawyer. It has an intellectual look on its face. It was wearing a black gown with a white *achkan*[21] underneath it. In the breast pocket of the *achkan* is a gold chain for a watch, and a huge law book in one hand. It seemed as if it was coming back from the court after the argumentative discussion of a case. All these toys were worth only two paise each. But Hamid has only three paise. How can he buy such expensive toys? And if the toy fell down, it would break into pieces. A little splash of water would permanently discolour it. What was the use of buying such toys?

Mohsin said, "My water-carrier would give me water daily in the mornings and evenings."

Mehmood said, "And my sepoy would guard my house. If a thief came, it will aim its rifle at him and make him run away immediately."

---

21. *Achkan*: A knee-length coat buttoned in front.

Noorey said, "My lawyer will put forward arguments and win many cases."

Sammi said, "And my washerwoman will wash clothes every day."

Hamid condemned the toys, "These are ordinary toys made of clay. In case they fall, they would break into pieces." But he is still looking at the toys with greedy eyes and wishes to hold them in his hands for some time. His hands unconsciously move towards them but children do not easily give their toys, particularly when their possessions are new. Hamid is filled with desperate loneliness.

After the toys, there come the sweets. Some of them buy *rewaris*, some *gulab jamuns*, and some *sohan halwa*. They are eating it joyfully. Hamid stood detached from the group. The unfortunate fellow has only three paise with him. Why doesn't he buy something to eat? He just stood looking at others with greedy eyes.

Mohsin lured, "Hamid, come and have some *rewaris*, it has such a pleasant fragrance."

Hamid was unable to believe him. This was a cruel joke, for Mohsin was not a generous person. Still, he goes to him, and Mohsin takes out a *rewari* from the bowl and extends it towards Hamid. When Hamid is about to take it, he puts it into his own mouth while Mehmood, Noorey and Sammi clap their hands and laugh loudly. Hamid feels ashamed.

Mohsin said, "Ok, I will definitely give you this time. I swear by Allah!"

Hamid replied, "Please keep it. Do you think I have no money?"

Sammi asked, "You only have three paise. What all can you buy with it?"

Mehmood mocked, "Come and take a *gulab jamun* from me, Hamid. Mohsin is a naughty boy."

Hamid said, "What is so special about sweets? There are so many bad things written about them in books."

Mohsin said, "But you too want to eat one, right? Then why don't you take out your money?"

Mehmood said, "I understand all his tricks. When all our money will be spent, he will buy sweets with his money and tease us."

After the sweets shops, there were shops that sold things made of iron, nickel and artificial jewellery. The boys have no interest in these shops. They all move forward but Hamid remains there and stops at the iron shop. The shop had many pair of tongs. He realized that his grandmother does not have a pair of tongs. When she baked *rotis*,[22] her hands got burnt. He thought that if he buys a pair of tongs for his grandmother, she would be extremely happy and her fingers would never be burnt ever. This would prove to be a useful thing in the household. What was the use of toys? It was just wastage of money. Happiness lasts for just a short while. Later, nobody even looks at them. They might break into pieces even before reaching home. But a pair of tongs is such a useful thing. You can easily make *rotis* with it. In case someone comes to borrow fire, you can hold a piece of burning wood and hand it over conveniently. *Amma* has no time to go to the market and she never has enough money to buy it. Thus, she burns her fingers daily.

Hamid's companions have moved ahead. They are drinking a refreshing sherbet at a charitable stall. Hamid thought, "All of them are so greedy! They bought so many sweets but no one even shared a single sweet with me. And then they say that I should play with them. They want me to do their work. Now I will see, how they will make me work for them. Let them eat these sweets, their teeth would rot, they would suffer from boils and pimples. They will get so addicted to sweets that they would steal money from their homes to buy them and get a good thrashing in return. The books do not tell lies. Why would my tongue be infected? *Amma* would come running towards me as soon as she sees the pair of tongs and would say, 'My child, you have brought a pair of tongs for me.' She would shower her blessings on me. She would then show it to her neighbors and the whole village would get to know that Hamid has brought a pair of tongs for his grandmother. And they all will say, 'He is such a nice boy.' But who

---

22. *Rotis*: Bread, especially a flat round bread cooked on a griddle.

will bless these notorious boys for buying toys? The blessings of elders reach the kingdom of God and are always heard. Why should I bother about Mohsin and Mehmood? I am poor and do not have any money but at least I don't go and beg from them. After all, some day my father and mother would return. Then I would ask them how many toys they want. I would gift them a basketful of toys and teach them that this is how one should treat their friends. And not like they do - buying *rewaris* for one paise and then tease the other person by eating it in front of him. All would laugh at me for buying the pair of tongs. Let them laugh! I won't give a damn about it."

He went to the shopkeeper and asked him, "What is the price of this pair of tongs?"

The shopkeeper looked at him and when he could not see any elder accompanying him, he said, "It is of no use to you."

"Is it for sale or not?"

"Why is it not for sale? Why have I brought it here?"

"Then why don't you tell me the price?"

"It's for six paise."

Hamid's heart sank when he heard the price.

"Tell me the final price."

"Ok. Make it five paise. Nothing less than that."

Hamid strengthened his heart and said, "Will you take three?"

After saying this, he immediately moved forward, afraid that the shopkeeper will rebuke him. But the shopkeeper did not scold him. Rather, he called him back and gave him the tongs. Hamid took it, placed it on his shoulders as if it was a rifle, and joined his companions with great pride. He was ready to face their critical comments.

Mohsin laughed loudly and said, "You idiot, why did you buy the tongs? What will you do with it?"

Hamid threw the tongs on the ground and said, "You may try doing that with your water-carrier. Its bones will crack in no time."

Mehmood said, "Is this a toy?"

Hamid said, "Why is it not? If I keep it at my shoulder, it will become a rifle. If I take it in my hand, it will become the tong of the *fakirs*[23]. I can also use it as a *manjira*[24]. If I like, I can destroy all your toys with just a single stroke of my tongs. Your toys can do no harm to my tongs. It is as brave as a lion."

Sammi had bought a small tambourine. He was impressed with the tongs and said, "Would you like to exchange with my tambourine? I bought it for two *annas*."

Hamid looked at the tambourine scornfully and replied, "My tongs can rip apart your tambourine. It is just a layer of some soft material that makes some noise on thumping. Just a touch of water can finish it off. But my brave tongs can stand against anything be it fire, water, storms or tempest."

Everyone was fascinated with the pair of tongs. But now no one has any money left with them. Moreover, they have now come quite far from the fair. It was well past nine and the sun was shining brightly. Everyone was in a hurry to reach home. Even asking their fathers won't prove beneficial as it was not at all possible to buy the tongs now. They all looked at Hamid with contempt and thought, "Hamid is so clever. That is why the rogue had saved his money."

Now the boys divided into two groups. Mohsin, Mehmood, Sammi and Noorey are on one side, and only Hamid is standing alone on the other side. A debate was going on. Sammi has turned a traitor and joined the opposite party. Mohsin, Mehmood and Noorey a few years elder to Hamid, but they were still terrified by Hamid's verbal blows. He has the force of justice and the strength of policy with him. On one side is clay and on the other iron. He is invincible and deadly. In case a lion came their way, the water-carrier would go haywire. The sepoy would run away leaving behind his clay rifle. And the lawyer would lie down on the ground with sheer fright and hide his face in his cloak. But the courageous pair of tongs, this Rustam-e-Hind, would grab the lion's neck and pluck out his eyes.

---

23. *Fakirs*: A Muslim (or, loosely, a Hindu) religious ascetic who lives solely on alms.
24. *Manjira*: A kind of a cymbal.

Mohsin tried his best to counter him, "Ok, but it cannot draw water."

Hamid held the tongs upright and said, "If the tongs would scold the water-carrier, he would go running and bring water to spray at his door."

Mohsin was defeated but Mehmood provided the reinforcements, "If he gets caught in a court case, then it would need the help of the lawyer."

Hamid was unable to counter this powerful argument. He asked him, "Who will catch him?"

Noorey said with excessive pride, "This sepoy who carries a rifle."

Hamid said in a teasing tone, "This poor man will dare to catch the Rustam-e-Hind. Really? Then come, let us have a wrestling match. The sepoy will run away the moment he would even see the tongs."

Mohsin thought of a new way to offend Hamid, "Your pair of tongs will burn in the fire every day."

He had thought that Hamid would not be able to reply. But this was not what happened. Hamid snapped back at him, "Dearest, only the brave ones have the mettle to jump in the fire. Seeing the fire, your lawyer, sepoy and water-carrier would run away. But jumping into the fire is a feat that only my Rustam-e-Hind can accomplish."

Mehmood again tried to enforce himself, "The lawyer would sit on table and chair while your tongs would be kept on the floor of the kitchen."

This logical comment aroused the spirits of Noorey and Sammi. What an intellectual statement was presented by Mehmood! The fate of a pair of tongs was that it would keep lying on the floor of the kitchen!

When Hamid was unable to think of a powerful retort, he took to cunningness, "My tongs won't remain in the kitchen. When the lawyer would sit on the chair, my tongs would drag him to the ground and insert his laws into his belly."

The argument was illogical; it seemed to be mere abuse. But the idea of putting the laws into his belly gained appreciation from everyone as it was new and unique in itself. The three knights were dumbfounded. Hamid had triumphed. His pair of tongs was finally established as the Rustam-e-Hind. And now Mohsin, Mehmood, Noorey and Sammi cannot deny this fact.

The respect that was naturally endowed upon the victor by the losers was given to Hamid as well. The others had spent three to four *annas* each but they were unable to buy any useful thing. But Hamid had won the game in three paise. It was the truth. The toys were temporary things that could break anytime. But Hamid's pair of tongs would last for several years.

The terms of a settlement were discussed. Mohsin said, "Let us have a look at your tongs and you can have a look at my water-carrier."

Mehmood and Noorey also presented their toys.

Hamid had no issues in agreeing to these terms. Everyone inspected the pair of tongs and all their toys were given to Hamid one by one. The toys were extremely pretty!

Hamid wiped the tears of the losers, "I was only teasing you all. How can the tongs made of iron compete with these beautiful toys? It seems as if they would come alive at any moment."

But Mohsin's party was not at all satisfied with this remedy. The impact of the tongs was extremely powerful. Mohsin, "But no one would bless us for buying these toys."

Mehmood said, "You crave for blessings? I am afraid that we may be beaten. My mother would definitely ask me if these clay toys were the only things that I could bring from the fair."

Hamid had to accept the fact that no one's mother would be so happy on seeing the toys as much as his grandmother would be pleased to see the tongs. He had only three paise to do everything and this use of the money would never draw any regrets. And now the pair of tongs was the Rustam-e-Hind and the king of all the toys.

On the way back, Mehmood felt hungry. His father gave him some bananas to eat. He shared it with Hamid while his other friends kept staring at him. This was the reward for the tongs.

III

At eleven o' clock the whole village was bustling with activity as the villagers had returned from the fair. Mohsin's younger sister came running towards him and snatched away the water-carrier from his hands. She jumped up with so much excitement that the water-carrier slipped from her hands and departed for heaven. This led to a fight between the brother and sister. In the end, both of them cried a lot. Their mother got so irritated by the noise that she slapped both of them.

The end of Noorey's lawyer was much more honorable. A lawyer was not supposed to be seated on the ground or kept at the niche in the wall. So, two pegs were fitted into the wall and a wooden board was fixed over it. It was then carpeted with paper and the lawyer was seated on the throne like Raja Bhoj. Noorey started fanning him. After all, there are electric fans and coolers for the lawyers in the courts, so he should at least fan him. The heat of the laws would fuse away the lawyer's mind so a bamboo fan was brought and Noorey started fanning the lawyer. It was never known, if it was the air from the fan or the fan itself that injured the lawyer, sent him from heaven to hell, and his body became one with the clay with which it was created. There was great mourning and then the remains of the lawyer were thrown into the garbage heap.

Now only Mehmood's sepoy was left. He was instantly assigned to guard the village. But a police officer was not an ordinary person that he would walk with his own feet. A basket was brought in which some red-coloured rags were spread so that the sepoy could comfortably lay down in it. Mehmood picked up the basket and began to walk in front of his door. His younger brothers shout, "Remain awake!" on the sepoy's behalf. But it was dark and Mehmood stumbled against something. The basket slipped from his hands and the sepoy, along with his gun, hits the ground and broke one of his legs. Mehmood found a medicine that could repair the broken leg. All he needed was the sap of the fig tree. The sap was brought and the leg was repaired but the operation was unsuccessful and thus, the other leg was also broken. But the sepoy could at least sit comfortably at one place. With one leg, it was difficult for him to either walk or sit. Now the sepoy has turned into an ascetic. He guards the place in the sitting posture. The fringed turban on his head has been removed and now you can make him whatever you wish to. He is sometimes used as weight as well.

Now, we should hear the story of Mian Hamid. Ameena heard his voice and ran towards him. She picked him up in her arms and started caressing him. Suddenly she saw the pair of tongs in his hands and was surprised.

"From where did you get this?"

"I have bought it."

"How much money did you give for it?"

"Three paise."

Ameena started beating her chest. She wondered what a stupid boy he was that he had not eaten anything since morning and just bought a pair of tongs with all the money he had. "Couldn't you find anything else in the fair that you bought this pair of tongs?"

Hamid felt guilty, "Your fingers get burnt while cooking, that is why I bought it."

Hearing that, the anger of the old woman changed into love. It was not the kind of love that could be spoken or expressed, through words. Rather, it was the silent affection that was filled with the sweet nectar of love. The child is well aware of the concept of sacrifice, generosity and understanding. Ameena thought, "When he would have seen others buying toys and eating sweets, he must have had an urge for the same. How was he able to control himself? Even then he considered the needs of his grandmother." Ameena's happiness knew no bounds.

This incident reversed the entire scenario. With his intense thoughtfulness and empathy, child Hamid played the role of an elderly and the poor old Ameena had transformed into a child as she spread her *dupatta*[25] and continuously gave blessings to Hamid while crying and shedding tears. Well, how would Hamid understand this mystery?

---

25. *Dupatta*: A length of material worn arranged in two folds over the chest and thrown back around the shoulders, typically with a salwar kameez, by women from South Asia.

The Chess Players

I

It was the time of Wajid Ali Shah. Lucknow was drowned in the colour of sensuality and luxury. The elders and the youngsters, the rich and the poor, all were occupied in the rave of the moment. While some were busy enjoying the gatherings filled with dance and music, others were happy being drowned in the puffs of opium. Love for pleasure dominated every aspect of life. Be it in the field of administration, literature, social system, art and craft, business arrangements, industries, cuisine and custom, everywhere sensuality ruled the game. The officials of the state were absorbed in fun and pleasure, the poets had drowned themselves in the mysticisms of love and separation, the artisans were busy creating the zari and chikan works and the businessmen were engrossed in perfumes and cosmetics dealings. The sensual pleasure reflected in everyone's eyes. Nobody was aware of the happenings of the world. At some place, the quails were fighting, rings were being prepared for the fights of the partridges. At other places, the game of chausar was going on, the attendants were shouting on the winning throw, the battle of chess had been pitched elsewhere. From the king to the pauper, everyone was engrossed in these pleasures. Even the fakirs did not eat *rotis* with the money they got as alms and instead spent it on opium or its extract. It has been established that playing chess and ganjifa sharpens the mind, develops mental abilities and helps solve complex problems. (This thought still exists today.) Thus, if Mirza Sajjad Ali and Mir Roshan Ali spent most of their time in the development of their mental faculties, then there isn't any problem. Both of them had ancestral properties and hence, there were no worries of sustenance. Both of them sat idle at home and enjoyed the pleasures of the world. What else could they do?

After having their breakfast every morning, both the friends would spread the chessboard, set up the pieces and engaged themselves in the warfare of chess. They would get so engrossed in this game that they would not even realize the time. From inside the house, someone would call, "The food is ready." And the answer would be, "We are coming, spread the mat." Both of them would not move and the cook would end up serving the food in the room itself, letting the friends enjoy the food while continuing the game. Since there was no elderly person in Mirza Sajjad Ali's house, the game was played in his house. Not only the members of his family but also the neighbors and servants passed critical comments, "This is a very ominous game that ruins the family. God forbid if someone gets addicted to it, he would be in ruins. A person engrossed in it becomes unfit to do anything. It is a very bad disease." Mirza's wife hated the game to such an extent that she even tried to find occasions to revile her husband. But she hardly got any opportunity. She would keep thinking about doing something but in the meanwhile, the chessboard would be set up for the game. And Mirza would come late at night, long after she had slept. She expressed her anger by scolding the servants, "Are they asking for betel leaves? Tell them to come here and get it themselves. They don't even have time to eat food? Go and throw it at their heads, let them eat it on their own or throw it to the dogs." But she could not say anything on his face. She had more complaints with her husband's friend Mir Sahib. She had even named him Mir, the brat. Perhaps, Mirza used to put all the blame on Mir Sahib to save his own skin.

One day, Begum Sahiba was suffering from a bad headache. She said to her maid, "Go and call Mirza Sahib. He must bring some medicine from the *Hakim*[1]. Run, be quick."

When the maid went and told this to Mirza Sahib, he said, "You go, I will just come."

The Begum was already hot-tempered. Hearing this, she lost her patience. She turned red and said to the maid, "Go and tell him that

---

1. *Hakim*: A physician using traditional remedies in India and Muslim countries.

he should come at once and take me to the *Hakim* , otherwise I will go on my own."

Mirza was playing a very interesting game. He would checkmate Mir Sahib in next two moves. He said irritatingly, "Is she on her deathbed that she cannot wait for a moment?"

Mir said, "You should go and talk to her. Women are delicate beings."

Mirza replied, "Oh yes! I should go because it will be checkmate in just two moves."

Mir explained, "Please don't be in such illusion. I have thought of a move that will turn the tables and defeat you. But you must go and see her. What is the use of hurting her?"

Mirza said, "I will go only after defeating you."

Mir replied, "Then I won't play at all unless you go and listen to her."

Mirza said, "I will have to go the *Hakim*. She is not suffering from any headache; it is just a way of troubling me."

Mir said, "So be it. But you need to look after her."

Mirza said, "Ok. Let me play just one more move."

Mir promised, "No, not at all. Until you go and listen to her, I won't even touch the pieces."

Mirza Sahib was left with no other option but to go to her. When he went inside, Begum Sahiba changed her tactics and groaning in pain said, "You love this wretched game so much that even if a person is dying, you will not leave the game! What kind of a man are you?"

Mirza said, "What can I do? Mir Sahib would not let me go."

Begum replied, "Does he think that everyone is as idle as him? Is there any anyone left in his family or has he finished them off?"

Mirza said, "He is an addicted person. When he comes, I am forced to play the game."

Begum said, "Why don't you drive him away?"

Mirza replied, "He is as old as me and superior in rank. I have to oblige him."

Begum warned him, "Then I will drive him away myself. If he gets angry, let him be. He is not feeding us. Hariya, go and pick up the chessboard and tell Mir Sahib that Mirza Sahib won't play anymore, so he must go home."

Mirza pleaded, "Oh please! Don't do such a thing. Do you want to humiliate me? Stop Hariya, where are you going?"

Begum said, "Why don't you let her go? Ok, you have stopped her; let me see how you can stop me."

And saying this, the Begum Sahiba angrily went towards the guest room. The color drained from Mirza's face. He pleaded his wife, "For God's sake, I bind you in the name of Hazrat Hussain. The one who goes there shall see me dead."

But the Begum was in no mood to listen. She went to the guest room but she could not muster the courage to face a strange man. When she peered inside, she saw that the room was empty. Mir Sahib had displaced the pieces and was strolling outside. Begum Sahiba came inside and overturned the chessboard; she threw some pieces on the floor, some fell outside and then she closed the door. Mir Sahib was outside the house when he saw that the pieces were thrown and heard the sound of the bangles and saw the door getting closed, he understood that the Begum was inflamed with anger. So, he went to his home.

Mirza said, "What have you done?"

Begum warned him, "If Mir Sahib came here again, then I will get him thrown out at once. If you had put such dedication in the worship of God, you must have achieved salvation. You are busy playing chess, while I remain occupied with the household works. Now tell me, do you still have any objection to going to the *Hakim*?"

Mirza left the house but instead of going to the *Hakim*, he went to Mir Sahib's house and told him the whole story.

Mir Sahib said, "When I saw the chess pieces being thrown away, I understood everything and ran to my home. She is quite short-tempered. But you have pampered her so much, that's not right. It is none of her concern about what you do outside the house. She is only responsible for a matter related to the household and has no right in any other matter."

Mirza said, "Never mind. But where shall we play now?"

Mir replied, "Why are you worrying? This is a big house. We can play anywhere here."

Mirza said, "But how will I make the Begum agree to this solution? When I remain at my house, she gets so angry. If I play here, then she would definitely kill me."

Mir said, "Oh let her shout! She will get used to it in a few days. But from now onwards you must deal with her in a tough manner."

II

For some unknown reason, Mir Sahib's wife considered it better if Mir Sahib remained away from the house. That is why she never criticized his love for the game and sometimes when Mir Sahib would get late, she would remind him and make him go to play the game. Mir Sahib was always under the illusion that his wife was very courteous and sober. But when the chessboard was spread in the guest room and Mir Sahib stayed at home all day, it troubled her. Her freedom was restricted. She hardly got any chance to take a glimpse of the outside world.

Mir Sahib's playing chess at home lead to whispering and murmuring among the servants. Up till now, they used to ward off flies the whole day. They were never bothered by the guests. But now they had to take orders. Sometimes they would be sent to get the betel leaves while sometimes they were ordered to bring the sweets. And the hookah would keep smoldering the whole day like the heart of a lover. They would go and complain to Begum Sahiba, "Begum Sahiba, Mir Sahib's chess has become a nuisance for us. We have blisters on our feet, running from here to there the whole day. Is this a game that starts in the morning and ends at night? It is all right to play for some time for leisure but to spend the whole day like this is not good. Well, we do not have any complaints, we are your servants and it is our duty to serve you no matter what. But this game is inauspicious. The one who plays it never prospers. A misfortune always struck their household. Everyone in the neighborhood is talking about Mir Sahib. We are his faithful servants and cannot tolerate his name being maligned. But what can we do about it?"

On this, the Begum Sahiba would reply, "Even I don't like this game, but he would not listen to me. What can be done about it?"

The elders of the neighborhood had begun to have many premonitions, "It's no good. When the rich people of our country are so obsessed then only God can save this country from destruction. This kingdom will be destroyed by chess. These are bad omens."

There had been great disarray in the kingdom. People were being robbed in broad daylight. No one was there to listen to their complaints. All the wealth from the villages were brought to Lucknow and spent on prostitutes, buffoons and sensual pleasures. The taxes of the English company were increasing day-by-day. Because of the lack of good administration, even the annual taxes could not be collected. The Resident warned them repeatedly but people were so drenched in sensuality that nobody took such warnings seriously.

Many months passed and the game of chess went on in the guest room of Mir Sahib. New strategies were created and new moves were devised. Sometimes there were arguments and accusations but soon the two friends reconciled and the game continued. Sometimes the chessboard would be overturned and an estranged Mirza would go to his home. But after a good night's sleep, all the resentment would vanish. In the morning, both friends would come again to the guest room.

One day when both of them were engrossed in a game of chess, an officer from the king's army came riding on a horse and asked for Mir Sahib. Mir Sahib was stunned. What was the problem? Why was he summoned? Nothing seems to be good now. He closed the doors of the house and said to the servant, "Tell him that I am not at home."

The horse rider asked, "Where is he if he's not at home?"

The servant replied, "I don't know. What's the matter?"

The horse rider said, "Why should I tell you? We need to notify him, maybe we need some soldiers for the army. Being a vassal is not an easy job. When he will have to go to the battlefield, then we will see his courage."

Servant replied, "You may please leave. I will deliver your message."

Horse rider said, "There's no need for that. I will come tomorrow and take him along with me. I have been ordered to bring him."

Then the horse rider went away. Mir Sahib was trembling with fear. He said to Mirza, "What will happen now, friend?"

Mirza said, "It's big trouble. I hope I am not summoned."

Mir said, "That wretched person has said that he would come again tomorrow."

Mirza replied, "This is disastrous. If we have to go to the battlefield then we will die without any reason."

Mir said, "The only solution is that we should not remain at home. Tomorrow onwards we will play the game in a deserted place by the bank of the River Gomti. Who will know about that place? And the fellow will have to return empty-handed."

Mirza exclaimed, "Wow! That's a great idea. We have no other solution."

Meanwhile, Mir Sahib's Begum was saying to the horse rider, "You gave him a good scolding."

He answered, "I know how to deal with such fools. All their intellect and courage has been destroyed by chess. Now they won't dare to remain at home."

III

From the next day, both the friends left their homes before dawn. Holding a small mat under their arms, carrying a box of chess pieces, they would go to the old mosque by the side of Gomti, which was built by Nawab Asaf-ud-Daula. They would buy tobacco, *chillum* and wine on their way and as soon as they reach the mosque, they would spread their mat, fill their hookahs and start playing chess. They would grow oblivious of their surroundings and no other words would be heard except 'check' and 'mate'. Even an ascetic was not as focused on his meditations as these two were in chess. When they felt hungry, they would go to an eatery and have their lunch. They would return and have hookah and would again get engrossed in the game. Sometimes they would even forget to eat anything.

On the other side, the political condition of the country had been deteriorating day-by-day. The city was in great turmoil and the people were fleeing to the villages with their families. But our players were not at all concerned. They came through narrow lanes, afraid that the king's men might recognize them and would be caught. They wanted to enjoy the benefits of being a vassal and earn thousands of rupees annually without doing anything.

One day both the friends were sitting in the ruined mosque. Mirza's position was somewhat weak. Mir Sahib was threatening him with 'check' after 'check' when they saw the company's soldiers towards them. The English army was coming to capture the city of Lucknow.

Mir Sahib said, "By God, the English army is advancing towards us."

Mirza replied, "Let them come. Check. Save your king."

Mir said, "There is artillery as well which has around five thousand soldiers. Their faces resemble the red monkeys, one would be afraid of even looking at them."

Mirza replied, "Don't make such excuses, cheat someone else, another check!"

Mir replied, "You are a weird person. The city has been struck with a disaster and you are only bothered with your 'checks.' Do you even realise that how will we run our homes if the city gets captured?"

Mirza said, "We will see to that when the time comes. Another check and then it will be checkmate."

The army marched away. It was around ten o'clock. Another game was set up. Mirza said, "Where shall we eat today?"

Mir asked, "It's a *Roza*[2] day today. Are you feeling very hungry?"

Mirza replied, "No! God knows what is happening in the city."

Mir said, "Nothing would be happening in the city. People would have eaten their lunch and would be sleeping peacefully. And the Nawab would be having fun in his harem."

Both of them started playing again. It was three in the afternoon. This time Mirza's game was weak. It was four o' clock when they say the army returning. Nawab Wajid Ali Shah had been caught and the army was taking him to a deserted area. There was no commotion in the city or any violence. Not even a drop of blood was shed. Till date, there was no such state, wherein the king was defeated in such a peaceful manner without any bloodshed. Rather, it was the heights of cowardliness. The king of Awadh was taken as a prisoner and Lucknow was drowned in sensual pleasures. This was the most pathetic condition of political downfall.

Mirza said, "Nawab Sahib has been captured by the tyrants."

Mir said, "Never mind that. Save your king!"

Mirza said, "Please wait, dear. I cannot concentrate on the game. Poor Nawab Sahib must be in so much trouble."

Mir replied, "Oh yes, he won't be able to enjoy his luxuries now. Check!"

Mirza said, "Not all your days are spent leisurely. He is in a painful condition."

Mir said, "Yes, that's right. Check again and then there would be a mate in the next move. You won't be able to escape this time."

Mirza replied, "By God, you are very cruel. Even after seeing such a calamity you feel no pity for the Nawab. Oh, poor Wajid Ali Shah!"

---

2. *Roza*: The fasting observed by the Muslims in the month of Ramzan.

Mir said, "First save your king and then mourn for the Nawab. Here, it's checkmate."

The army marched away taking the king as the prisoner. And then Mirza set up another game. The wound of defeat is bad. Mir said, "Come on, let us sing an elegy to mourn the fall of Nawab Sahib." But Mirza's loyalty towards the king had vanished with his defeat. He was eager to take revenge for his defeat.

IV

It was evening. Bats had begun to scream in the ruins. The swallows had returned to their nests. But both the players were adamant to continue the game as if two soldiers were fighting in combat. Mirza had been defeated three times in a row and even the fourth one did not seem to be on his side. Every time he decided to play carefully but unfortunately, a single bad move made him taste defeat again. With every defeat, the feeling of revenge aggravated. On the other hand, Mir Sahib was thoroughly enjoying himself and sang ghazals and teased Mirza, as if he had found some hidden treasure. Mirza got irritated but to overcome the embarrassment of his defeat, he would praise him. As his position grew weaker, he started losing his patience and got irritated at every petty matter, "You should not change your moves. What is this that you make a move and then change it? Make a move in a single go. Why do you keep holding the piece? Keep it aside. Do not touch the piece until you decide the move. You take half an hour to make one move. This is not allowed. Did you change your move again? Please put the piece back."

Mir Sahib's wazir was about to be taken. He said, "When did I make the move?"

Mirza said, "You have already made the move. Please keep the piece there only."

Mir said, "Why should I keep it there? I had never let go of the piece."

Mirza said, "If you do not let go of the piece till the judgment day, then won't it be counted as a move? When you saw that your wazir would be taken, you started cheating."

Mir accused, "You are a cheater. Winning or losing is a matter of fate. No one wins by cheating."

Mirza said, "Then you have been checkmated in this game."

Mir asked, "Why would I be checkmated?"

Mirza said, "So you keep the piece back to the place where it was."

Mir said, "Why should I put it there? I will not keep it there."

Mirza said, "Why won't you keep it there? You will have to do that."

The dispute was increasing. No one was ready to refrain. They started cursing and abusing each other. Mirza said, "You must have known the rules if someone in your family would have played chess. The ones who peeled grass, what knowledge would they have about chess? Nobility is on a different plane. Just by becoming a vassal, one cannot become a nobleman."

Mir retorted, "What? Your ancestors must have peeled grass. We have been playing this game since many generations."

Mirza continued mocking, "Oh please! You have worked as a cook in the house of Gazi-ud-din Haider all through your life and you consider yourself a noble? It is not so easy to become a nobleman."

Mir said, "Why are you blackening the names of your ancestors? They must have been cooks. We have been dining with the kings since time immemorial."

Mirza said, "Hey you grass cutter! Don't make such tall claims."

Mir warned, "Watch your words, otherwise, you will be in trouble! I am not used to such insults. If someone stares at me for long, then I pluck out their eyes. Do you have such courage?"

Mirza said, "Oh! So you are challenging me? Do you want to see my courage? Then come and fight with me. Let us see who is the courageous one."

Mir said, "Don't be under the impression that you can defeat me."

Both friends took out their swords. It was the era of Nawabs. People used to carry their swords and daggers with them. Both of them used to love pleasure but were not cowards. They were devoid of all political emotions of loyalty and patriotism. They did not wish to die for the king or their kingdoms. But they did not lack any courage. The fight began and swords clashed, making the sounds of metal striking against metal. Both of them were wounded and fell down, and died writhing in pain. They had not shed a single drop of tear for their king but they had laid down their lives in defense of the wazirs of chess.

It was dark, the chessboard was still spread. The chess pieces were sitting on the thrones in seeming like they were lamenting the death of the two warriors. Silence reigned all around. The broken arches of the ruins, the destructed walls and the dust-laden pillars were watching these corpses and cursing their fate.

The Salt Inspector

I

When a new department was established to put a ban on the open trading of salt, people started trading it illegally. A lot of crooked methods were created to achieve this purpose – some bribed while others smuggled. The officers were having a great time. People even gave up the honorable position of a *patwari*[1] and sought employment in this department. Even lawyers yearned to occupy the position of an inspector in this department.

This was the time when people perceived English education and Christianity as the same thing. As Persian was the dominant language of that time, people who were well versed and well-read in the Persian language were appointed to the highest positions.

During this time, *Munshi*[2] Vanshidhar had also completed his studies and was looking for a job. He had read the unrequited love story of Zulaikha and rated the love stories of Majnu and Farhad way above the achievements of Nal and Neel and the discovery of America.

His father, an experienced old man, advised the young man, "Son! You know the sad plight of our house. We are under heavy debts. There are young girls in the house who will soon reach a marriageable age. I am just an old tree that would collapse at any moment. Now it is time for you to take up the responsibilities on your own shoulders, as you are the owner of the house. While searching for a job, get least bothered by the position and status that entails with the job. It is like the mausoleum of the pir. Most importantly, keep an eye on the offerings that you would get. Therefore, you must search for a job that gives you additional benefits along with your income. The monthly

---

1. *Patwari:* A government official who keeps records regarding the ownership of land.
2. *Munshi:* A secretary.

salary is like the full moon, visible just for a single day and gradually wanes away by each passing day until it completely disappears from the sky. The additional income is like a flowing stream that will quench all your thirst. Salary received from a man won't promise any increment but God might bless you with some additional source of income that would bring you prosperity. You are smart enough to take decisions and I don't think there is any need for me to handhold you. There is a great need of discretion in this matter. You must learn to use your understanding. Act wise and while making a decision, keep in mind the needs and the opportunities available which would act to your benefit. Always remember, it becomes an authoritative right to be tough with a person who needs favors from you. But it is difficult to tame the one who does not need any. That is the only advice that I can give you to survive in the world."

After this, the father gave his blessings. Vanshidhar was an obedient son. He listened attentively to his father's advice and then left his home. In this vast world, patience was his friend, intellect his guide and self-reliance his aid. Fortune favored him and he was selected for the prestigious post of the Salt Inspector. He earned a good salary and there was no limit to his additional income. When the old *Munshi* heard about this, his happiness knew no bounds. His creditors softened their behavior towards him and the hope of bringing on old festivities was revived. The neighbors grew extremely jealous of him.

II

It was a wintry night. The constables and security guards of the salt department were completely drunk. It had been six months since *Munshi* Vanshidhar took charge of the work. He had won the hearts of everyone with his behavioral efficiency and had become a trustworthy person.

The Yamuna river flowed about a mile away from the Salt Department's office building. A boat-bridge was built over the river. The inspector had shut the doors and was sleeping peacefully. Suddenly he woke up to the commotion of bullock carts and shouts of boatmen.

He was perplexed to see the carts crossing the river at this hour. Surely there was something going on. His logical conclusion further strengthened his suspicion. He got up and dressed himself in his uniform, put his pistol in his pocket and rode towards the bridge on his horse. He saw that a long queue of bullock carts was moving across the bridge. He asked angrily, "Whose carts are these?"

There was silence for a few moments. Then the men whispered among themselves and one of them replied, "They belong to Pandit Alopidin."

"Who is Pandit Alopidin?"

"Of Daatagunj"

Munshi Vanshidhar was shocked. Pandit Alopidin was the most reputed landlord in this area. He had a huge business with a turnover of lakhs of rupees. Every trader in the area was indebted to him. He had established business and had several workers employed in his service. The English officers used to come to his area as guests and engage their time in hunting. The hospitality went on round the year.

Vanshidhar asked, "Where are the vehicles going?"

"Kanpur"

When he asked about the contents of the vehicles, a pin-drop silence ensued. When he got no answer, he asked loudly, "Are you all dumb? What is inside these vehicles?"

When he didn't get an answer, he went near the vehicle, inspected it and found salt in huge quantities.

III

Pandit Alopidin was following the convoy in his royal chariot, lying half-asleep and half-awake. The news of this accidental disaster reached Pandit Alopidin. Some of the cart drivers came and told him,

"Panditji, the salt inspector has stopped our carts. He is standing by the river bank and is calling you."

Pandit Alopidin had an unwavering faith in Goddess *Laxmi*. He used to say that Goddess *Laxmi* ruled not just the earth but also the heaven. Justice and ethics were mere playthings of Goddess *Laxmi*, as she could make them dance to her tune. Strutting his head with pride, he said, "You go, I am coming." Saying this, he took out a *paan*[3] and ate it. He covered himself in a quilt and said, "Greetings Babuji! Tell me what blunder did I commit, to have compelled you to stop all my vehicles from crossing the bridge? You must be kind to Brahmins like us."

Vanshidhar replied, "By the order of the government."

Pandit Alopidin laughed and said, "I don't know about any government order. You are the only government that I know of. Both of us are like family, how can I go against you? Why did you bother to come here? I was coming to meet you. How can we pass through this place and not make an offering to the God who resides here?"

Vanshidhar was not at all affected by such temptation of wealth. Honesty was all that he believed in. He replied harshly, "Don't take me as one of those who sell their honesty for a few rupees. You are under arrest and you are bound to come with us. That's it! Let's not waste our time by beating around the bush. The decision has been already made. *Jamadar*[4] Badlu Singh, I order you to take him into custody."

Pandit Alopidin was stunned. Chaos hustled among the cart drivers. Perhaps this was the first time in his life when Panditji was compelled to listen to such rude remarks. Badlu Singh went forward but could not muster the courage to hold his hand. Panditji had never seen such righteousness insult his wealth before. He took Vanshidhar as a clumsy young man who had not engrossed himself in worldly pleasures yet. So he requested in a humble tone, "Babu Sahib, I request you not to do that, I would be ruined. All my reputation would turn to dust. What would you get by insulting me? I am not a stranger to you."

---

3. *Paan*: Betel leaves prepared and used as s stimulant.

4. *Jamadar*: A minor official or a junior officer.

Vanshidhar firmly stood by his decision and said, "I don't want to hear anything."

Alopidin felt the ground slipping from under his feet. This came as a blow to his prestige and self-respect. But he still had full confidence in the power of money. He said to his assistant, "Please gift one thousand rupees to Babu Sahib. He is behaving like a hungry lion."

Vanshidhar got angry and said, "One thousand rupees? Even one lakh rupees won't tempt me to divert from the path of truth."

Alopidin was frustrated to see such perseverance of righteousness and the sacrificial spirit that was rare even among Gods. Both the powers of righteousness and wealth were at war with each other. From one to five, five to ten, ten to fifteen…and finally, twenty thousand rupees were offered to the inspector. Vanshidhar's honesty was unshakeable. It stood like a mountain against Panditji's numerical strength.

Depressed, Alopidin said, "I cannot go beyond this. You may do as you wish."

Vanshidhar shouted at his *jamadar*. Badlu Singh cursed the inspector in his heart and moved towards Pandit Alopidin. Panditji drew back in fright. He spoke in an extremely humble tone, "Babu Sahib, please have mercy on me, I am ready to compensate with twenty-five thousand."

"It is impossible."

"Thirty thousand?"

"No way!"

"Not even if I offer you forty thousand?"

"Not even forty lakhs. Don't you understand? Badlu Singh, take this man into custody immediately."

Righteousness had trampled over wealth under its foot. Alopidin saw a healthy man advancing towards him with the handcuffs. He looked around helplessly with pleading eyes. Then he fell down unconscious.

IV

As soon as dawn came, the same story could be heard from everyone – be it old or young. Every single being was commenting on Panditji's conduct and criticizing him as if he was the only sinner in the world.

The milkman who sold adulterated milk, the officers who made false entries, and the Babus who travelled in trains without tickets, the moneylenders and traders who made fraudulent documents – everyone was looking down upon Panditji as if they had never sinned before.

When the accused Alopidin arrived at the court the next day, his head hung low out of shame. This created a commotion in the city. Such was the density of the crowd, that one would be unable to mark the difference between the walls and the roof.

Pandit Alopidin was considered as the most powerful of all. The officers were his devotees, clerks his servitors, the lawyers and attorneys his obedient servants and orderlies, peons and watchmen as his voluntary slaves.

The moment people saw him, they ran towards him from all directions. People were surprised, not because Alopidin had committed this deed, but because they wondered how did he come into the clutches of law? He was a man of wealth and had the capability to make anything possible. Then why would the police catch him? Every person was sympathizing with him.

An army of lawyers was immediately prepared to fight for the case. On the grounds of justice, began a battle of righteousness and wealth. Vanshidhar was standing silently. He had no defense except the force of the truth and no weapons except the bare facts on his side. There were some witnesses but he knew that they could be easily lured with money.

Vanshidhar felt that even justice was not on his side. It was the court of justice, but it severely reeked with partiality. But justice and partiality had nothing in common. Where there was bias, one could never expect justice there. The case soon came to a close.

The Deputy Magistrate's judgment stated, "The evidences against Pandit Alopidin are false and misleading. It is impossible that such a reputed man would stoop so low for the sake of a little profit. It might be possible that *Munshi* Vanshidhar is not completely wrong but because of his rude and inconsiderate behavior, a good man had to go through such an ordeal. It is good that he is alert and attentive towards his work but his obsession with honesty had corrupted his ability to think. He needs to be more careful in the future."

The lawyers heard this decision and leapt with joy. Pandit Alopidin came out with a smile on his face. His near and dear ones began to rain money all around him. The sea of generosity was on a high tide and the waves had shaken the very foundations of the court.

When Vanshidhar came outside, satirical comments started showering on him from all sides. The peons mocked him by saluting him again and again. But at this moment, every harsh word or gesture was fueling the fire of his pride.

Perhaps he would not have walked with such pride if he had won the case. He was proud to have upheld his principles and stand with honesty by his side. He lost respect for the people who were disloyal to their job and used their prestigious titles to extract money.

Vanshidhar was paying the price of making wealth as his enemy. Hardly a week had passed, when his termination letter arrived. He had been punished for doing his duty with complete honesty. With utter grief and sorrow, he went back to his home. His father was extremely angry with him. Even after thoroughly guiding him, the boy paid no attention to his advice, "He would always have his way. He wants me to face the demands of the wine-seller and butcher and live like a saint in my old age, and that too in such a meager salary! But this boy had to insult and display his honesty everywhere. His thoughts are so poor. All his education has been wastage and nothing else."

When Vanshidhar came home in his dejected state after a few days, the old man grew furious and started beating his head and said, "I feel like breaking your head as well as mine." Out of anger, he uttered many harsh words and if Vanshidhar had not vanished from his sight, his anger would have aggravated wildly. The old mother was also unhappy. All her wishes to visit Jagannath and Rameshwaram had turned to dust. Even his wife was so upset that she did not even talk to him for several days.

A week had passed. It was evening. The old *Munshiji* was busy praying. Suddenly, a decorative chariot stopped at their door. It had green and pink curtains, a beautiful pair of well-built oxen with a blue bell and copper horns. It was accompanied by many servants, carrying sticks on their shoulders.

When *Munshiji* ran out to welcome the visitor, he saw that it was Pandit Alopidin. He bowed his head in salutation and started flattering him, "We have been fortunate that you have come to our house. You are our God. Please forgive us! What can we do if our son turned out to be a brat? God must keep one sonless rather than giving one such a shameless son."

Alopidin said, "No brother, you must not say that."

Munshiji replied surprisingly, "Then what should I call such a son?"

Alopidin said in an affectionate voice, "How many people are there in this world that are loyal to their work and are ready to sacrifice everything to maintain their righteousness? Rather than tarnishing, these people enhance the glory of their family and ancestors."

Pandit Alopidin said to Vanshidhar, "Inspector Sahib, do not consider it as mere flattery, I do not need to put so much effort to flatter anyone. The other night you took me into custody with the power of your authority but today I have willingly come into your arrest. I have seen thousands of people and have come across many top officials but only you were the one who defeated me. With the power of wealth, I had made everyone a slave. But I was wrong. Sir, with your permission, I would like to make a request."

When Vanshidhar saw Alopidin advancing towards him he got

up from his seat and welcomed him courteously, with his self-respect intact. He thought that this fellow had come there to insult and humiliate him. He did not even try to apologize and did not like the smarmy attitude of his father. But when he heard his words, all the bitterness of his heart vanished.

He glanced at Panditji's face which radiated sincerity. This humbled his pride. He said shyly, "It is your generosity that you are saying such things to me. Please forgive me for my insolence. The laws of righteousness had bound me, otherwise, I am your humble servant."

Alopidin said humbly, "You had not accepted my request the night of my arrest, but today you would have to accept my request."

Vanshidhar said, "What can I do for you? I will try to serve you in the best possible manner."

Alopidin took out a stamped paper and kept it in front of Vanshidhar. Then he said, "Please accept this job and sign this paper. I am a Brahmin, I won't leave until you have accepted my request."

Vanshidhar read the paper and his eyes sparkled with tears of gratitude. Pandit Alopidin had appointed him the permanent manager of his entire wealth and property. Along with an annual income of six thousand rupees, he was offered daily expenses, a horse for commutation and a bungalow to live in with the assistance of a few servants. He said in a trembling voice, "I lack words to praise such generosity! But, I do not deserve such a high post."

Alopidin said with a smile, "I am in need of an undeserving candidate like you."

Vanshidhar replied, "I am your servant. It would be my good fortune to work for a famous and noble person like you. But I do not possess the knowledge, the wisdom, or the temperament that would make up for my weaknesses. For such a great work you need an experienced and far-sighted man."

Alopidin took out a pen, handed the pen to Vanshidhar and said, "I don't need scholarship, talent, sensibility, experience or work efficiency. I know the value of these attributes. Luckily, I have been given the jewel that is superior to talent and scholarship. Now I request you to sign the paper without thinking about anything else. I pray to God that may he keep you steadfast, fearless and rude and completely committed to his righteousness no matter what came his way. "

With twinkling eyes, Vanshidhar looked towards Panditji and a feeling of devotion and reverence filled him. He signed the paper with trembling hands. At last, righteousness triumphed over evil and Panditji joyfully hugged Vanshidhar.

A Wintry Night

I

Halku came in and said to his wife, "Sahna is here. Please give me the money. I'll pay the dues and get rid of him."

Munni was sweeping the floor. She turned around and said, "We are left with three rupees. If you would give the last of our money, then how would we buy a blanket? How would you guard the crop in the cold nights of winter? Go and tell him that we would clear our dues during the harvest season. We don't have any money now."

Halku was in a dilemma. The month of *Poos*[1] was coming; it was the peak of winter and it would not be possible to sleep in the open field without a blanket. But he knew that Sahna won't agree. He would threaten and abuse him. It was better to face the winters without a blanket and get rid of this trouble now.

Thinking along these lines and carrying his heavy weight (that disproved the meaning of his name), he went to his wife and persuaded her, "Please give me the money. At least let us get rid of him. I promise to arrange some money for the blanket through other means."

Munni moved away from him and said with arching eyes, "I know about your other means. Please elucidate it in detail. Would someone donate a blanket to you? I have no idea how much more we owe him. There's no end to it. Why don't you stop tilling the land? Toil hard and kill yourself, and then hand over the harvest to him and that shall be the end. It seems like we are born to be buried under debts. We will serve as labor to fill our stomach. Tillage is of no use to us. I won't give any money. No, I won't."

Halku sadly replied, "So you want me to silently face his abuses?"

1. *Poos:* The tenth month of the Hindu Calendar.

Munni said in an agonizing tone, "Who gave him the right to abuse you? Is he the king?"

But the moment she uttered these words, her taut eyebrows got lowered. The bitter truth in Halku's words seemed to be a fierce animal that was staring at her. She went up to the niche in the wall, took out the money and placed it in Halku's hands. While handing him the money, she said, "You must stop tilling the land from now on. Our daily labor is enough to feed us peacefully, without being browbeaten. What's the use of tilling? We earn something by hard labor and then put that money into this fire as well. And on top of that, we have to face such continuous bullying."

Halku took the money and walked towards the door as if he was handing over his heart to Sahna. He had saved these three rupees with much difficulty by saving bit by bit from his daily wages, in order to buy a blanket. But today, he was about to lose his hard-earned money. With every step, he sank deeper under the weight of his helplessness.

II

A wintry night of *Poos*! Even the stars of the sky seemed to be shivering through the cold. Halku was lying on the edge of his field, under the shelter of the sugarcane leaves, on a bamboo cot with a thick cotton sheet wrapped around him. He was shaking with cold while his pet dog Jabra was whining under the cot with his mouth pushed into his stomach. Neither of them was able to sleep.

Halku fixed his knees into his neck and said, "Hey Jabra, are you cold? I had told you to sleep on the straw bed at home. But you followed me out here. Now, you shall have to face the biting cold, I am helpless. Now you have to repent for your faithfulness."

Jabra wagged his tail and after a long whine, he yawned and became quiet. Perhaps, Jabra's mind guessed that his master was unable to sleep due to his repeated cries.

Halku took out his hand and caressed the cold body of Jabra and said, "Don't come with me tomorrow, otherwise you might freeze to death. These strong west winds are bringing the wintry iciness with them. I must fill another *chillum*[2] in order to pass this night somehow. I have already smoked eight *chillums*. This is the only pleasure I get of being a peasant. There are some fortunate people who drive away from the cold by wrapping themselves around thick quilts, sheets and blankets. The cold does not even dare to come near them. Such strangeness of life! We, the peasants, labor hard while others enjoy at our cost."

Halku got up and filled his *chillum* with a cinder from the pit. Jabra also stood up.

While smoking his *chillum*, Halku said to Jabra, "Would you like to have some *chillum*? It does not drive away the cold, but only relaxes your mind."

Jabra looked at Halku with eyes that overflowing with love.

Halku, "Just face the cold for tonight. Tomorrow I shall put the straw bed here for you. When you'll sit on it, you won't feel cold."

Jabra placed his legs on Halku's knees and brought his mouth near Halku's mouth. Halku could feel his warm breath.

After smoking the *chillum*, Halku lay down. But whenever he decides to fall asleep, the next moment his body starts to shiver. He twisted on his sides, but couldn't drive away the cold. No matter what he did, the cold didn't leave his body like an evil spirit.

Unable to drive away the cold, he tenderly lifted up Jabra, patted his head and made him sleep in his lap. The dog was stinking badly but holding the animal close to his body, gave him a feeling of peaceful satisfaction that he had not felt in months. Jabra was perhaps feeling that heaven was right here; and Halku's pure soul had not a trace of loathing towards the dog. He would have embraced his friend or brother in a similar manner. He was no longer hurt by the abject plight that had landed him into this situation. No, this unique friendship

---

2. *Chillum*: A hookah; a straight conical pipe used for smoking cannabis.

had opened the doors of his spirit and every pore of his being was shining brightly.

Suddenly Jabra heard the footsteps of an animal. This special affection had ignited a new enthusiasm in him. Seemingly unaffected by the cold breeze, he came out of the shed and started barking. Halku tried to cajole him to return to him but Jabra kept on barking. He would return for a moment and then go back at once. Protecting Halku was his duty and this was jumping out of his heart like an unsatisfied desire.

III

Another hour passed. The night began to trigger the draughts of cold wind. Halku sat up, brought his legs closer to his chest and then hid his head in them. But still, there was no respite from the biting cold. It seemed that all the blood in his body had frozen, and ice flowed through his veins. He looked up at the sky to ascertain the remaining time left for the night to pass. The *Saptarishi*[3] constellation was still half-way up. Once the constellation reaches directly above his head, it will be morning. More than one-fourth of the night was still left.

There was a mango orchard near Halku's field. The leaves of the tree had started to fall. A heap of dry leaves had gathered in the orchard. Halku thought of collecting the leaves and lighting a fire to get rid of this biting cold. But he thought that if someone saw him gathering leaves at this hour, people might consider him as a ghost. There is also a possibility of some wild animal hiding in the heap. Nevertheless, he decided to gather the leaves as the cold was becoming intolerable.

He went to the neighboring *arhar*[4] field, uprooted some stalks and tied them together to make a broom. He took a piece of smouldering

---

3. *Saptarishi*: The Indian name of the Ursa Major or the Great Bear constellation. It consists of 7 bright stars arranged in a pattern that resembles a big bear or a big kite with a tail.
4. *Arhar*: Yellow lentils.

dung cake in his hand and walked towards the orchard. Jabra saw him and came to him wagging his tail.

Halku said, "It is impossible to stand the cold any more Jabru. Let us go to the orchard, collect some leaves and burn them to warm ourselves. Once we do that, we shall come back and sleep here. The night is still a long way."

Jabra droned to express his agreement and started walking towards the orchard.

The orchard was dark, the cruel wind was mercilessly trampling upon the leaves and the dewdrops were continuously dripping from the trees.

All of a sudden, the wind brought a waft of the fragrance of the henna flowers.

Halku said, "What a fine smell it is, Jabru! It must have tickled your nose as well."

But Jabru had found a bone in the field and was busy gnawing at it.

Halku placed the smoldering piece on the ground and started gathering the leaves. In a few minutes, a big heap of leaves was created. His hands were stiff with cold and his feet were bare. He raised a mountain of leaves and decided to burn it to escape the biting cold.

The fire was lit and in a few moments, the flames leapt up and touched the leaves of the tree above it. In the unsteady brightness of the fire, the trees of the orchard seemed to carry the unbounded darkness on their heads. In this limitless sea of darkness, this light appeared to be a rocking boat.

Halku was sitting in front of the fire, warming himself. Soon he took off his cotton sheet, tucked it to his side and then spread out his legs as if challenging the cold, "Do what you can." After conquering the infinite power of cold, it was not possible for him to repress his triumph.

He said to Jabra, "Hey Jabra, are you still feeling cold?"

Jabra whined.

"Why didn't we think of this before? Hadn't this idea struck my mind, we would have suffered so much."

Jabra wagged his tail.

"Come on, let's jump over this fire and see who can cross it over. But do remember son, in case you burn yourself I won't be able to provide any kind of treatment."

Jabra looked at the fire with frightened eyes.

"Don't say anything about it to Munni, otherwise she would argue with me."

Saying this he jumped over the fire in a single swift, the flames touched his feet but without any harm. Jabra only circled around the fire, and then came and stood beside him.

Halku said, "Come, come, this is not right. You must jump over it."

Saying this, he jumped over the fire again and came to the other side.

IV

The leaves had burnt out. The orchard was once again in darkness. The fire was reduced to embers which the wind occasionally ruffled and then it would again fall under the ashes.

Halku wrapped himself with the cotton sheet, sat beside the warm ashes and began humming a song. His body had grown warm but the moment cold rose around him, laziness suppressed it.

Jabru barked loudly and ran towards the field. Halku felt that a herd of animals, maybe *neelgais*[5], had invaded his field. The noise of their running and tramping around was clearly heard. It seemed like they were grazing in the field, as the sound of munching became more evident.

He mumbled to himself, "No, when Jabra is around, no animal can dare to enter the field. He would bite them away. I must be imagining things. I was surely mistaken."

He shouted loudly, "Jabra! Jabra!"

---

5. *Neelgais*: A large Indian antelope.

But Jabra kept on barking and did not return back to him.

Then he again heard the sound of grazing. It was impossible for him to ignore it now. Waking up, after settling in a comfortable position, was a torture to him. The thought of chasing away the animals in this bitter cold seemed unbearable to him. Thus, he did not budge.

He shouted loudly, "Liho! Liho! Liho!"

Jabra barked again. The animals were ruining the field. The harvest was completely ready and this year, it was going to be a good harvest. But these rowdy animals were bent on destroying it.

Halku got up and walked a few steps. Suddenly, the wind biting like the sting of a scorpion, hit him and he was forced to return to the dying fire and scoured through the ashes to make his body warm.

While Jabra was barking himself hoarse, the neelgais were devouring the field, and Halku was sitting beside the warm ashes with calm resignation. Listlessness had bound him from all sides.

He covered himself in his sheet and went to sleep on the warm ground.

When he woke up in the morning, the sun was shining brightly, and Munni was waking him up, "You came here and slept, and there the whole field has been destroyed."

Halku woke up and said, "Have you been to the field?"

She said, "Yes, all the crops have been ruined. Who sleeps like this? What was the use of camping here all night?"

Halku quickly reeled off an excuse, "Here I was dying with such a severe stomach ache, and you're bothered about the crops."

Both walked up to their field. They saw that the whole crop was trampled upon, and Jabra was lying under the shed almost lifeless.

Both of them looked at their field. While Munni was sad, Halku was happy.

Munni replied anxiously, "Now, we shall have to work as laborers to pay off the tax."

Halku replied, "So what? At least I won't have to sleep here on a cold night."

Violence is the Absolute Religion

I

There are some people in this world who, despite being servants to none, are servants to all. They have no work of their own but still, do not have a minute to spare. Jaamid was one such person. He had no concerns in the world. Neither did he have any friends nor any enemies. If anyone said something to him with a smile, he would get him as a free slave. He enjoyed working for others. If someone in the village fell ill, he would take care of him. If you ask him, he would accompany you in the middle of the night to the doctor, would go on a search for the best of herbs in the forest. It was not possible that he would see a poor person being exploited and remain silent. And then even if someone killed him, he would not stop his intercession. He had got into hundreds of such situations. He would often get into an altercation with the constable. That is why people considered him an idiot. And it was a fact as well. Who would consider a person who takes upon himself the burden of another, who would run for miles to douse some fire as an intelligent being? To summarize, others were benefited by his actions but he was never benefited. So much so, that he was dependent on others even for his daily meals. But he was a passionate man.

II

In the end, when people reproached him a lot saying, "Why are you destroying your life? You would die for others, but is there anybody who is concerned about you? If you fell ill for a day, there is nobody to give you some water; when you serve others, they give you some food like alms; the moment their work is over, they won't even turn back and look at you." Jaamid realized the truth at last. He actually had nothing that he could call his own. He woke up one day and started walking in one direction. After two days, he reached a city. The city was huge with tall buildings, wide, clean roads, big markets, innumerable temples and mosques which were almost equal to the number of houses.

In the village, there was neither a mosque nor a temple. The Muslims prayed on the roof of a house while the Hindus offered water to the Gods under a tree. Jaamid was amused to see the high status of religion in the city. In his eyes, there was nothing more important than religion. He thought, "How honest and true these people are. They must be so kind and compassionate, that is why God has given them so much." He looked at each passerby with respect and bowed his head. He felt as if each person was like God.

He kept exploring the city and soon it was evening. Tired, he went and sat in the courtyard of a temple. The temple was very big. A dome was shining brightly at its top. There was marble all around, but in the courtyard, there was a lot of garbage and cow dung. Jaamid could not stop himself when he saw the temple premises in such a bad condition. He searched for a broom but could not find one. Exasperated, he started cleaning it with his own cloth.

After some time, the devotees started coming for the evening prayers. When they saw Jaamid cleaning the area, they started talking amongst themselves.

"After all, he is a Muslim."

"He must be a low caste person."

"No, even they do not clean their own cloth. He must be a mad man."

"Hope he is not a spy from the other side."

"No, he appears to be a poor man."

"He must be someone from Hasan Nizami."

"He must be cleaning for the cow dung. (To Jaamid) Don't take the cow dung, ok? Where do you stay?"

"I am a traveller from another land, sir; what will I do with the cow dung? I saw *Thakurji's* temple and came and sat here. There was garbage lying all around. I thought devotees would come here soon, so I started cleaning the place."

"You are a Muslim, right?"

"*Thakurji* belongs to all, be it a Muslim or a Hindu!"

"Do you believe in *Thakurji*?"

"Who would not believe in *Thakurji*, sir? If I would not believe in the creator, then whom would I believe?"

The devotees started discussing-

"He is a villager."

"Trap him. He should not escape."

III

Jaamid was trapped. He was treated well. He was given a good house to stay in. He got good food to eat twice a day. People always surrounded him at all times. Jaamid knew a lot of Hindu devotional songs and sang well. He started singing at the temple every day. When devotion was accompanied by an elegant voice, then what else was needed? The people swayed to his songs. Many people started coming to the temple just to hear him sing. Everyone was convinced that God himself had sent this prey.

One day a huge gathering was called at the temple. A bed sheet was laid out in the courtyard. Jaamid's head was shaved off. New clothes were given to him. A *havan*[1] was conducted. Jaamid was made to distribute the sweets. He was even more impressed by the benevolence of the people. How good these people are! They are treating an outsider like me so well! This is called true religion. Jaamid had never received such respect in his life ever before. The same homeless young man who was called an idiot by all had now become the leader of the public. Hundreds of people came just to

---

1. *Havan*: Doing prayers by lighting the holy fire.

catch a glimpse of him. Stories of his knowledge were spread far and wide. It was published in the newspapers, that a big Muslim preacher was cleansed and made a Hindu. The straightforward Jaamid did not understand the real meaning of all this respect. What would he not do for such good-hearted, well-natured people? He prayed every day and sang devotional songs. Even in his village, he sang regularly at various religious occasions. The only difference was that in the village no one respected him while here, everybody was his devotee.

One day, Jaamid was sitting with a few devotees and reading a scripture when he suddenly saw a young man across the road with a *tilak*[2] on his forehead, beating an old helpless man.

The old man was crying and pleading him for mercy. He fell at the young man's feet and started saying, "Master, please forgive my mistake". But it had no effect on the young man. Jaamid suddenly felt a surge of anger. He could not sit idle after seeing such a horrible scene. He jumped up and came out, and stood in front of the young man and said, "Why are you hitting the old man, brother? Don't you feel pity for him?"

The young man replied, "I would break his bones."

Jaamid asked, "After all, what is his fault? Tell me something."

The young man said, "His hen came into our house and spoiled it."

Now Jaamid turned to the old man and asked, "So, did he teach his hen to spoil your house?"

The old man replied, "I swear, I always keep it tied. Today, I made a mistake. Master, please forgive me; you are continuously thrashing me."

The young man said, "I have not yet beaten you. Now I would beat you, and bury you alive."

Jaamid stopped him and said, "If you bury him alive, then you will also not live long. Do you understand? If you raise your hand again, it won't be good for you."

The young man was proud of his strength. He slapped the old man again and Jaamid caught him by his neck. They started wrestling.

---

2. *Tilak*: Vermillion mark on the forehead.

Jaamid was also a strong young man. When Jaamid pushed him and the young man fell on the ground, all the devotees sitting inside the temple came out and started beating Jaamid. Jaamid was confused. Nobody was asking anything. Nobody was saying anything to the young man. Everybody was beating Jaamid. In the end, he fell down. Then the people started talking amongst themselves.

"He cheated us!"

"Shame on your religion. One should never expect anything good from them. A crow will side with a crow. A bad man is expected to do bad things. Nobody cared for him, he was sweeping the temple. He didn't even have a cloth to cover him. We gave him respect and transformed him into a man from an animal. Even then, he failed to become one of us."

"That is the basis of their religion."

Jaamid was lying by the roadside groaning in pain. He was not sad because he was being hit. He has suffered such pain before. He was sad as he was unable to understand why these people started beating him mercilessly? Where has all their goodness gone? I am the same person. I have committed no mistake. I did what anybody would and should have done under these circumstances. Then why did these people torture me like this? Why did the Gods suddenly become devils?

He was in this state of confusion the entire night. In the morning, he got up and started walking.

On his way, Jaamid met the same old man. Seeing him, he said, "You saved my life yesterday. I heard those devils tortured you. I ran away on seeing an opportunity to escape. Where were you? Here, the people are waiting to meet you since last night. *Kaazi*[3] *Sahib* had gone out searching for you in the night itself but was unable to find you. We were a minority last night that is why they were able to hit us. It was the time for prayers and everybody was in the mosque. If they had even the remotest idea, a thousand people would have arrived with sticks. I swear by Allah, I would rear three hens from today. *Kaazi Sahib* has said, 'If that young man turns up again, then I should go and

---

3. *Kaazi*: A judge in the Muslim community.

73

tell him. Either he would run away or his bones would be broken.'"

The old man took Jaamid to *Kaazi* Jorawar Hussain. Seeing Jaamid, the *Kaazi* came forward, embraced him and said, "Oh! My eyes were searching for you. You defeated so many unbelievers yesterday. After all, their blood is impure. What can I say about those unbelievers! I heard they wanted to convert you. But you defeated their plans. Islam needs people like you. The name of Islam shines because of young men like you. The mistake was that you did not wait for one more month. You should have let the marriage happen and then it would have been fun. A girl for free, and wealth along with it! You made a mistake."

A string of devotees kept coming for the whole day. Everyone wanted to have a glimpse of Jaamid. Everybody was praising his courage and religious fervor.

IV

It was night and three hours had passed. The number of devotees had reduced. Jaamid had started learning the religious scriptures from *Kaazi Sahib*. For that purpose, he had prepared the room next to him. He had finished his readings for the day and was about to go to sleep when he heard the sound of a horse carriage stopping at the door. Devotees of *Kaazi Sahib* often came there. Jaamid thought that it must be one of them. When he looked out, he saw a woman getting off the carriage. The driver was unloading her luggage.

The lady looked here and there and then said, "No, I am sure, this is not the house. Perhaps you have forgotten."

The horse driver said, "You don't understand. I have told you that Babu Sahib has changed his house. Please come upstairs."

The lady hesitated and said, "Why don't you call him? Call out!"
The horse driver said, "Why should I call out when I know it is Sahib's house. Then what is the use of shouting? He must be sleeping. His sleep would be disturbed. Don't worry. Please go upstairs."

The lady went upstairs. The driver also followed her with the luggage. Jaamid stood silently. He could not understand the secret. Hearing the noise of the horses, *Kaazi Sahib* came on the terrace. On seeing a woman, he closed all the windows and took out the sword that was hanging on the wall and stood at the doorway waiting for her.

As soon as the lady reached the terrace, she was shocked to see *Kaazi Sahib*. She tried to turn back immediately but *Kaazi Sahib* caught her and dragged her inside the room. By this time, Jaamid and the horse carriage driver had both reached upstairs. Jaamid was surprised to see this. The secret had become more interesting and secretive. This storehouse of knowledge, the epitome of justice, religion and vision, was now exploiting an unknown woman. With the driver, he also entered the room.

Kaazi Sahib was holding both her hands. The driver closed the doors.

The woman looked at the driver with bloodshot eyes and asked, "Why have you brought me here?"

Kaazi Sahib shined his sword and said, "First you sit down quietly. You will get to know everything."

The woman shouted, "You seem to be a Muslim teacher. Has your Allah taught you to kidnap daughters and daughter-in-laws of others and keep them forcefully in your house and disrespect them?"

Kaazi replied, "Yes. It is the order of Allah to bring the unbelievers into our fold. If they don't do it willingly, then we will bring them in forcefully."

The woman said, "What if someone does this to your daughter or daughter-in-law?"

Kaazi replied, "It is happening. We will do exactly what you do to us. By accepting Islam, you don't lose your respect. It only increases. Hindus have taken upon themselves the task of destroying us. They want to remove even our last remnants from this country by deceit and greed. If you do this to Muslims, will we keep quiet?"

The woman said, "Hindus never torture anyone. Tired of your

atrocities, the lower caste people might be taking revenge on you. But no true Hindu would favor that."

Kaazi Sahib thought for a moment and said, "True, earlier these tricks were done by Muslims at the lower level. The decent people considered it bad and tried to stop them. With increasing education and social etiquettes, this would have vanished, but now the entire Hindu community is waiting to finish us. Then what is the way out for us? We are weak and so we have to resort to these things to survive. But why are you so afraid? You won't have any problems here. The respect that Islam gives to women is far more than that which is given by any other religion. A Muslim man would give his life for his woman. You would get married to my young friend Jaamid who is standing here. Then you would lead a peaceful and a happily married life."

The woman said, "I consider you and such religious system pathetic. It would be better that you leave me; otherwise, I would raise my voice, and all your show of being a religious preacher would vanish."

Kaazi warned her, "If you open your mouth, I would kill you. Do understand that."

But the woman was adamant. She said, "Life has no value in front of one's self-respect. You can take my life, not my respect."

Kaazi said, "Why are you so insistent?"

The woman went near the door and said, "I am warning you, open the door." Jaamid was standing silently until now.

As soon as the woman moved towards the door, *Kaazi Sahib* pulled her by her hand. Jaamid opened the door quickly and said to *Kaazi Sahib*, "Leave her."

Kaazi said, "What nonsense are you talking?"

Jaamid said, "Nothing. It would be better if you let her go."

When *Kaazi Sahib* did not let go of the woman and the driver also tried to hold her, Jaamid pushed *Kaazi Sahib* and ran out of the room, holding the lady by her hand. The driver jumped after him, but Jaamid pushed him so hard that he fell on his face. In a moment, the lady and Jaamid were on the street.

Jaamid asked, "In which street is your house?"

The woman said, "In Adhiyaganj."

Jaamid said, "Let me take you home."

The woman said, "What can be a bigger favor than that? I would never forget your kindness. You saved me today! Now I understood that good and bad people exist everywhere. My husband's name is Pandit Rajkumar."

At that moment, he saw a horse carriage coming their way. They were about to climb into it when *Kaazi Sahib* hit Jaamid with a stick but the stick hit the carriage. They quickly got in and the horse cart started moving.

There was no problem in finding the house of Pandit Rajkumar. As soon as Jaamid called out, the Pandit came out worried and on seeing the woman, said, "Where were you, Indira? I could not find you at the station. I got a little late. What took you so long?"

Indira went inside the house and said, "It is a long story. Let me catch my breath and then I will tell you. You just understand that if this Muslim youth would not have helped me today, then I would have lost everything."

Panditji got more interested in listening to the story. He went inside with Indira, but he came out in a minute and said, "Brother, you might think I am acting; but in you, I see my God. I am unable to understand how can I thank you. Please come and sit down."

Jaamid said, "No, please give me your leave."

Pandit said, "What can I do in return for your kindness?"

Jaamid replied, "Please do not take revenge for this incident on some poor Muslim. That is my only request".

Saying this, Jaamid stood up and left for the city. The poisonous air of the city seemed to be suffocating him. He wanted to reach his village as fast as possible where religion meant compassion, love and brotherhood. He now hated religion and religious people.

Splashed!

Early in the morning after finishing my bath and my prayers, I applied a vermilion *tilak* on my forehead, put on my yellow *dhoti*[1] and my wooden sandals, tucked the almanac under my arm, picked up my stout staff, my Foe's-Skull-Breaker, and set off to a client's house. I was supposed to decide the most auspicious hour to get married. Once it is decided, the prestigious family would most likely gift me a large coin at the very least and refreshments on top. My meals, I must add, are no ordinary meals. Mere clerks and petty officers never find the courage to invite me. A month's sustenance for them is a day's refreshments for me. In this matter, I admire the merchants and bankers, who feed well with such an open heart, that the body is suffused with bliss. I accept invitations only after considering the client's generosity. If someone looks worried while he feeds me, I lose my appetite. What good one receives by feeding someone if you have to cry while you do it? I cannot digest such a half-hearted meal. The client should be bountiful while offering, and must keep on exhorting, "Here, Shastriji, have some more sweets," and I must keep saying, "No, no, *Jajman*[2] , no more now!"

It had rained heavily one night, and pools of water had dotted the streets. I was walking deeply engrossed in my own thoughts when suddenly a car splashed past. Large muddy drops hit my face. When I glanced down, my *dhoti* looked as if someone had stirred a bucket of mud and flung it at me. My clothes were ruined, my body dirtied, and to say nothing of the money lost. If I could catch those people in the car, I would have taught them a lesson that they would have never forget. But all I could do was stand there helplessly bubbling in anger. I couldn't go to the client's house dressed like this and my own house was over a mile away. Seeing me in such a mess, the passerby were clapping

---

1. *Dhoti*: A cloth worn by men.

2. *Jajman*: One of the fixed circle of persons in a Hindu caste system..

their hands and ridiculing me. I had never felt so embarrassed. What should I do? If I went home, what would my good wife say?

Quickly, I decided what had to be done. I gathered ten to twelve stones from the street and waited for another car. After all, I had the Brahman's force within me! In less than ten minutes, a car came into sight. Ah! It was the same car. Perhaps it was on its way back after picking up the master from the railway station. As it drew near, I let loose one of the stones and flung it with all my strength. The *Sahib's* hat flew off and landed on the other side of the street. The car slowed down. I fired off another stone. This one smashed the window, and a piece of glass hit the cheek of the *Sahib*[3] Bahadur and drew blood. The car stopped, and the *Sahib* stepped out and walked up to me. He drew his fist and said, "You pig, I'll get you arrested." As soon as I heard that, I dropped my almanac on the ground, grabbed *Sahib* around the chest, and tripped him with my leg. He fell backwards with a thud into the muddy street. Quickly I straddled him and laid into his neck and face, delivering a score of blows in quick succession until the *Sahib* got dizzy. Meanwhile, his wife had got out of the car in high heels, silk *sari*, powdered cheeks, painted lips and darkened eyebrows. She began to poke at me with her umbrella. I let the *Sahib* go and reached for my staff and said, "Deviji, please don't thrust yourself into men's affairs; you might be injured, and that would cause me grief."

The *Sahib* found his chance and, rising carefully to his feet, kicked me in the knee with his boot. Enraged, I picked up my staff and hit the *Sahib's* leg. He went down like a chopped tree. *Memsahib*[4] ran at me brandishing her umbrella. I gently pulled it out of her grasp and threw it aside. The driver had been sitting in the car all this time. Now he too climbed out and attacked me with a cane. I brought my stick down on him as well, and he went sprawling. By now, a sizeable crowd had gathered to watch the fun. The *Sahib*, lying on the ground, spoke up, "Rascal! I'll get you arrested."

---

3. *Sahib*: A polite title or form of address for a man.
4. *Memsahib*: A polite title or form of address for a lady.

I hefted my staff again and was tempted to thump him on the skull. But the *Sahib* quickly folded his hands and said, "No, no, sir, I won't go to the police, forgive me."

I said, "Yes, don't talk of the police otherwise I'll crack your skull right here. At most, they will put me away for six months, but I will cure you of this habit permanently. Blinded by sheer pride, you drive a car and splash people as you go. You don't even care to look if anyone is walking alongside!"

One of the onlookers said, "Sir, these drivers don't know what they're doing, they just splatter mud as they go. When someone gets soaked, they watch the fun and laugh at him. You did very well to fix at least one of them."

I shouted at the *Sahib*, "Are you listening to what the people have to say?"

The *Sahib* turned threw an angry look upon that man and said, "You speak a lie, an absolute lie."

I scolded him, "Your arrogance hasn't abated much, should I give you a few more blows?"

The *Sahib* whimpered, "Oh no, sir, no, he speaks the truth. It's true! Now you are happy?"

Another bystander said, "Now, he would say what you want to hear, but as soon as he's back in his car, he'll start up his antics all over again. While driving, they think they're some nawab's nephew."

Another gentleman advised, "Tell him to spit and lick it up."

"No, let him pinch his ear and do sit-ups," said another.

Someone from the crowd added, "And the driver too. These are worse rogues. If a rich man is proud, that's one thing, but why should the drivers act so? As soon as his hands touch the steering wheel, a curtain descends over his eyes!"

I accepted this proposal. Both the driver and the owner must pinch their ears and do sit-ups while the *memsahib* counts, "Listen, *memsahib*, you'll have to keep the count. A hundred sit-ups and nothing less!"

Two men pulled the *Sahib* up by his arms and two others pulled up the driver. The driver had a wounded leg but still began to do the sit-ups. But *Sahib's* arrogance had still not lessened. He sat down and began to curse. By that time, I had become furious. I was adamant of not letting him go without making him do a hundred sit-ups. I told four of the men to push the car off the edge of the road.

No sooner said than begun. Instead of four, fifty came and began to shove the car. The roadway was built on a high embankment with the land below it on either side. If the car goes off the road, it would be smashed to a heap. The car was almost at the edge when the *Sahib* groaned and said, "Sir, please don't break the car, I'll do the sit-ups."

I ordered the men away, but it had already become a source of entertainment for them. No one paid any heed. Only when I ran at them with my staff raised did they leave the car and disperse; and the *Sahib*, closing his eyes, began to do the sit-ups.

After he'd done ten sit-ups, I asked the *memsahib*, "How many so far?"

The *memsahib* huffily answered, "I did not count."

"In that case the *Sahib* will stay here all day, groaning like this, I won't let him go. If you want to get him home safely, start counting. Then I'll set him free."

The *Sahib* understood that he wouldn't be saved without suffering the penalty, and he resumed his sit-ups. One, two, three, four, five...

Suddenly another car was seen coming. The *Sahib* saw it too. He rubbed his nose and said, "Panditji, you are my father! Take pity on me. I'll never sit in a car again." I felt merciful and said, "No, I'm not stopping you from sitting in a car; all I'm saying is that you should remember that others are human beings too when you are in it."

Seeing the second car speeding along, I signaled. All the bystanders picked up a stone or two. This car was being driven by the owner himself. He slowed down and was trying to slip away when I stepped forward, grabbed his ear and shook him vigorously, then slapped him soundly on both cheeks and said, "Don't splash mud with your car! Understood? Go quietly on your way."

This gentleman began to chatter, but when he saw the crowd standing with stones in their hands, he silently drove away.

A minute later another car appeared. I told the men to bar the way. The car stopped. I bade farewell with four slaps but surprisingly, this poor fellow was a true gentleman. He endured the slaps and drove away without a word of abuse.

Suddenly someone shouted, "Here comes the police!"

In an instant, everyone disappeared! I too clambered off the road, stepped into a little lane and disappeared.

God's Justice

I

In Kanpur district, there was a landlord named Pandit Bhrigudutt. *Munshi*[1] Satyanarayan, a devout person of good character, was his employee. He used to handle Pandit Bhrigudutt's business documents worth lakh of rupees and thousands of tons of wheat. But his character was impeccable. A responsible employee is always respected than other workers. Every opportunity, be it happy or sad days, Panditji interacted with him with great kindness. Slowly, Panditji started trusting *Munshiji* blindly and stopped checking the accounts altogether. It was possible his entire life, he would not have worried about the accounts, but fate is always cruel. At Kumbh Mela[2] in Prayag, Panditji went to take a bath but never returned. Nobody knew if he slipped a pit or was devoured by a wild animal, but nothing more was heard of him. Furthermore, with Panditji's missing, *Munshi* Satyanarayan's powers grew considerably. Panditji left behind a helpless widow and two small children, who lived in Panditji's house. One day after the cremation rituals, the sorrow-stricken widow called *Munshi* and said, "Lala, Panditji has left us in the lurch. Now, this boat can cross the river only if you help us. All the crops have been sown by you, and I leave it all on you. These are your children too, please adopt them. Till the time the master was alive, he considered you as his brother. I am sure that you will continue to live as per his faith."

Satyanarayan cried and replied, "Sister-in-law, it has been my misfortune that my brother is no more. Otherwise, he would have made me a man. I have eaten his salt and I wish to die here. Don't worry about anything. I will continue to serve you until my death. But

---

1. *Munshi*: A secretary.
2. *Mela*: A fair.

I have a request: whenever I scold someone, please scold him as well. Otherwise, they won't obey me."

II

After this incident, *Munshiji* controlled the business for many years. He was very good at his work. There was no problem at all. The entire district started respecting him. People forgot all about Panditji. He attended courts and committees, and the district officials thought of him as the landlord. He was respected amongst other landlords too, but an increase in respect is a costly affair as well. And Bhanukunwari, like other women, held on to the money. She was not used to the behavior of men. Panditji always gave gifts and rewards to *Munshiji*. He knew that after learning, loyalty was the biggest quality in a man. Moreover, he used to handle and check the accounts himself. It was only a check for namesake, but it was an added deterrent because the biggest enemy of loyalty and integrity was an opportunity. Bhanukunwari was not aware of these things. Therefore, in the midst of opportunity and lack of money, how could *Munshiji's* integrity remain intact?

Close to Kanpur city, right on the banks of the river Ganges, there lay a crowded and fertile village. Panditji wanted to construct a concrete bank, a temple and a house in that village, but he was not able to do so. Coincidentally, the village was put up for sale. Thakur, the landlord of this village was stuck in some litigation and wanted some money to fight the case. *Munshiji* heard about it. He immediately went over and after a few quick negotiations, an agreement was made. The agreement was registered and *Munshiji* gave the money to Thakur. For ease of work and convenience, *Munshiji* did all the paperwork in his name. Since Panditji's children were minors, it would have been problematic to register the documents in children's names. There would have been a lot of problems in the paperwork if it was done in their names and the delay would have resulted in the loss of the property. *Munshiji* took the papers and came to Bhanukunwari. She was behind the veil and the news was read out to her. Bhanukunwari thanked him with her eyes wet. The intention to construct a temple and a concrete bank was finalized.

Munshiji went to the village the very next day. The villagers came with offerings for the new master. A feast for the rich men of the town was organized. People toured the Ganges in a boat. A spot was selected, away from the crowd for the construction of the temple.

III

Although there were no corrupt feelings in *Munshiji's* mind when the village was bought, the seeds of corruption were sown within the next three to four days and it started growing. *Munshiji* kept the accounts of this village separately and did not think it to be necessary to inform the mistress about it. Bhanukunwari did not consider it right to interfere in these matters; but listening to the other employees, she was afraid that *Munshiji* would betray her. She hid these feelings from *Munshiji*, suspecting whether the other servants were plotting to cause harm to her.

Many years passed by. Now the seed of corruption sown had taken the form of a tree. Bhanukunwari started seeing the signs of this in *Munshiji*. In *Munshiji's* heart, the law won over righteousness, and he had decided that the village was his. He used to think, "Yes, I owe Bhanukunwari thirty thousand rupees." But the embers were burning on both sides. *Munshiji* was well armed and was waiting for the attack and Bhanukunwari was looking for an opportunity. One day, she mustered some courage, called *Munshiji* inside and said, "Lalaji, when will you start the work on the temple at 'Bargada'? It has been eight years since it has been bought, and it would be nice if the work could start as soon as possible. Who knows about life? Whatever is to be done, please do it now."

By taking up this issue in this manner, Bhanukunwari gave a good account of her cleverness. *Munshiji* could not say anything and was impressed. He thought for a moment and then said, "I intended to do that many times, but I did not get a suitable piece of land. The land by the side of the Ganges is in the custody of the villagers and they are not willing to leave it."

Bhanukunwari said, "How come I am hearing about this now? It has been eight years, and you have never discussed this with me. I don't even know which district it is, how much is the profit, what kind of a village is it, is anything there or not. You are doing whatever needs to be done, but I should also be aware of it."

Munshiji stabilized himself. He understood that it was not easy to beat such a clever woman. If the village is to be taken, then why be afraid? He said openly, "You did not show any inclination, and I thought it right not to disturb you unnecessarily."

This deeply pained Bhanukunwari's heart. She came out from behind the veil and looking directly at *Munshiji*, said, "What are you saying? Did you take the village for me or for yourself? Did I give the money or not? The expenditure on its purchase, was it yours or mine? I don't understand what you are talking about."

Munshiji replied slowly, "You know that the village was bought in my name. The money was certainly yours, and I will return that. I paid for the other expenses. And I have kept an account of it all."

Bhanukunwari was trembling in anger and said, "You will certainly pay for this cheating. You cannot deprive my children so cruelly. I had no idea that you had a dagger hidden in your heart, otherwise, why would such a situation arise? Anyway, from now onwards, you will not touch any of the accounts. I will take whatever is mine. Please go and think in solitude. Nobody gets anything by committing sin. You must have thought that my sons are orphans, so you will be able to take all the wealth. Don't be under such an impression. I will get even the price of a single brick from selling your house."

Saying this, Bhanukunwari again went behind the veil and started crying. Women always cry after getting angry. Lala Sahib did not know what to say. He got up from there, went to the office and started turning the papers this side and that side, but Bhanukunwari followed him to the office and scolded him, "Don't touch any of my papers, otherwise it will not be good for you. You are a poisonous snake, and I don't want to see your face again."

Munshiji wanted to do some paperwork, but he was helpless. He threw the keys of the treasury, threw the account books, slammed the door shut behind him and left like the wind. He did try his hands in cheating but was not aware of the consequences of it.

The next day when the other servants heard of this, they were very happy. They were helpless in front of *Munshiji*. They went to Bhanukunwari and started aggravating her thoughts. Everyone agreed that *Munshi* had cheated Bhanukunwari. The salt of his master will burst out of his bones.

Preparations for a legal battle started from both sides. On one side was the body of justice, and on the other side was the soul of justice. Nature got the courage to fight against man.

Bhanukunwari asked Lala Chhakkanlal, "Who is our lawyer?"

Chhakkanlal looked here and there and then said, "The lawyer is Sethji. But Satyanarayan would have already approached him. We need a good lawyer for this case. Mehra Babu has a good reputation these days. He speaks at the speed of a motorcar. Lord! What more can I say? He has helped a lot of people escape from being hanged. No lawyer dares to open his mouth in front of him. If you say, should we hire him?"

Chhakkanlal's interest created doubt in her mind. Bhanukunwari thought for a while and said, "No. First, let us ask Sethji. After that, we will see. You go and call him."

Chhakkanlal cursed his luck and went to Sethji. Sethji had looked after all legal issues of Panditji for a long time. He heard the case and was silent. He considered Satyanarayan to be a good man. He felt sad at his downfall and came immediately. Bhanukunwari started crying and told him the whole story. She called her sons and said, "You save these orphans. I give them to you."

Sethji suggested a compromise. He said, "It is not good to fight against each other."

Bhanukunwari said, "It is good to fight against injustice."

Sethji said, "But our side is weak."

Bhanukunwari again came out from the veil and said in a surprised tone, "Is our side weak? The world knows that the village is mine. Who can take that from us? No. I can't compromise. You look at the papers. For the sake of my children, you take this pain. Your efforts will not go in vain. Satyanarayan's intentions were never wrong. Look, in the account statement where the village was bought, there is an expenditure of thirty thousand shown. If he has written it as a loan, then you would be able to notice if he had paid the interest for that amount. I would not compromise with such a cruel man."

Sethji understood that there was no use of explaining to her. He looked at the papers and started preparing for the legal battle.

IV

Munshi Satyanarayan returned home fuming. When his son asked for sweets, he hit him badly. He started shouting at his wife asking her why she had let the son come near him. He scolded his old mother and said, "Can't you even take care of a child? I slog the entire day and come home in the evening and then you want me to play with the children? Don't I have any other work in this world?" After spreading such unpleasantness in the house, he left. Later on, he started thinking, "I made a great mistake. What a fool I am! All the papers were with me for so long. I could have done whatever I wanted to do. But I did not. Today when things were revealed, it struck me. If I had wanted, I could have made fresh account books, in which there would be no mention of the village or its payment, but because of my foolishness, the money coming into the house was all gone. How could I know that the witch would behave with me like this and would not even let me touch the documents?"

An idea struck him and *Munshiji* suddenly jumped up. He thought, "Why not get the workers on my side?"

Although due to his harsh behavior in the past, the workers would not directly talk to him and are against him at this moment. But there was no one amongst them who would not fall for temptation. Tempting them with money is all that was needed, but from where would he get so much money?

"My misfortune! If I had known these two or four days back, there would have been no problem. Who knew that witch would hit me like this? Now there is only one way; somehow I would have to make the documents vanish. This needs to be done secretively, but it needs to be done urgently."

If for once you decide to bow down before bad thoughts, then there's no rising again. If you fall into the depths of sin once, then you only keep going down further. *Munshi* Satyanarayan, who was a thinker, was now only trying to retrieve the situation somehow.

Munshiji thought, "Is it easy? For this, how much cleverness, courage and intelligence are required! Who says that stealing is easy? If I get caught, then there was no other way but to die."

After a great deal of thought, he could not muster the courage to do it himself. He struck upon an easier idea, "Why not set the office on fire? A bottle of kerosene and a cloth is all that is required. I will get some hoodlum involved. But how do I know if the documents are kept in that room itself? The witch would have kept it with herself. No, the mistake of setting the office on fire would be shameful."

For a long time, *Munshiji* kept tossing and turning. He kept thinking of new methods; based on his own arguments he would keep discarding the thoughts. The state of his ideas was like the monsoon clouds that form and disperse when the wind blows.

But in this state of mental instability, there was one strong thought, somehow, the documents have to be obtained. The task was difficult, but if he had no courage, why did he set out for all this? Can a property worth thirty thousand rupees be considered worth peanuts? Whatever, it was not possible to gain it without becoming a thief. After all, even thieves are human beings. If he succeeds, then he would rule the world. And if he failed, then he would lose his life.

V

It was ten in the night. *Munshi* Satyanarayan put a bunch of keys below his waist and set out in the dark. Seeing a bundle of grass stacked at the door, he got frightened. It seemed to him as if somebody was sitting there. He stopped and carefully looked around. There was no one around. He mustered some courage and moved ahead.

Who am I afraid of at my own door? And who am I afraid of even in the street? I am going my way! Nobody can look at me with a suspicious eye. Yes, if I am caught stealing, then there is something to fear. And in that case, there should be a way out.

Suddenly he saw Bhanukunwari's guard coming his way. He got afraid. He leapt into a street by the side and stood there for a long time. When that guard left, he came back to the street. That guard was his servant until that day's morning. He thought, "I had abused him so many times. I had even kicked him. But today, I am afraid of him."

He again took refuge of logic. It was as if he had come drunk. Supposedly he saw, what can he do? Thousands of men walk on the street. I am one of them. Can he read my mind? Does he know what's going on in the mind? He would have given a salute looking at me and he would have talked to me, but I was so afraid that I did not even show my face. He explained this to myself and moved ahead. It is true that a mind caged in the web of sin is like the leaves of autumn that sheds at the slightest breeze.

Munshiji reached the market. Most of the shops were closed. Cows and pigs were sitting on the roads. Only the sweet shops were open and some vendors were selling jasmine flowers. All the sweet shop owners knew *Munshiji* and as they passed by them, he bowed his head. He changed his way of walking and moved fast. Suddenly he saw a chariot coming along his way. It was the chariot of the lawyer, Seth Ballabhdas. He had gone in it a thousand times with Sethji to the court but when he saw it today, it frightened him, like the vehicle of the God of Death. He went into an empty shop. Suddenly the pig got up thinking that he had come to evict it. By then the chariot had passed and *Munshiji* was relieved. This time, he did not take the help of his logic. He realized that it was no use to pretend, and it was good that the lawyer had not seen him. He can read minds and would have read my intentions from my face.

Some learned men say that the natural instincts of a man lean towards sin, but it is just a hypothesis and not a fact borne out of the experience. The experienced truth is that man is always afraid of sin and we can directly perceive how man hates sin.

After walking for a while, *Munshiji* found a street. This was one of the routes to Bhanukunwari's house. The street was lit by a dim lantern. As expected by *Munshiji*, there was no sign of the guard. In the stable, the lower caste people had organized a dance session. Women were dancing, beautifully dressed and adorned in jewels. The men were playing the drums and singing:

> 'Nahi ghare shyam, gheri aaye badra.
> Sovat rehun sapan ek dikhaoon rama.
> Khuli gayee neend, dhharak gaye gajra.
> Nahi ghare shyam, gheri gaye badra.'

Both the guards were watching this. *Munshiji* quietly went to the lantern and just like a cat pouncing upon the rat, he leapt up and blew it off. One step was over, without much difficulty. He got some courage. He reached the verandah of the office and listened. There was silence all around. Only the sound of the lower caste people could be heard. At *Munshiji's* heart was pounding; his head was tense, his limbs were trembling and he was breathing heavily. Every part of his body was alert. All his manliness, agility, courage and intelligence were at its peak.

91

The same old lock was on the office door. He had brought its keys after a thorough search of the market. The lock opened, the doors protested with a weak noise. Nobody heard anything. *Munshiji* entered the office. A lamp was burning inside. Seeing *Munshiji*, it moved a bit, as if it was stopping him from entering.

Munshiji's legs were trembling. His heels were raised. The weight of sin was heavy.

Munshiji started turning the files. Where was the time to go through them in detail? He collected all the files into a bundle, kept it on his head and moved out quickly. Carrying that bundle of sin, he vanished through the street. Through the bad, smelling and dark alleys, he was running barefooted carrying the bundle of selfishness and falsehood. It was as if a sinful soul was moving along the streets of hell.

After running some distance, he reached the banks of the river Ganges. The stars' reflected on the river just like the dim shimmering of the light of religion in the most sinful of hearts. On the bank of the river, a few *Sadhus* were lying. *Munshiji* threw the bundle into the river forcefully. This created a commotion in the sleeping waves and then there was silence once again.

VI

There were two women in *Munshi* Satyanarayan's house, his mother and his wife. Both were illiterate. Hence, there was no need for *Munshiji* to drown in the Ganges or to run away somewhere! Neither did they wear any inner garments, nor socks, and nor could sing on the harmonium. They did not even know how to apply soap. Hairpin, jacket and such things were unheard by them. The wife had no self-respect and the mother had no sense of respect. The wife listened to the taunts of the mother-in-law. The mother-in-law hated bathing or cleaning the house. The daughter-in-law was just like a doll made of clay. If she needed some money, she would ask the mother-in-law.

Both the women were unaware of their rights and were living like domestic animals. They would not buy any food from the market. They would make the *rotis* themselves. If they had eaten the sweets from the shop of Agra, they would have known what taste was all about. The old woman knew about some old herbal medicines and would keep cutting grass or weeds for the medicines.

Munshiji went to his mother and said, "*Amma*[3]! What will happen now? Bhanukunwari has shown the door to me."

Mother got frightened and said, "Shown the door?"

Munshi replied, "Yes. And I am innocent."

Mother asked, "What happened? Bhanukunwari was not like that."

Munshi said, "There was no issue. The village that I had bought in my name was taken away from me. Yesterday, there was an argument between the two of us. I told her that the village is mine. I have bought it in my name, and you have no rights over it. When I said this, she got agitated and kept saying whatever came to her mouth. She dismissed me right there and threatened me, 'I will fight with you and get that village back.' They will file a case against me. The village is mine and I have rights over it. Not one, let them file a thousand cases, but the decree will be mine."

Mother looked at the daughter-in-law and said, "But you had bought this village with their money and for them."

Munshi said, "That was then. Now I can't leave that village. It gives such good returns. She can't do anything to me. She can't take that money back from me. She has one hundred and fifty villages. Yet she is not satisfied."

Mother said, "Son, if somebody has more wealth, would he throw it away? You have changed your integrity, and that is not a good thing. What would the world say? And whether the world says anything or not, it is for you to understand that you should not cheat somebody whom you have served for all these years. What did Narayan not give you? You have enough to eat, wear, there is enough money, and you

---

3. *Amma*: One's mother.

have children, what more do you want? Listen to me, and don't let this blot of sin remain on you. Don't take this village. Goodness is only in one's own toil. Anything that you take by unfair means shall be wasted away."

Munshi replied, "I have heard many such things. If the world ran on these thoughts, then nothing could be done. I have served them for a long time, and it is because of my work that they were able to add four to five villages to their wealth. Till the time Panditji was alive, there was respect for my integrity. I did not have to cheat him since he gave me enough on his own. It has been eight years since he passed away, and I swear, I never got anything since then. Don't they know that this man, who is working with so much honesty, also deserves to get something? Don't say it in that way, give it as a gift, give it anyway, but she thought that she has bought me on this twenty rupees salary. I waited for eight years. Now should I continue slogging for the same twenty rupees and leave my children at the mercy of somebody else? I have got a chance now, so why should I leave it? Why should I die with the unfulfilled dream of being a landlord? Till the time I live, I will eat myself and after me, my children will enjoy."

There were tears in the mother's eyes. She said, "Son, I have never heard such things from you ever before. What has happened to you? You have children. Don't play with fire."

The daughter-in-law looked at the mother and said, "We don't need such money. We are happy with our normal food."

Munshi replied, "All right, then you have that food. I wish to eat better."

Mother said, "I won't be able to see all this. I would drown in the Ganges and die."

Wife intruded and said, "If you want to sow all these thorns, then send me to my house. I will take the children with me."

Munshi got irritated and said, "Your intelligence has gone to the dogs. Lakhs of government servants take bribes and kill each other in this way. Neither does anything happen to their children nor do they die of the plague. Why does sin not eat them away, and will eat only me? I have always seen truthful people in pain. I will enjoy the fruits of whatever I have done. You do what you want."

In the morning, when the office opened, all the documents were gone. *Munshi* Chhakkanlal went to the house confused and angry and asked the mistress, "Did you take all the documents?"

Bhanukunwari replied, "How do I know? It must be where you had kept them."

There was commotion in the house. Guards were beaten up. Bhanukunwari suddenly suspected *Munshi* Satyanarayan, but in her understanding, the task was not possible without the support of Chhakkanlal. A report was given to the police. A priest was called in to find the name of the thief. Maulvi Sahib threw the dice. He said that it was the work of some old enemy. He also said that someone from the house had betrayed them. This continued till night. Then there were discussions as to how the case could be fought without the documents. Their side was weak at the beginning itself. Whatever strength there was in it, was due to the documents. Now that evidence was also gone. There was no strength in the case at all; but Bhanukunwari said, "We will not lose. If somebody snatches our thing, it is our duty to fight. The one who sits idle is a coward". Sethji got the news of this calamity, and he also said that there was no strength in the case now. There were only assumptions and logic. If the court agrees, then it was fine, or else one would have to accept defeat. But Bhanukunwari did not agree. Two brilliant barristers were called in from Lucknow and Allahabad. The hearing of the case started.

Thousands of people gathered to watch the hearing. The main reason for so much interest among people was that Bhanukunwari watched the proceedings from behind a veil. That was because she did not have any faith in her servants now.

The prosecution barrister gave an emotional speech. He painted the picture of the past of Satyanarayan. He showed how loyal, efficient and hardworking he was; and it was natural for the late

Pandit Bhrigudutt to have complete trust in him. He then proved that Satyanarayan's financial status was never such that he could have collected so much money. Then, in the end, he talked about *Munshiji's* selfishness, cunningness, cruelty and breach of trust in a manner that everybody present started abusing *Munshiji*. Thereafter, he painted a sympathetic picture of Panditji's two young children. How pathetic it was that such an honest man did not hesitate to put a dagger through the neck of the young fatherless children of his erstwhile master. Due to this, all the glory of his past actions faded into oblivion. Because they were not pure pearls but artificial glass pieces which were shown only to gain the trust of his master. It was a beautiful nest, to trap a gullible and good master. If we had the documents with us today, then *Munshiji's* truth would have been readily evident; but the fact was that the documents vanished immediately after *Munshiji* was dismissed. It is all right to forgive your enemy once, but this man had done cruelty to children for whom anybody would have shown kindness. Many rich men of the city were the witnesses, but all hearsay things were not of much value.

The case hearing continued on the second day.

The defense lawyer started his defense. In his speech, there was more humor and sarcasm than seriousness, "It is an assumption that whatever the servant of a rich man buys is a result of using the money of the master. By this principle, the government should confiscate all the property of government employees. We have no problem in accepting that we could not have collected so much money and that we took the money as a loan from the master. But instead of asking for the money, we are being asked for the property itself. If the documents of loan are shown, it will become absolutely clear that the loan has been completely repaid. My friend has rightly said that the documents being absent at this time is in itself a proof. I also support his argument. If I take a loan and get married, will you ask for my new bride as repayment?"

"My able friend has accused us of doing injustice to two orphan children. If the intentions of Satyanarayan were bad, then the best opportunity for him was when Pandit Bhrigudutt had died. Why would he delay it so much? If you trap a lion and then do not catch its children immediately and instead allow them to grow up, then I do not consider the person to be a wise man. The truth is that whatever Satyanarayan had owed to the family has already been repaid by him on account of having served them for so long. For eight years, he served Panditji's children with all his devotion. The reward he is getting for his simplicity is too heart rendering and sad. In this, there is no fault of Bhanukunwari. She is a nice lady, but she has the inherent qualities of her caste. An honest man is by nature clear and straight in his speech; he does not need to add spices to his talk. That is why *Munshiji* is being defamed. That is the root cause of this case, and nothing else. Bhanukunwari is present here. Can she say whether there was any discussion of this village during the last eight years? Were its profit, loss or anything related to it ever asked or discussed? Assume that I am a government servant. If I come to the office and start talking about the business of my wife and my friends, I might end up losing my job, and possibly spend some time at Bareilly's guesthouse. Why should there be any discussion about a village over which Bhanukunwari had no rights?"

After this, a lot of witnesses were presented, and most of them were landlords of the nearby villages. They gave statements that they had seen Satyanarayan usurping money by giving receipts to the village laborers.

By then it was dusk. The court decided to give its decision within a week.

VII

Satyanarayan had no doubts about his victory. The prosecution witnesses were broken and there was no evidence at all. Now, he would be counted amongst the landlords and would also be called rich, in a few days. But due to some reason, he was hesitant in seeing eye-to-eye with the eminent people of the town. Seeing them, his head bowed down. He was afraid that they would ask him something about the case. He went to the market and the shopkeepers would talk to each other in hushed tones and people would look at him in a strange way. Till then, people considered him to be a wise and good man and the rich men looked at him with respect. Though *Munshiji* had not heard anything against himself, he felt that the truth was not hidden from anybody. He might win in the court, but his standing had gone down. Now people would consider him as selfish, corrupt and a cheat. Even the people in his own house started looking at him with disrespect. His old mother had not drunk a drop of water for three days. His wife begged him to have mercy on his sons, "The result of a bad deed is never good. Give me poison first."

The day when the decision of the court was to be announced, a vegetable seller woman came with some vegetables at the door of *Munshiji's* house and called out to his wife, "Daughter-in-law! We heard something in the market. If you don't mind, shall I tell you? Whomsoever I meet says that *Munshiji* has cheated Panditji's wife and snatched something. I don't believe it. If Lala Babu had not managed things, then Panditji's wife would have been left with nothing. Not even a piece of land would have been left. He was the only one who managed everything. Then why will he cheat her? Has anybody brought anything with him that he would take to the other world? The result of bad things will be bad only. Man may not see it, but God sees everything."

His wife felt very bad. She wished the earth to split open, and let her be consumed by it. Women are shy by nature. They have more self-respect. They can't bear curses and a bad reputation. She bowed her head and said, "How would I know these things? I have heard it from you today. What vegetables do you have?"

Munshi Satyanarayan was listening to this conversation from his room. After she had left, he came and asked his wife, "What was that witch saying?"

His wife turned away from him and looking at the ground, said, "Did you not hear that? She was praising you. Look behind you and you will realize how many people say such things and how many I have to avoid meeting."

Munshiji returned to his room. He did not reply to his wife. His soul was filled with shame. The man who was always respected, who always walked with self-respect, who was discussed with awe by everybody, he would not be shameless for eternity. *Munshiji*, in his hysteria, had thought that he would manage to do all this without anybody knowing about his bad deeds, but his wish was not fulfilled. There were many problems. To remove them, he had to do a lot of things. But even those things were to be done to save him from shame so that people wouldn't say that he had cheated his mistress. Even after trying so hard, he could not save himself from shame. The shame that came with these bad wishes could not be borne. *Munshiji* started thinking, he will get the money and all the pleasures, but he would not be able to save himself from shame. The decision of the court would not save him from shame. What is the result of prosperity? Fame and respect. If I lose them, what will I do with prosperity? After losing the strength of the heart, suffering shame from the world, after becoming a shameful man in the eyes of the society and after sowing the seeds of disharmony in his own house, what use would that wealth be to him? And if there really was a power of justice and if it punishes him, then he will have no other option but to be defamed in front of the whole world. If a truthful man faces problems, then the world sympathizes with him. But calamities that befall a bad man becomes the source of sarcasm for the whole world. In that state, God is called unjust; but the bad fate of cruel men actually signifies the justice of God. Oh, God! Please save me! Why don't I go and fall at Bhanukunwari's feet and request her to withdraw the case? Sad! Why did this idea not strike me before? If I had gone to her by yesterday, then it would have been all right. But what can be done now? Today, the decision would be announced.

Munshiji kept thinking about this for a long time, but could not decide what he should do.

Bhanukunwari was convinced that the village was gone now. The poor lady was left clenching her fist. She could not sleep the whole night, and was angry at Satyanarayan, "Oh sinner! You are taking my property worth fifty thousand rupees in front of everybody and I am not able to do anything. The people who are in charge of justice these days are blind. They cannot see the thing that the whole world can. They only see through other's eyes. They are slaves of evidence. Justice is that, which proves the truth; not that they get cheated by the evidence themselves, and get trapped in the web of cheats. That is why these cheats and bad souls have gained courage. Anyway, let the village go if that happens; but Satyanarayan, you won't be able to show your face anywhere in town now."

This thought calmed Bhanukunwari a bit. Human nature is such that they get more pleasure by the losses of their enemies than by their own gains. You have taken one village of mine, and God willing, you will never be happy with that. You will burn in hell yourself, and there will be nobody to light even a lamp in your house.

The day of the decision arrived. There was a huge crowd of people along with the lawyers and court workers. At the correct time, the judge arrived. There was silence in the courtroom. The people moved ahead in anticipation.

The judge announced, "The case is dismissed. Both sides to bear their expenses themselves."

Although the decision was as per the expectations, there was a commotion among the people when the judge announced it. With a sad expression, the people slowly came out discussing the case.

Suddenly Bhanukunwari came out from behind the veil and stood in the witness box. The people who had gone out started coming back inside and watched Bhanukunwari with interest and amusement.

Bhanukunwari said in a trembling voice to the judge, "Lord! If you give me permission, I want to talk to Satyanarayan."

Although this was against the law, the judge gave his permission.

Then Bhanukunwari looked at Satyanarayan and said, "Lalaji, the judge has announced the decree. Congratulations for the village. But integrity is everything to a man. Tell me honestly, whose village is it?"

Thousands of people, on hearing this, started looking at Satyanarayan with great amusement. *Munshiji* was lost in his thoughts. In his heart, there was a battle raging between promise and alternative. Thousands of people were looking at him. The truth would not be hidden from anybody now. He could not lie in front of so many people. With shame, he closed his lips. He only had to say 'mine'. That was nothing, but society gives the punishment for the most heinous crimes, and he was afraid of receiving that. By saying 'Yours', things would have gone bad. The case that was won would be lost. But the reward for the most righteous thing could be expected. Hope won over fear. He felt that God had given him a chance to redeem himself. I can still become a man of respect. I can still save my soul. He came forward, bowed before Bhanukunwari and said, "Yours!"

Thousands of people said, "The victory of truth!"

The judge stood up and said, "This is not the justice of law; it is God's justice."

Don't think this to be a story; it is based on a true incident. Bhanukunwari and Satyanarayan are still alive today. The people were stunned by the moral courage of *Munshiji*.

The victory of Godly justice over human justice was the talk of the town for many months. Bhanukunwari went to *Munshiji* and brought him back. She handed over the entire business to him and after a few days, wrote off that village in his name. *Munshiji* did not think it right to keep it and offered it to God. Now the profit out of the village is used to help the desolate people and students.

Shroud

I

A father and son were sitting outside the hut in front of a diminishing bonfire. Inside the house, the son's young wife was crying due to labor pain. Her soul-rendering cries were so intense that the two of them would startle hearing it. It was a wintry night and nature was drowned in silence while deep darkness had engulfed the whole village.

Ghisu said, "I think she won't be able to survive. The whole day has passed. You should go in and check her condition."

Madhav replied irritatingly, "If she has to die, then it should happen soon. What will I do by seeing her?"

"You are a heartless man. Up until now, you have been living peacefully with her and now you would betray her?"

"I cannot bear to look at her suffering."

They belonged to the lower caste and were the most infamous people in the village. Ghisu worked for one day and then rested for three days, while Madhav was so lazy that if he worked for half an hour, then he would spend an hour smoking the *chillum*. This was the reason why they never got any work. Even if there was little food left in the house, they would still think that there is no need to work. When there was no food left, they remained hungry for days. Ghisu would cut some wood and Madhav would sell it in the market. Until the time the money lasted, both of them wandered around and enjoyed. It was a village of farmers, there was a lot of work there for any hard-working man. But Ghisu and Madhav were only called when there was no one else available and the people were left with no other option and had to remain content by getting the work of one person by making the payment of two. They led a very extraordinary life. There was nothing in their house except for some earthen pots. They wore torn clothes to cover up their body. Free from the troubles of the world, they were deep into debts. They were abused and flogged but they never bothered about it. They were extremely poor and even without any hope of return, people still lent them money. They would steal potatoes and peas from other people's fields, roast them in the fire, and eat them. Otherwise, they would uproot some sugarcane from someone's field and pass the night sucking it. Ghisu had spent sixty years of his life in this way, and now Madhav, like an ideal son, was following his father's footsteps. Ghisu's wife had died a long time back. Madhav had got married last year. Ever since his wife had come, she had laid down the foundation of the organization in this family and used to fill their house. Ever since her arrival, the two of them had grown even more inactive. They even developed arrogance. If someone called them for work, they would demand double the amount of wages.

Ghisu said while peeling the potatoes, "Go and check on her at least once! I think she is haunted. Even the *Ojha*[1] asks for a rupee as his fees."

Madhav was afraid that if he went to check on his wife's condition, his father would finish off more than his share of the potatoes. He said, "I am afraid of going inside."

"What are you afraid of? I am here."

"Then why don't you go and see her?"

"When my wife died, I had not moved from her side for three days. And won't she feel ashamed of seeing me? I have never even seen her face. Should I see her like that? She will not be in her senses to cover her properly. It would be uncomfortable if I go inside."

"What if a child is born? There are no provisions in the house."

"Everything will fall into place. Let the child come first. The people, who would not lend us any money now, will call us and give us the money. I had nine children and we never had anything in the house, but God provided for all of them."

Ghisu lived in a society where being hardworking was not always beneficial. In his village, farmers worked hard all their life but were

---

1. *Ojha*: A village doctor who removes evil spirits.

less well off than other people who took advantage of their miseries. Rather, we may say that Ghisu was much wiser than the farmers were. He was not a part of the stupid hard-working farmers but belonged to the category of the parasites that lived off them. But he was not disciplined enough to follow the rules and regulations of the idlers. Therefore, the other people in this category were landlords while he was detested by the whole village. But he was still satisfied that even though he lived in poverty, at least he did not have to work like the farmers and no one could take advantage of his simplicity.

Both of them started eating the hot roasted potatoes. They had not eaten anything since yesterday and had no patience to let them cool. Thus, in the process, they burnt their mouths. After unpeeling the outer covering of the potato, it burnt the tongue and the palate and it was better to swallow it down rather than keeping that ember in the mouth. The stomach had many things to cool the potatoes, and therefore, both of them swallowed it at full speed although their eyes were watered due to this process.

At that moment, Ghisu was reminded of his landlord's marriage that he had attended twenty years ago. The satisfaction that he felt after the feast was something to remember for a lifetime. The memory was still fresh in his mind. He said, "I will never forget that feast! Since then I did not eat such delicious food and that too without any restrictions on the quantity. The bride's family had provided *puris*[2] fried in *desi ghee* for everyone. There were curd, *chutney*[3], three kinds of dry vegetable dishes, one curry vegetable dish and many sweets. It is just not possible to describe the delicious taste of the food and it was available in abundance. Everyone ate to their hearts' content. People ate so much that no one was even able to drink a drop of water. But those who were serving put down fresh *kachoris*[4] in our plates. We said that we have had enough and we do not need anything else

---

2. *Puris*: A small, round piece of bread made of unleavened wheat flour, deep-fried and served with meat or vegetables.

3. *Chutney*: A spicy condiment of Indian origin, made of fruits or vegetables with vinegar, spices, and sugar.

4. *Kachoris*: (in Indian cooking) a puri stuffed with spiced lentils, potatoes or beans.

but they forcefully fed us. And when everyone washed off their hands and rinsed their mouths after eating, then they served us the mouth fresheners. But I was just not in my senses to have a *paan*[5]. It was so difficult to stand that I went to my bed and rolled into my blanket. The landlord was a large-hearted man!"

Madhav enjoyed all these delicacies in his imagination and said, "Nowadays no one gives such feasts."

"Who will give such a feast now? Mine was a different era altogether. Now everyone wants to save money. Do not spend in marriages, do not spend in funerals. Where will they store all this money that belongs to the poor? They want to earn and collect the money but do not wish to spend it."

"You must have eaten at least twenty *puris*?"

"No, I had eaten more than twenty."

"Had I been there, I would have eaten fifty."

"I would not have eaten less than fifty. I was a young and strong man. You are not even half of what I was back then."

They finished the potatoes, drank some water and fell asleep in front of the fire covering their bodies with their *dhotis*[6] as if two large pythons were sleeping together.

Madhav's wife was still crying out of pain.

II

In the morning when Madhav went inside the hut, he found that his wife had turned cold. Mosquitoes were buzzing over her face. Her stony eyes were looking at the roof and her whole body was covered in dust. The child had died in her womb.

Madhav ran out to his father. And then both of them started beating their chests and cried loudly. When the neighbors heard their

---

5. *Paan*: Betel leaves prepared and used as a stimulant.
6. *Dhotis*: A garment worn by male Hindus, consisting of a piece of material tied around the waist and extending to cover most of the legs.

wailing they came running towards them and started consoling these unfortunate men.

But there was no time to cry. A shroud and wood were to be arranged for the cremation. There was no sign of money in the house just as there is no trace of meat in the nest of the eagle.

Both father and son went to the landlord for help. He despised both of them. He had beaten them up on several occasions, sometimes for stealing and sometimes for not coming to work on time. He asked them, "Hey Ghisua! Why are you crying? I don't even see you these days. I think that you do not want to live in this village anymore."

Ghisu touched his head to the ground and said with teary eyes, "My lord! We are in great difficulty. Madhav's wife died last night. She was in pain all night! We both sat by her side and did everything to save her but she did not survive. We have no one to look after us, master. We are ruined. I am your servant, only you can help me now! All the money was spent on her treatment. Now only you can help us with her cremation."

The landlord was a kind man but taking pity on Ghisu was similar to trying to color a black cloth. He wanted to throw him out of the house. Ghisu never came even after calling him so many times, and now when he is in need, he came to beg for help. But this was not the time for anger or punishment. He gave him two rupees but not even a single word of consolation escaped his mouth. He did not even look at Ghisu out of sheer disgust.

When the landlord had given two rupees then how could the trader and moneylender dare to refuse him? Ghisu knew how to extract money in the situation. Some gave two *annas* while some gave four *annas* and within an hour, Ghisu had collected a handsome amount of five rupees. From somewhere they got the grains and from somewhere the wood for cremation. In the afternoon, Ghisu and Madhav went to the market to buy the shroud. And here people started cutting the bamboo to prepare the funeral pyre.

The tender-hearted women of the village came, saw the body, and cried at its wretched condition.

III

On reaching the market, Ghisu said to Madhav, "We have collected sufficient wood for her cremation."

Madhav replied, "Yes, we have sufficient wood. Now we need the shroud."

"Let's buy cheap material."

"Yes, you are right! By the time we go for cremation, it will be night. Who will see the shroud then?"

"It is such an odd ritual, someone who did not get a good cloth to wear all her life needs a new shroud on death."

"The shroud will burn with the body."

"Absolutely right! If we had these five rupees earlier, we could have used it for her medication."

Both were trying to understand each other's feelings. They kept wandering in the market. They looked at all kinds of clothes, silken and cotton but did not like anything. It was already evening when both of them reached a liquor shop. They went inside and kept standing there for a while in a dilemma. Then Ghisu went to the shopkeeper and said,

"Sir, give me a bottle of liquor."

Then they ordered some snacks and fried fish and sat down to drink. Soon they were intoxicated.

Ghisu said, "We would have gained nothing by buying the shroud. It would have burned with her and turned to ashes in the end."

Madhav looked at the sky as if he was making the Gods a witness of his innocence and said, "It is the way of the world. Otherwise, why would people give thousands of rupees to the Brahmins? Who knows what happens in the next world?"

"The rich have money. Let them waste it. We have nothing to waste."

"But what shall you say to other people? Won't they ask for the shroud?"

Ghisu laughed, "We will say that we lost the money. We tried to search for it but could not find it. They won't believe us but still, they will give us the money again."

Madhav laughed at their unexpected luck and said, "She was a very good woman. She died but still made sure to feed us even after death."

More than half of the bottle was now empty. Ghisu ordered for some *puris*, *chutney*, pickle and meat. The shop was just opposite the liquor shop. Madhav brought all the food items in two plates. One-and-a half-rupees were spent and only some money was left with them.

Right now, they were eating the *puris* majestically, the way a lion eats his prey in the jungle - without any fear of answerability and without any worries of defamation. They were used to and had won over these emotions way before.

Ghisu said philosophically, "When our soul is pleased, then won't it bless her?"

Madhav bowed his head with respect and said, "It will definitely give her blessings. Oh God! You can hear all our prayers. Please take her to heaven. Both us are blessing her with our hearts. We had never eaten anything like the food that we ate today."

After a while, a question arose in Madhav's mind. He said, "Father, we will also go there someday?"

Ghisu did not respond to this innocent question. He did not want to think about death and spoil the happiness that he was enjoying.

"If she asks us why did we not give her a shroud, what will we say to her?"

"We will not reply."

"She will definitely ask."

"How do you know that she won't get any shroud? Do you take me for a fool? You think that I do not have any sense. She will get a shroud and for that matter, a good one."

Madhav did not believe him. He said, "Who will give her the shroud? You have spent all the money. She will question me. I was the one who married her."

Ghisu got angry and said, "I am telling you that she will get a shroud, why don't you believe me?"

"Then you only tell me who will give her the shroud?"

"Those people who gave us the money this time will give. But yes, we won't get the money now."

As the evening progressed into night, the liquor shop got more and more lively. Someone sang, someone bragged and some people hugged their companions. Others made their friends drink some more.

The environment was full of intoxication and unimaginable beauty. Just one drink intoxicated many of them as if the intoxication of air was ruling over them. Life's miseries pulled them to this place, where, for some time, they could forget all their troubles.

Both father and son were still happily enjoying their drink. All the people were looking at them with envy. They are so lucky that they were sharing a full bottle of liquor.

After eating to his heart's content, Madhav gave away the remaining food to a beggar who was looking at him with hungry eyes. And for the first time in his life, he experienced the joy of giving.

Ghisu said, "Take it and bless the giver. It is the earning of his wife, who is dead, but your blessings will reach her. Bless her with all your being."

Madhav again looked towards the sky and said, "She will go to heaven father, she will be their queen."

Ghisu stood up and said cheerfully, "Yes son, she will go to heaven. She never tortured anyone, never dominated anyone. Even in her death, she fulfilled our greatest desire. She will definitely go to heaven. Not these people who deprive the poor and fill their vaults with money; they torture the poor and then go to the temple to hide their sins."

Intoxication leads to sudden mood swings and thus, the mood of gratitude soon changed to sadness and depression.

Madhav said, "But father, she had to bear a lot of sorrow in her life."

He suddenly covered his face and started wailing.

Ghisu pacified him, "Why are you crying, son? Be happy for her as she has left this materialistic world and finally attained salvation. She was very lucky to leave this wretched world quickly."

And then both of them started singing:

"Procuress! Why are you looking at me with your shining eyes? Procuress!"

All the drunkards were looking at them while they were still engrossed in their singing. Then both of them started dancing. They jumped, danced, made faces, and acted and then finally they fell unconscious.

The Flirtatious Editor

I

Following the death of his beloved wife, Pandit Chokhelal Sharma, the editor of Navras, had developed a particular devotion towards the ladies. His romantic inclinations and artistic passions had also become sharper. Well-written pieces from men were discarded; but submissions by the women, irrespective of their quality, were immediately accepted. Along with the acceptance letter, women often got went a personal note from the editor, praising the piece with profuse admirations such as: "Reading your story moved me deeply", "My own past floated in front of my eyes", "The profundity of your emotions is like a lustrous pearl in the ocean of writing, and its glow will never die." And their poems! One is a whirlpool that had caught his heart, while another is a melody from a universal flute, the sweet suffering of the infinite, the silent song of a still night. An ardent desire for a meeting often accompanied these passionate compliments: "If you should ever happen to come this way, don't forget to meet me. I would think myself fortunate to be able to meet face to face the person who is the creator of such poems."

The writers who received such passionate encouragement were overjoyed. Their pieces, like wretched beggars, had knocked the doors of many but had been turned down by dozens of journals and magazines with their hopes dashed. But how well they were received here. For the first time, there was an editor who could recognize their true talent. They would perceive all other editors to be egoists and criticized them for believing as if they own all authority of the world. Getting a small editorship somewhere seems to be like being granted a kingdom. If ever these people got into bureaucracy, it would be a reign of terror! Thank God, the government doesn't pay any attention to their opinions. It's a good thing that they passed the ordinance. Go on, you editors, go on hating women the way you do! That's why they're punishing you. Now Sharmaji is also an editor, not an idler, the editor of a world-famous magazine, Navras, which held sway over all magazines.

Subscriptions for Chokhelalji's magazine shot up. Everyday a deluge of gratitude notes filled the editor's mailbox. Women writers revered him. They began to write personal letters to him, with news of family weddings, engagements, births and deaths. Some desired him to pray for them, some needed a few words of consolation, and others craved his advice on some domestic situation. And every month five to ten women came to meet him in person. When Sharmaji found out about their arrival, he would personally welcome them, put them up for a day or two with great enthusiasm and showered them with royal treatment. He got free passes, so he could take them to the theatre. By the time they left, the women were completely charmed. It is rumored that he had developed an intimate friendship with several women writers, but this cannot be spoken with certainty. All we are sure of is that the women who came to meet Sharmaji were highly devoted to him. He seemed like a lonely monk in the cottage of literature. He has managed to keep the hopelessness of his widower's life secrets deep inside; his agony silent, hidden, as he drinks at the sweet fountain of love. Some women had made it their religion to fill the void in their dear editor's life. If a hungry man can be given a little honey from their cupboard, then it is they who are blessed. Some women parceled him jars of pickles, someone *laddus*[1]; another knits him a woolen prayer-mat with her own hands. One woman came regularly every month to sew his torn buttons for him; others brought him delicacies cooked at home, two or three times a month. Now he belonged not to one woman, but to everyone. It would be hard to find a fiercer advocate for women's rights other than him. Men were always quick to criticize him. He got sympathy and respect from women alone.

---

1. *Laddus:* An Indian sweet made from a mixture of flour, sugar, and shortening, which is shaped into a ball.

One day the editor received a poem fired with a woman's intense, explicit passion. Perhaps other editors would have found the poem indecent, but Chokhelal had become extremely liberal in his views. It was written in beautiful handwriting. The woman's pen name was enchanting. He formed an immediate mental picture of her. Slight by build, eyes that would plead him, red lips, skin of gold, hands quick to gesture, all enhanced by a sensitive nature; a woman dry and firm at first glance, like a sweet or toffee, yet quick to melt and cling. He read her poem several times, and every time a thrill ran through him:

Do you think you'll leave me and go?

Can you go?

I'll lay my arm around your neck

I'll tighten my noose around you

I'll rest my hand on your thigh

And lay my head there.

Do you think you can leave me and go?

Can you leave?

I'll bring myself to your lips

You'll drink the nectar in that cup

And dissolve yourself in it.

Sated, you'll lay your head in my lap.

Do you think you'll leave me and go?

'Kamakshi'

With every reading, Sharmaji found a new strain of delight in the poem. He laid it on his desk and immediately turned to his typewriter and pounded out a letter to Ms. Kamakshi.

"I can't describe how I felt when I read your poem. Such a thirst has entered my mind that it turns me into an arid desert. I don't know how to quench my thirst. The only hope I have is that I will find the nectar to satisfy me from the same place that gave me the thirst. Like a fettered animal, my mind wants to rip off its shackles and run. I can see the soul that gave birth to the emotions in the poem: such a bottomless reserve of love, a love that finds joy in surrendering itself. I'm not flattering you when I say that I haven't read a poem like this in years, it has raised a tornado in me that has twisted the roof off my peaceful widower's life. You've set fire to the thatched hut of my soul, and I cannot believe that it can be only a moment's pleasure on your part. Behind your words, I can see a heart that has known the red-hot anguish of love, been fired in the oven of desire. I would be thrilled to meet you in person. My humble cottage, with its gift of love, waits to welcome you."

"With love," etc.

A reply arrived on the third day. Kamakshi had expressed her gratitude in very thoughtful terms and provided the date and time of her arrival.

II

Today Kamakshi would make her auspicious appearance.

Sharmaji woke up early and shaved, bathed with soap and besan, picked out a *dhoti* of fine *khadi*[2], put on a loose, frilled *kurta* of the finest silk, and carried a cream silk shawl. He walked into his office with such an air of splendor that all the workers were taken aback. He had asked them to make sure the office was cleaned thoroughly. New flowerpots graced the hallway; fresh bouquets had been arranged on the table. Her train arrived at nine, it was eight-thirty and she would arrive at the office by nine-thirty. He could not concentrate on his work. Repeatedly, he looked at the clock on the wall, and then picked up a small mirror from his desk drawer. Then he returned to pacing up and down the room. He had noticed a few strands of grey in his moustache, but he did not have scissors to remove them. No matter. It'll contribute to his image. When love is accompanied by reverence, it becomes a beloved visitor bearing a gift. For young men, love is an expensive business, but for greater souls or those who've approached greatness, love brings with it many things of value. Younger men have

---

2. *Khadi:* An Indian homespun cotton cloth.

to buy costly presents to make an impression, but the great or semi-great need only to grant their blessings.

Exactly at nine-thirty, an attendant comes in with a card. It said: "Kamakshi."

Sharmaji asked him to show the lady in and turned again to glance into the mirror. Then he picked out a thick file from a shelf and opened it. He was engrossed in the study when the woman stepped in through the door. Sharmaji seemed completely unaware of her presence.

The woman approached his desk slowly, and suddenly Sharmaji, surprised, lifted his head as if she has jerked him out of meditation. He stood up to welcome her, but this is not her, this cannot be the woman he had imagined!

A fat, swarthy, middle-aged woman, unsteady on her feet, stared back at him as if she would gulp him down, swallow him whole. Sharmaji's enthusiasm and his passion froze in an instant. The drops of honey that he had gathered in his heart froze into shards of stabbing glass. For a moment, he couldn't speak, he couldn't hear. Then he blurted out, "An editor's life is an animal's life! There is no time even to lift one's head from work. On top of that, I have overworked myself into terrible shape. I have a blinding headache since last night. How can I help you?"

Kamakshi had a large folder in her hands. She kept it on the desk and wiped her face with a handkerchief. Then she said in a soft voice, "That's terrible. I was going to visit a friend of mine, and I thought I would stop to meet you, but if you're unwell, I'd be happy to stay a few days and maybe lighten your load a little. I can help you with your editorial work. Your health is of vital importance to all women everywhere! I can't leave you in this state."

Sharmaji felt that the blood had frozen in his veins, his pulse faltered. He thought, "If this witch stayed here, his life would be hell. She thinks that she is a poet and this kind of poetry! Heights of indecency! It is indecent. Immoral. Completely putrid with filth. From a younger, prettier woman, the poem would have been an arrow of love. From this witch, it is waste from a sewage pipe. Where does she get the right to write poems like that? Why does she write these poems? Why isn't she sitting in a corner somewhere singing *bhajans*[3] to Lord Ram? And she says, 'How can I leave you and go?' To which I say, why the hell would anyone want to be with you? He'd see you coming from afar and hide somewhere. And the poetry, there's no head or tail to it, it's completely formless, no sense of rhythm, nothing! And she thinks it is poetry! If poetry could come out of a body like hers, donkeys would sing! Camels would dance! The old hag doesn't even know that to write poetry you need youth, beauty, a certain delicacy and a refined sensibility. The woman looks like a she-devil! If someone met her in a dark alley, they'd be scared witless; and she writes passionate poems. No matter how hungry someone is, will he eat dung? And the witch has brought along a huge sheaf of more matter! More filth! Reams of it!"

He glanced at the thick folder and said, "No, no, I don't want to trouble you. It's not really serious. I'll be fine if I rest for a while. Your friend must be waiting for you."

"Oh, there's no need to be shy. I can leave in five or ten days time, no harm would be done."

"There's not the slightest need for that, ma'am."

"I don't want to flatter you on your face, but you have a rare quality of a gentleman that I've never seen in anyone else. You're the first great man who has liked my creations; I'd been quite disheartened. Your letter encouraged me to write some more poems. You could keep these if you like. I've started writing a play as well. I'll mail that to you as soon as it is done. I'd be happy to read a few poems to you if you have a moment. I might never get the opportunity again! I don't know if they're any good, but I hope you'll like them. They're in the same strain as the first one."

She did not wait for permission; quickly she pulled open the folder and began reading a poem. Sharmaji felt as if someone was beating him on his head with a shoe. Several times nausea almost overcame him. He felt as if a thousand donkeys have gathered around his ears and were braying in concert. Kamakshi had a voice as melodious as

---

3. *Bhajans*: Devotional songs.

a koel's, but Sharmaji hated it. He began to develop a real headache. Will this donkey leave, or will she go on forever? Can't she tell from my face the way I feel? And still, she keeps going! With a face like that, I would hate her poems even if she were Mahadevi Verma or Subhadra Kumari.

He couldn't restrain himself any longer. He said, "How can I begin to describe your poems? Why don't you leave these with me, I'll read them when I find sometime. I'm really busy right now."

Kamakshi said in a compassionate voice, "You work so hard even with your delicate health? I feel so sorry for you."

"That's very kind of you."

"Will you have sometime tomorrow? I thought maybe I could bring the first act of the play."

"I'm sorry, I have to drive up to Prayag tomorrow."

"Can I go with you? I could read it to you in the car."

"I'm not sure when I'm going to leave."

"When will you be back?"

"I'm not sure yet."

And then he picked up the phone and said, "Hello, extension 77."

Kamakshi waited for him for half an hour, but Sharmaji seemed so engrossed in important matters on the phone that he could not tear himself away.

Disappointed, Kamakshi left quietly, whispering that she'll certainly come back again. Sharmaji took a breath of ease and picked up the sheaf of poems and dropped them in the wastebasket. He said to himself, "Dear God, I hope I never see her again. Bad woman! She ruined my day."

He called his manager and said, "That poem of Kamakshi won't run."

The manager was astonished. "The form's already on the machine."

"Doesn't matter. Take it off."

"The issue will be very late."

"Let it be. That poem won't run."

Captain Sahib

I

For Jagat Singh, going to school was as distasteful as drinking fish oil or eating sour food. He was a young man who loved wandering around the village. Sometimes he would roam around the guava trees and eat the guavas while the gardener kept cursing him. At other times, he would tour the riverbanks and go to the villages on the other side by crossing the river in the boat. For him, hearing abuses was fun and he never let go of a single opportunity to get slashed by abuses. To clap behind and startle a horse, mimic the walk of old men were his means of entertainment. The lazy do not work but become the slaves of bad habits, and to maintain bad habits one needs money. Whenever Jagat Singh got a chance, he would steal money from the house. If he did not get ready cash, he would shamelessly steal utensils or clothes. He would take glass bottles and sell them in the market. There were several antique items in the house, but he ensured that nothing would be left. He was so adept at this art that one would be surprised at his sheer cunningness and sharpness. One day, he climbed to the top from the sides of his two-storied house and took away a brass utensil. Nobody in the house was aware of this.

His father Thakur Bhakt Singh was the *Munshi*[1] of the town post office. He had secured this post after a lot of turmoil, but he could not fulfill any of the intentions with which he had come there. Instead, he was at a loss because the vegetables and fruits that he used to get for free in the village were not available there. Furthermore, no one could be suppressed or taken advantage of.

Under such circumstances, Jagat Singh's antics made him angry. He would beat Jagat Singh many times. Though he was well built,

---

1. *Munshi*: A secretary in South Asia

Jagat Singh suffered the beatings silently. Had he caught his father's hands, his father would not have been able to move. But Jagat Singh would not do such a thing. There was no effect of the beatings, threats and abuses on him.

Whenever Jagat Singh entered the house, a huge commotion would take place. His mother would come to scold him, his sisters would abuse him as if some wild bull had entered the house. His family members hated him. They would become angry at his very sight. These rejections made him shameless. He was unaffected by the trouble. He would sleep anywhere when he was sleepy and would eat whatever he got.

As the members of his family started finding out things he had stolen, they became even warier of him. For one whole month, he could not steal anything and became a debtor of the *charas*[2] gang. The *ganja*[3] shop owner and sweet shop owner started talking to him harshly. It was difficult for poor Jagat to move about. He would always be on the lookout for an opportunity to steal something but he could not succeed. But then, an opportunity struck him. One day, Bhakt Singh left the post office in the afternoon and put an insurance premium to be sent by registered post, in his pocket. It kept it with him as he didn't trust the peons and wanted to save the document from any prospective prank that could be played by them. But when he reached home, he forgot to remove it from his pocket. Jagat Singh was waiting for such an opportunity. When he searched the pocket for money, he found the envelope. It bore tickets worth several *annas*. Many times, he removed the stamps and sold them at half the price.

He immediately took the envelope. Had he known that the envelope contained currency notes, he would not have stolen it. So when he opened the envelope and found money inside, he was in a dilemma. The torn envelope clearly declared his misdeed. His state was that of a hunter who had gone hunting for a bird and had killed a man instead. His heart was full of regret, shame and sadness, but he

---

2. *Charas*: Hand-made hashish. It is made from the extract of the cannabis plant.

3. *Ganja*: Cannabis or marijuana.

did not have the strength to bear the punishment for this mistake. He kept the notes in the envelope and went away.

It was summertime. Everyone was asleep in the afternoon, but Jagat could not sleep. He had bad times ahead and there was no doubt about it. It was not safe for him to stay in the house. He thought of escaping somewhere for five to ten days. By then the anger would subside. But he has to plan to go somewhere far off, or his escape won't be possible. He could not hide in the town for long. Somebody would give his whereabouts away, and he would be caught. But to go someplace far, he needed some money. Why not take one note from the envelope? His misdeed would be revealed anyway that he had opened the envelope. Then what harm would be caused by taking ten rupees? Father had the money, and he would give it. Thinking this, he took a ten-rupee note from the envelope. But then another thought came to his mind. If he took the money and opened a business in another town, it would be even better. Then he would not have to steal every time. In a few days, he would come back with lots of money, and surprise everybody!

He again took out the envelope. It contained two hundred rupees. A milk shop could easily be run with two hundred rupees. After all, what else is used in Murari's shop other than a few brass utensils and two to four big buckets? But he lives so well! He buys *charas* worth hundreds of rupees. He played cards and put bets of ten rupees every time. If the shop was not profitable, how else can he do all that? In those happy dreams, he got so lost that his mind went out of control, like a man losing his hold in a current and drifting away with the waves of thoughts.

He left for Bombay that evening. The very next day, there was a case of negligence and cheating filed against *Munshi* Bhakt Singh.

II

A band was playing at the Bombay Fort ground and the energetic and beautiful *jawans*[4] of the *Rajput*[5] regiment were marching. Just like the winds give shapes and sizes to the clouds, an officer was giving new shapes and sizes to the formation of the troops.

When the exercise was over, a young man came to the officer. The officer asked him, "What is your name?" The young man saluted and said, "Jagat Singh."

"What do you want?"

"Please enroll me in the army."

"Are you afraid of death?"

"Not at all. I am a Rajput."

"You will have to work very hard."

"I am not afraid of that either."

"You may get imprisoned during the war."

"Gladly"

The captain realized that he was a courageous, smart and energetic young man, and enrolled him in the army immediately. On the third day, the regiment moved to Aden. As the ship moved away, Jagat's heart was left behind in his homeland. Until the time the land could be seen, he kept looking at it. When the land could be seen no longer, he took a deep breath and started crying. For the first time in his life, he remembered his near and dear ones. That small town, the shop where he could get *ganja*, the tours with friends, all came floating in front of his eyes. Who knew, if he would meet them again or not. At one point of time, he became so emotional that he almost jumped into the sea.

---

4. *Jawans*: A male police constable or soldier.
5. *Rajput*: A member of a Hindu military caste claiming Kshatriya descent.

III

Three months passed since Jagat Singh came to Aden. The new sights kept him attracted for many days, but the old thoughts came back often. He remembered his loving mother, who saved him from his father's anger, his sisters' taunts and rejection by relatives. He remembered the day he had fallen ill. There was no hope of his surviving, but his father was not concerned and his sisters were not bothered. It was only his mother who sat by his side through many nights and made him feel better with her loving words. Those days, he had seen her crying silently at night. She herself was unwell, but she had served him forgetting about her own health. Will he be able to see his mother again? In anger and disappointment, he would go to the seashore and keep staring at the water for hours together. He wanted to send a letter home; but out of fear and shame, he stopped himself from doing so. In the end, he could not stop himself. He wrote a letter and asked for forgiveness for his sins. He assured his mother with these words, "Mother, I have done many wrong things, and you were unhappy and angry with me. I am ashamed for all that I have done and assure you that if I live, I will certainly become worthy in life. Then you will not be ashamed to call me your son. Please bless me so that I can fulfill my promise to you."

He sent the letter and expected a reply from that day onwards. A month passed but there was no reply. He was worried. Why was there no reply? Is mother not well? Perhaps, father did not let her reply out of anger. Is there some other problem? Under a tree in the camp, some soldiers had made a temple of *Shaligram*[6] . Some devoted soldiers offered water to the idol. Jagat Singh always made fun of them; but today, he went up to the idol, and stood there for a long time with his head bowed. He was in deep meditation when the office peon called out to him and handed over a letter addressed to him. When Jagat Singh took the letter, his entire body trembled. Praising God, he opened the envelope and found a letter inside. It read- "Your

6. *Shaligram:* A stone which is the symbol of Lord Vishnu.

father has been punished for five years for cheating. Your mother is on her deathbed. If you can get leave, come home."

Jagat Singh immediately went to Captain Sahib[7] and said, "Sir, my mother is not well. Please give me leave."

The captain looked at him with harsh eyes and said, "You can't get leave now."

"Then accept my resignation."

"Your resignation also can't be accepted."

"But, I can't stay here for another minute."

"You will have to stay. You will have to go to war very soon."

"War has been declared! Oh! Then I won't go home. By when will we leave?"

"Very soon, in two to four days."

IV

Four years passed. There was no warrior like Captain Jagat Singh in the regiment. His courage increased in difficult situations. Jagat Singh would overcome situations where everybody's courage failed. He would always be ahead in battle; on top of that, he was very humble, serious and cheerful and therefore, all his officers and subordinates held him in high esteem. It was as if he was reborn. The officers trusted him so much that they discussed every issue with him. Anybody, if asked, would speak of his exploits: how he had set fire to the tent of the Germans, how he saved their captain from the fire of machine guns, how he saved an injured subordinate and brought him back carrying him on his shoulder. It was as if he did not have any love for his life. It was as if he was searching for death itself!

But every night, when he got time, Jagat Singh sat by himself and remembered his near and dear ones. A few drops of tears fell from his eyes. He sent a big portion of his salary home, and there was no week when he did not write a letter to his mother. He was worried about his

---

7. *Sahib:* A polite title or a form of address for a man.

father who was suffering due to his misdeeds. When would the day come, when he would fall at his feet and beg for his forgiveness, and he would bless him and forgive him?

V

Four years and three months had passed since Bhakt Singh had been in jail. There was a huge crowd in front of it. The term of many prisoners was getting over. People from their household had come to take them home. But old Bhakt Singh was sitting in his cell with his head bowed and sadness in his heart. His spine had bent. His body had become a skeleton. It seemed as if a clever sculptor had made a statue of a famine-ravaged man. His term was also getting over, but nobody had come to take him. Who would come? Who was there to come?

An old inmate came to him, shook his shoulders and said, "Tell me Bhagat, has anybody come from home?"

Bhakt Singh said, "There is no one at home."

"You will go home on your own?"

"I do not have a home anymore!"

"Then will you stay here only?"

"If these people do not kick me out, then I will stay here."

Today, after four years, Bhakt Singh remembered his wayward son. The son because of whom his life was destroyed, pride was lost and his family was destroyed. His very memory was hateful for him. But today, in the midst of despair and helplessness, his thought was straw of hope. He thought, "I don't know how he is? However bad he is but, after all, he was my son. He was the heir of the family. If I die, at least he will shed a few tears and give me some water on my deathbed. I never behaved well with him. I acted like *Yamraj*[8] whenever he played some prank. Once, I had hung him upside down for coming into the kitchen without washing his feet. I had slapped him so many times for speaking rudely. I did not give him any respect. This is the

8. *Yamraj:* The Hindu God of Death.

punishment for my misbehavior. If the chains of love are weak, how can a family be saved?"

VI

It was morning. The sun of hope came out. How soft and sweet were its rays today! The winds were cool, the sky was beautiful, the trees were green and the chirping of the birds was sweet. Nature was colored in the color of hope; but for Bhakt Singh, there was only darkness.

The jailor came to the main hall. The prisoners stood in a line. An officer started calling each prisoner by name and gave the release order. The faces of prisoners were exuding happiness. The man, whose name was called, walked up to the officer, took the release order, saluted him and then left after hugging his inmates. His near and dear ones would come forward and hug him. Some were giving money, others were distributing sweets and some were rewarding the jail officials. Today the puppets of hell had become Gods of humility.

In the end, Bhakt Singh's name was called out. With his head bowed, he walked up to the jailor slowly, took the release order and walked towards the jail door, as if there were huge sea waves coming forward to engulf him. He came outside the door and sat down on the ground. Where would he go?

Suddenly he saw an army officer on a horseback, coming towards the jail. He was wearing a khaki uniform and was sitting on horseback with a strange sense of pride. Seeing him, the soldiers stood in a line and saluted him.

Bhakt Singh thought, "He is a lucky man for whom this caravan is coming. And here I am who does not have any place to go."

The army officer looked around and then after getting off the horse, came straight to Bhakt Singh and stood in front of him.

Bhakt Singh looked at him carefully and then stood up surprised and said, "Oh Jagat Singh, my son!"

Crying, Jagat Singh fell at his feet!

A Tale of Two Oxen

I

Amongst the animals, the donkey is considered the most idiotic animal. When we wish to say that a person is extremely stupid, we address him as a donkey. However, it cannot be decided if the donkey is actually a fool or is it his innocence and tolerance that has earned him this title. A cow hits with her horns and a calved cow automatically transforms herself into a lioness. The dog is a very poor animal but sometimes even he gets agitated but it is unheard and unseen of a donkey getting angry. You may hit him as much as you can, give him the most decayed grass but still you will not find even a shadow of discontentment on his face. He may bray with pleasure during the month of *Baisakh*[1], but we have never seen a donkey in a happy state. His face always bears the look of desolation that never changes during any situation be it good or bad. The characteristics of the sages have reached their pinnacle in this simple being but still people call him an idiot. Such a drastic insult of virtues!

Perhaps, simplicity is not suitable for the world. You may see that the Indians are being severely mistreated in Africa. Why are they not allowed to enter America? Poor fellows do not drink, save their money for bad times, work hard, do not fight with anyone, suffer from resentment but never utter a word, and still, they are infamous. It is said that they have lowered the principles of life. They might have been called civilized if they had learnt the concept of retaliation. Japan has set an example by establishing itself as a civilized nation with just one victory.

However, the donkey has a younger brother that is considered just a bit less stupid than he is. And he is called the ox. The way we use the

---

1. *Baisakh:* The second month of the Hindu calendar.

word 'donkey', in a similar manner we use the word 'heifer's uncle.' Some people may say that the ox is supreme in stupidity but we do not hold such opinions. The ox sometimes hits hard and sometimes proves to be recalcitrant. There are many other ways through which he depicts his dissatisfaction and therefore, his position is lower than that of the donkey.

Jhuri had a pair of oxen – Hira and Moti. They were handsome, sturdy and had a great stature. While residing with each other for so long, the oxen had developed a sense of companionship. They used to sit together and discuss their issues in a silent conversation. It is difficult to understand how one was able to read the mind of the other. They definitely had some secret power that was denied to a man who was considered the most powerful living being in the world. Both of them licked and smelled each other in order to show their affection. Sometimes they used to entangle their horns not in the spirit of violence but in a humorous manner as if they were involved in a friendly combat. Without this spirit, friendship grows weak and the sense of trust is lost. When these oxen were yoked to a cart or a plough, they tried their best to take the maximum load on their neck.

After the day's toil, when they would be released in the evening, they licked each other and got rid of their tiredness. After the trough was filled with fodder, they rose simultaneously, lowered their mouths together into the trough and sat together. If one would remove his mouth from the trough, the other would follow him.

One day, it so happened that Jhuri sent the oxen to his in-law's house. The oxen were unaware of where they were sent and thought that their master had sold them. It cannot be said whether they felt offensive at being sold or not, but Jhuri's brother-in-law, Gaya had a tough time getting them to his home. If he goaded them from behind, they moved from right to left, if he pulled them forward using the nose strap they pushed it backwards. If he whipped them, they lowered their horns and howled.

If God had given them the voice they would have asked Jhuri, "Why are you sending us away? We have left no stone unturned to serve you well. If the hard work was not enough, you could have put us to more work. We were even ready to die working for you. We never complain about the fodder, and ate whatever you gave us. Then why did you sell us to this cruel man?"

In the evening, they both reached a new place. They were extremely hungry but when they were taken to the manger, they did not lower their mouths into it. Their heart was heavy with pain. The place that they took as their home was left far behind today. The new home, new village, new people were strangers to them.

Both consulted each other in their mute language, looked at each other through slanting eyes and laid down. When the whole village was asleep, they broke their tether and started towards their home. The ropes were quite strong and it could not be estimated that any ox would be able to break them. But these oxen had been empowered with such strength at this moment that the ropes broke away in a single stroke.

When Jhuri woke up the next morning, he found the two oxen standing beside the manger and the broken pieces of ropes were dangling around their necks. Their feet were soiled with mud and their eyes reflected the love they felt for their master.

As he saw the oxen, his heart was filled with love. He ran towards them and hugged them tightly. This scene of embracing and kissing was extremely delightful.

The boys gathered around them and welcomed them with claps and cheers. In the history of the village, this event was not extraordinary but it was still important. The youngsters decided that brave animals must be honored. Someone brought *rotis* from his home, the other brought *gur* , and another brought seedcake while someone brought fodder.

One boy said, "Nobody has such faithful oxen."

The other supported him, "They returned alone from such distance."

The third one said, "These are not mere oxen. They must have been humans in their previous births."

No one dared disagree with this statement. When Jhuri's wife saw the oxen at the door, she grew angry. She said, "These oxen are so ungrateful that they did not work there for a single day and shirked away from the place."

Jhuri could not withstand such blame on his oxen and said, "Why are they ungrateful? They must have not been given any fodder, so what could they do?"

His wife said authoritatively, "Only you know how to feed the oxen properly, other people do not know anything, right?"

Jhuri said, "If they had been given proper fodder, they would not have run away."

The wife got irritated and replied, "They ran away because those people are not a fool like you who just caresses the animals. If they feed them properly, they tend to make them work hard. But these two are sluggards and therefore ran away. Let me see now how they get to eat seed cake and wheat husk. I shall only provide dry fodder for them; they may eat it or go to hell."

And thus, the attendant was strictly instructed to give only dry fodder to the oxen.

When the oxen put their mouths into the manger, they found the fodder tasteless without any oil or juice.

What should they eat? With hopeful eyes, they looked towards their master. Jhuri said to the attendant, "Why don't you put some seed cake into it?"

"Mistress will kill me if I do that."

"Do not let her know and put it secretly."

"No master, later you would be on her side and put all the blame on me."

II

The next day Jhuri's brother-in-law again came to take the oxen away. This time he yoked them to the cart.

Many times, Moti tried to push the cart into a ditch but Hira controlled it. He was the tolerant one.

In the evening, they reached the place and Gaya tied them with thick ropes and thrashed them for running away. Then he again fed them with dry fodder, whereas his own oxen were given seedcake and dry *rotis* as well.

The oxen had never been insulted like this before. Jhuri had never hit them even with the lightest stick. Both of them sprang up at his one command. And here they had been beaten. It was a case of injured self-respect and moreover, they were fed with dry fodder.

They did not even look into the manger.

On the second day, Gaya yoked the oxen to the plough, but they refused to budge. He thrashed them continuously and got tired but the oxen did not move their feet. At one point, when the cruel man repeatedly hit at Hira's muzzle, Moti lost his temper. He ran away with the plough breaking the rope, the plough and all the straps attached to it. If they had no ropes in their necks, it would have been impossible to catch them.

Hira said in their silent language, "It is useless to run."

Moti replied, "He would have killed you!"

"Now we will get badly thrashed."

"Let it be. If we have been born as an ox, then is it possible to avoid thrashing?"

"Gaya is running towards us with two men carrying sticks."

Moti said, "If you say then I will give him a taste of his own medicine since he is bringing the stick."

Hira advised him, "No brother, you need to stop."

"If he hits me then I will throw him down."

"No, it is against the dharma of our breed."

Moti was forced to refrain himself. Gaya reached them and took them away. Fortunately, he did not thrash them at that moment otherwise Moti would have counter-attacked. They observed his attitude and Gaya and his assistants realized that it was better to remain in control at that time.

Again the dry fodder was brought for them and they kept standing silently.

In the house, people had started their dinner. At this moment, a little girl came out with two *rotis* and fed them one *roti* each. With that one *roti*, their hunger could not be reduced but their hearts seemed to be satisfied. Even this place has some kind-hearted person. The girl was the daughter of Bhairo. Her mother was dead and the stepmother ill-treated her. Perhaps that was the reason that she had developed a soft corner for the oxen.

Now both of them were yoked for the whole day, beaten, tethered to the stake in the evening, and fed by the little girl. This token of affection was so powerful that even after eating dry fodder, they did not grow weak. But their eyes were filled with the thirst of rebellion.

One day Moti said, "It has become intolerable now, Hira!"

"What do you want to do?"

"I will toss one of them with my horns."

"But do you know that the sweet little girl who feeds us daily is the daughter of the master of this house. You will make her an orphan."

"So shall I throw the mistress, she is the one who thrashes the girl."

"But why do you forget that we are not allowed to use violence against women."

"You are too stubborn to let me move out of this place. Should we break away the ropes and run away?"

"Yes, that's a good idea and I would have accepted it. But how shall we break away such thick ropes?"

"I have a solution. First, we must chew some portion of the rope and weaken it, and then it will break away at one stroke."

In the night, when the girl left the place after feeding them, both of them started chewing the ropes. But they were unable to get hold of the thick ropes. They tried repeatedly but failed.

Suddenly the door opened and the little girl came outside. Both the oxen lowered their heads and started licking her hand. She caressed them and said, "I shall release you and then you should run away secretly, otherwise these people will kill you. Today they are planning to put a headstall through your noses."

She opened the knots but they remained still and stood there.

Moti said, "Why don't you move?"

Hira replied, "We can go but what will happen to this little child? Everyone will suspect her and she will be in so much trouble."

Suddenly the girl shouted, "The oxen of Jhuri uncle are running away! Oh Dada, Dada! The oxen are running away, come out quickly."

Gaya was utterly confused as he came out of the house. He tried to catch hold of the oxen but they were speeding up. Gaya followed them but they increased their pace. Gaya shouted along the way and then returned to get some more villagers for help. This gave a chance to the animals to escape. They ran straight with full speed, without even recognizing the route. The route known to them was lost. They wandered away to strange and unknown villages. They halted near a farm and pondered over their next step.

Hira said, "I think that we have lost our way."

"You ran with such a speed. We could have brought him down."

"If we had done that then what would have the people said? They may discard their dharma but why should we do that?"

Both of them were hunger-stricken. They were near a field of peas and started feeding on it, wary of any danger.

When they had their fill, they experienced freedom and started jumping around the field. They belched and then locked their horns together and started pushing each other. Moti pushed Hira with such force that he fell into a ditch. Hira got angry, gained his balance and retaliated the blow. When Moti realized that the romp was turning into a fight, he stepped aside quickly.

III

Suddenly they saw a bull running towards them. Yes, indeed a bull came and stood before them. The two friends looked at him. The bull was a magnificent one. Fighting him was equivalent to inviting death but there was no way out of it as well. He was advancing towards them with a terrible look on his face!

Moti said, "We are doomed. Is survival possible? Think a way out."

Hira said in a tensed tone, "He is too proud of himself. There is no chance of his listening to our pleas."

"Should we run away?"

"That would be cowardice."

"Then you may die at his hands. I am going."

"And what if he chases you?"

"Then think of a solution quickly!"

"We must attack him together. I shall attack him from the front and you should hit him at the rear, only then will he run away. If he hits me, you should put your horns in his stomach. It might prove to be dangerous but that's the only solution."

Both the friends risked their lives and jumped towards the bull who was not experienced in fighting against two enemies together. He was used to fight only one animal at a time. The moment he hit upon Hira, Moti attacked on his rear side. When he turned towards him, Hira attacked him. The bull wanted to defeat them one by one but the oxen were experts in fighting. They gave him no chance to attack. When he made a decisive move to finish off Hira, Moti pushed his horns into his stomach. As he turned to retaliate, Hira pushed his horns on his rear. The poor animal was wounded badly and thus, he ran away. Moti and Hira chased him and the bull fell down, gasping for breath. Then both of them pitied his condition and left him alone. Relishing their victory, they walked along the road.

Moti said, "I wanted to finish him off."

Hira retorted, "We must not use violence against a fallen enemy."

"This is rubbish. An enemy should be hit in such a manner that he never rises again."

"I think we should now think about reaching our home."

"First we should eat something, we can think later."

A field of peas was right before them. Moti entered it against Hira's advice. They had just begun eating when men surrounded them with sticks in their hands. Hira was at the edge and escaped easily. But Moti was in the irrigated part of the field where his feet were caught in the soft soil. He was unable to move and was caught. When Hira saw that Moti was in trouble, he returned. He could not leave his friend alone and the guards caught him as well.

In the morning, both the friends were locked inside the *kanjihauz*,[2] the municipal yard for stray cattle.

IV

It was the first time in their lives that the whole day had passed and they had not been given even a grain of food. They were unable to understand the nature of their new master. Gaya was better than this one. The *kanjihauz* housed many other animals like buffaloes, horses, goats and donkeys but there was no fodder in front of anyone. All of them were lying on the floor as if they were dead.

Many had grown so weak that they were unable to stand on their feet. Hira and Moti continuously stared at the door but no one came with the fodder. Then both of them started licking the salty mud of the walls but that could not alleviate their hunger.

When night had fallen and still they got no food, a spark of revolt was ignited in the heart of Hira. He said to Moti, "I cannot stand it any longer."

Moti replied with his head hanging down, "I feel as if I am dying."

"Come, let us destroy this wall."

2. *Kanjihauz*: A kine-house; the place where stray cattle are kept.

"I don't think I have strength enough to do that."

"You were very proud of your power. What happened now?"

"All my pride has gone!"

The wall of the courtyard was built of mud. Hira was a powerful ox, the moment he hit the wall with his sharp horns, a portion of the wall came loose. This encouraged him and he continuously ran towards the wall and hit it hard. With every hit, some chunks of mud came off the wall.

At that moment, the security guard of the *kanjihauz* came there with a night lamp, in order to count the animals. When he saw the disorderly behaviour of Hira, he thrashed him with his stick and tethered him.

Moti said, "What did you get by being thrashed?"

"At least I could witness my strength."

"What is the use of this strength if it makes you tethered?"

"But I will keep doing it, no matter how many ropes bound me."

"You will get killed."

"I don't care! We shall be anyways dead if we remain here. Think about it, if the wall would have fallen, so many lives could be saved. So many animals are locked up here. No one has any power in their bodies. If they remain like this for some more days, they will fall dead."

"Yes. You are right. Then I will also apply all my strength."

Moti also rammed his horns into the wall, a chunk of mud came off and this encouraged him. Then he pushed the wall with his horns as if he was fighting with an enemy. After about two hours of continuous toil, the upper portion of the wall had fallen. He pushed with some more effort and half of the wall collapsed.

As soon as the wall had fallen, the half-dead animals suddenly came alive and the three mares bolted away at once. After that, the goats ran away and then the buffalo too made her way out. But the donkeys remained there.

Hira asked them, "Why don't you run away?"

One of the donkeys answered, "What if they catch us again?"

"What's the harm in running away when you have the opportunity?"

"We are afraid. It is better to stay here only."

Half of the night had passed. Both the donkeys were still in a dilemma whether they should run away or remain there, while Moti was busy cutting off the ropes that bound his friend. When he accepted defeat, Hira said to him, "You run away and leave me here. We might meet again somewhere."

Moti said with tear-filled eyes, "You think that I am so selfish. We have been together since so many days. Now when you are in trouble, should I abandon you and run away?"

Hira said, "You will be badly thrashed; those people will understand that you are responsible for this act."

Moti said with pride, "The crime for which you are tethered, why should I bother if I get a beating for it? At least we saved the lives of nine to ten animals. They all will bless us."

After saying this, he pushed the donkeys out with his horns, came back, and slept beside his friend.

With the first light of the dawn, the *Munshi* , the security guard and the other employees came and there is no need to describe the ruckus that they created. It would be enough to say that Moti was severely beaten and he was also tethered with a thick rope.

V

For one week, both the friends remained bound in the *kanjihauz*. Nobody gave them even a straw of fodder to eat. Yes, they were given water once a day. That was their sole diet. They had grown so weak that they were unable to stand and even their hump bones became visible. One day they heard a drum beating in front of the place and by afternoon, 50 to 60 people gathered there. At that time, both friends were brought out. People saw their faces and turned away uninterested. Who would buy such weak oxen?

Suddenly a bearded man with blood-red eyes and a cruel demeanor came there and prodded their haunches with his fingers while talking to the *Munshi*. Both the friends were terrified at the look of the man. There was no doubt as to who he was and what were his intentions. Both of them saw each other with fearful eyes and lowered their heads.

Hira said, "Why did we run away from Gaya's house? Now we shall lose our lives."

Moti said in a disdainful tone, "It is said that God is merciful to all, but why does He become merciless in our case?"

"For God, our lives and deaths make no difference. Well, it is good that we die; at least we will be near Him for some days. Once He saved us in the form of that girl. Why will He not save us now?"

"This man is a butcher for sure."

"Why do you worry? Our flesh, skin, horns and bones will become useful for someone."

After being sold, the two friends accompanied the bearded man. They were terrified to the core. They were unable to walk steadily, but they continued to run out of fear. Whenever they slowed down, they were hit with a stick.

On the way, they saw a herd of cattle grazing in the green fields. All the animals were happy. Someone jumped, someone leisurely chewed the cud; they had a blissful life, but they were so selfish. They were not at all concerned about their two brothers who were in the clutches of a butcher.

Suddenly, both of them realized that the route was familiar to them. Gaya had taken them to his house through the same route. The same fields, the same gardens, the similar villages; this made them move faster. All the tiredness, all the weakness suddenly vanished. And behold! They had reached their own village. This was the same well where they used to drive the water-wheel.

Moti said, "Our house is near."

Hira said, "God has been kind upon us."

"I will run away to my home."

"But will he let us go?"

"I will push him down."

"No, no, let us run away to our place."

Both of them frantically ran towards their house jumping like calves. That was their fold. Both of them came running to their place and stood there. The bearded man followed them.

Jhuri was basking in the sun. When he saw the oxen, he came running to them and embraced them one by one. Their eyes were filled with tears of joy. One of them was licking Jhuri's hand.

The bearded man came and held the oxen by their ropes.

Jhuri said, "These are my oxen."

"How can these be your oxen? I bought them in an auction at the *kanjihauz*."

"I think that you have stolen them. Leave without a word, these oxen belong to me. They can be bought only if I sell them. Who has the right to auction my oxen?"

"I will report to the police."

"These are my oxen. The proof is that they have come to my doors."

The bearded man tried to take the oxen by force. At that time, Moti advanced towards him lowering his horns. He fell backwards but Moti continued his advance. He ran away and Moti chased him out of the village. Once outside, he started threatening him; he abused him and threw stones at him, but Moti stood facing him. The villagers were enjoying the show.

When the bearded man accepted defeat and left the place, Moti returned with pride.

Hira said, "I was afraid that you will kill him in your anger."

"He won't come again."

"In case he comes, I will teach him a lesson. Let me see how he takes us away."

"What if he shots you?"

"I will die, but I won't be of any use to him."

"Nobody cares about our lives."

"Just because we're so simple."

In a short while, their manger was filled with fodder, seedcake and grain, and both of them began to eat. Jhuri stood there patting them. He embraced both of them.

Just then, Jhuri's wife came running from the house and kissed the foreheads of the oxen.

Fact

I

That secret always remained undiscovered in Amrit's heart. It was never revealed to Purnima by his eyes, his tone or his attitude towards her. She had always thought that she was just like an ordinary neighbor and a friend to him. She never thought about any possibility of sharing any other relationship with him. There were a lot of instances when Amrit happened to be there helping her and this never made her question or give a second thought to the occurrences. For instance, when she goes to draw water from the well, Amrit would coincidentally come there and take the pitcher from her hands and help her fill the pitcher. Whenever she went to feed her cow, he would take the fodder away from her hands and put it in the manger. When she went to the market to buy groceries, he would meet her on the way and help her carry the groceries.

There was no other man in Purnima's family. Her father had passed away many years ago and her mother was left alone in the world to fend for herself. Before going to school, Amrit would go to her house and ask them if they wanted anything from the market. He had some farms, some cows and a vegetable garden as well. He would give her food grains and vegetables without letting his parents know about it but Purnima always thought that these hospitalities were just because of his humanitarian nature. What else would she understand? After all, people living in the same village, even if they were not related by blood, were considered brothers and sisters according to the old customs.

One day, Purnima told him, "I get anxious when you remain in the school for the whole day."

Amrit replied in a straightforward manner, "What can I do? My exams are near. I cannot miss school now."

"Sometimes I wonder how will I see you when I leave and why would you come to my house then?"

Hearing this, Amrit asked, "Where will you go?"

Purnima replied shyly, "Where all your sisters have gone, where all girls go one day."

Amrit said dejectedly, "Oh, that thing!"

Then he fell silent. He had not yet thought that someday Purnima would also get married and leave. He never got any time to ponder over these matters, he was happy being with her and that was all that mattered. If a person thinks about his future continuously then he can never remain happy in the present.

Amrit knew that she would get married someday but even sooner than he expected, a marriage proposal came for Purnima. The boy belonged to a rich and well-known family. Purnima's mother was very happy and accepted the proposal immediately. She had seen too much of poverty in her life and now the most important thing for her was wealth. And she knew that Purnima would get all the comforts in this family. It seemed like she had been waiting for such a proposal all her life. Earlier, she used to worry a lot about her daughter's marriage. Her heartbeat would increase pondering upon Purnima's marriage. But now, God had put an end to all her worries and problems in a single stroke.

When Amrit heard the news, he was devastated. He immediately ran towards Purnima's house but stopped himself when he realized that he had no reason to go there. He wondered why was he being punished? What was his fault? He came back to his house and lay down on the bed. Purnima will go. How will he live without her? This emotion gave way to the stunning silence that comes after a storm. He was deeply crestfallen. He thought now that Purnima is leaving, she won't care to meet or bother about him. And when did she ever care about him? He was the one who took care of her and her needs all day and night. Purnima never even asked about his well-being. And now her pride knows no bounds. She would soon be the wife of a rich man.

Let her be. Amrit can also stay without her. This is what you get in this world for loving someone with all your heart!

But all these thoughts were embedded deep in his heart and were absolutely pointless. He did not have the courage to go and say to Purnima's mother, "Purnima is mine. Only I will marry her." He knew that it would create havoc in the village. Such a thing was never even heard of, not even in the stories.

Purnima hadn't seen him all day and had grown so restless, waiting for his arrival all day. She wondered why Amrit passes my door but never comes in. Whenever they came face to face with each other, he would not speak to her and leave quickly just to bump into him. She takes the pitcher to the well, thinking that he would come but he never came.

One day, unable to control her emotions any longer, she went to his house and asked him, "Why don't you come to meet me nowadays?" Her voice was choked with emotions as she realized that soon she would leave the village and these people behind.

Amrit remained silent as if nothing had happened. He replied in a careless tone, "My exams are near. I don't have any time."

He waited for a while and then continued, "I thought that now that you are to be married…" he wanted to say, "why should I love you more" but he thought that it would be foolish to say such things.

If a patient is nearing his death, we do not stop his treatment by thinking that he would definitely die. Rather, as his health starts declining, we do all that is our power to save him. And when he is actually on his deathbed, then we do every possible thing to make him feel better. He changed the topic and said, "I have heard that you are getting married into a very rich family."

Purnima ignored the last words of his statement and said in a sorrowful tone, "What is my fault? I am not going off my own accord. Every girl has to get married someday that is why I have agreed to go."

She reddened with shame as she said these words. Perhaps she had said more than she wanted to.

Love is like a game of chess. You have to be careful about every step you take. Amrit looked at her in a way as if he was trying to draw some meaning from her words. It would have been so much better if he could look into her heart and get a confirmation of her feelings. All the girls talk about marriage in a similar sad tone as if they were sacrificing their lives. But one day they wear beautiful clothes and extravagant jewels and go to their husband's home in a palanquin. Amrit was not satisfied with her reply.

Then he said hesitantly, "Why would you remember me once you leave?" He was ashamed to ask such a question and wished that he could lock him up into his room. He could not muster the courage to even look at her face. He was afraid that she had understood the feelings he had for her.

Purnima lowered her head and said in an affectionate tone, "Do you think that I don't care for you? I am innocent and still, you are angry with me. You should have shown some sympathy and consoled me, no! Do I have any option? My own family is sending me to a stranger's place. What would happen to me there? Isn't this problem big enough to worry me that you are additionally pouring your anger into it?"

Her voice choked again. Today, when he saw the sorrowful state of Purnima, Amrit realized that she also has anguish hidden in her heart. His trivialness and selfishness seemed to blacken his face. Purnima was saying the truth. Also, there was an insult and reprimand in her words. Why would she complain to strangers? It was his duty to console her in this sorrowful state. She was also feeling lost and deprived of his love. But she was sacrificing her life in order to fulfill her duty. A new ideal of love was put in front of her that demanded a sacrifice that would burn her forever.

He said in a shameful tone, "Please forgive me Purnima! It was my mistake, rather my foolishness."

II

Purnima got married. Amrit put all his efforts in the preparations of the marriage. Her husband was an elderly, stout, crude man who was extremely arrogant and bad-tempered. Nonetheless, Amrit kept showering hospitality towards him and treating him like God as if his blessings would take him to heaven. He did not get any time to talk to Purnima, neither did he tried to get an opportunity to talk to her. Whenever he saw her, he found her weeping. And he tried his best to convey through his eyes the compassion he had for her and consoled her in the best possible way.

On the third day after her wedding, Purnima left for her husband's home. Amrit went to the temple that day and prayed with extreme devotion for her future happiness. When the grief was so fresh, then why would he bother? Sorrow destroys the diseases of the soul. But he still felt a vacuum in life. He thought that he had no aims or desires and his life was nothing but a tragedy.

III

Purnima came home after three years. Meanwhile, Amrit had got married as well but seemed to be leading an aimless life. His mind had cultivated an undefined lust but he was unable to give any shape to it. That lust had stayed intact inside him like the mercury in the thermometer. With Purnima's arrival, the mercury reached its maximum temperature. She had a two-year-old son. Amrit played with him throughout the day. He used to take him for morning and evening walks and brought him different kinds of toys and sweets. He used to bring milk and *halwa*[1] for him every morning and then bathe him and wash his hair. He used to clean his boils and pimples and applied balm on them. He had taken all these services on his head. The child had also grown attached to him and would not leave his side

---

1. *Halwa:* A sweet Indian dish consisting of carrots or semolina boiled with milk, almonds, sugar, butter, and cardamom.

for a single moment. Sometimes he even slept with Amrit and even when Purnima came to call him, he did not go with her.

Amrit asked, "Who is your father?"

The child would reply, "You!"

Amrit embraced him lovingly after hearing the reply.

Purnima had grown into a beautiful woman now. The innocent bud had bloomed into a mesmerizing flower. But she had also become very proud and had started using cosmetics to beautify herself. She had even started wearing costly *saris* and gold jewels that made her look even more attractive. It seemed as if she ignored Amrit. She would only talk to him when the need arose and even when she spoke to him it seemed as if she was doing him a favor. Amrit loved her son so much and fulfilled all his demands but his efforts seemed worthless in her eyes. She thought it was his duty to serve her and he was bound to fulfil his duty. He did not deserve any gratitude for doing all these things for her.

Whenever the child cried, she would threaten him that if he cried then Amrit would never talk to him if he cries and the child would get pacified.

Whenever she needed anything she would call Amrit and order him as if he was her servant. And Amrit would obediently follow all her orders.

She stayed for six months and then returned to her husband's home. Amrit went to see them off at the railway station. When she sat inside the train, Amrit gave her the child. Amrit's eyes were filled with tears but he looked aside and rubbed his eyes to hide his tears. How could he show his tears to Purnima? He wondered when they will meet again.

Purnima said arrogantly, "My child will search for you for many days."

Amrit said in a choked voice, "I will always remember him."

"Do write to me sometimes."

"I will."

"But I won't reply to your letters."

"I will not expect you to... but do remember me."

The train started moving. Amrit kept looking at her window. After the train had gone a bit further, he saw that Purnima took her head outside the window and looked at him and then showed her son to him.

Amrit wanted to reach Purnima at that moment. He was so happy that it seemed that he had achieved his objective.

IV

Purnima's mother passed away that year. Purnima was travelling at that time and could not meet her mother for the last time. Amrit put great efforts to get her the best medical treatment and after her death, he completed her last rituals as if she was his own mother. Now, he was the owner of his house since his father had also passed away a few years ago. Nobody could question him regarding the expenditure for her cremation.

Purnima was left with no reason to return to her mother's home. She got busy with her own life. She was the mistress of her house and could not leave the house to anyone else. She gave birth to two more children. The elder son had grown up and was now studying in a school. And the younger one was studying at a nearby *madarsa*[2]. Amrit would send his servant once a year to find out about their well-being. Purnima was happy and content and that was sufficient for him. Amrit's sons had also grown up and he was occupied with the matters of the household. He was now more than forty years old but he still missed Purnima. He had preserved many sweet memories of her in his heart.

---

2. *Madarsa*: A college for Islamic instruction.

V

Suddenly one day, news reached Amrit that Purnima's husband had passed away. But it was surprising to know that he felt no remorse. He had always thought that her elderly husband was not a good match for Purnima. She must have not expressed her real feelings due to her duty and helplessness. Amrit had always felt that she was not in love with her husband even though he was so rich. After all, in this country, many beautiful girls are compulsively married to unsuitable partners. If Purnima had been in some other country then many young and eligible bachelors would have been ready to marry her and she wouldn't have landed up with an elderly husband. His dead desires for her came alive once again. He was no longer hesitant and neither was he bound to remain quiet as before. And moreover, now Purnima too was free from all responsibilities. Her plight must have made her more kind. Her wantonness and carelessness must have taken their leave. She would have become a matured woman who would understand his love and be ready to receive it. He would go to her house to express his condolence and bring her back. And he would always serve and take care of her as much as possible. He would feel satisfied if she would be near him. He just wanted the reassurance of her love and affection.

Twenty years ago, he had known a different Purnima. Then, she was young; she had a beautiful body, red cheeks, delicate limbs and intoxicating laughter. The same beauty still resided in Amrit's heart without much change. The changes seemed to be even more beautiful to him. There would definitely be changes due to age but he could not think of any changes in her body that would reduce her beauty in any way. Now he had very little desire for her physical beauty, he was more interested in her sweet words. He wished to see the love for him in her eyes and wanted her to trust him completely. He genuinely loved her and decided to make up for the mistakes that he had committed in the past.

VI

By chance, one day Purnima herself came there with her younger child. She had a widowed maternal aunt who stayed with her mother. She was still alive and this is how the empty house was settled again.

When Amrit heard the news, he rushed to meet her as if pulled by a magical force. He was carefully taking along the beautiful memories of his childhood with him. At that time, his condition was similar to that of a little kid who saw his companion and rushed towards him with his broken toys to play.

But when he saw her face, all his excitement and zeal was reduced to ashes. He was stunned and kept standing in front of her. Purnima stood there with a bowed head. She was wearing a white *sari* and her face was veiled. Her back had bent, she looked extremely weak and tears were continuously flowing down her cheeks. Her face had turned pale and she looked like a dead body in a shroud.

Purnima's maternal aunt came there and said, "Sit down, son! Look at her condition, she has become as weak as a thorn. Her tears never stop flowing. She eats only one meal a day without salt, milk or butter, only plain dried *rotis*. She has no desires left in her. Moreover, she fasts often, sleeps on a mat on the ground. She remains indulged in prayers late in the night. Her kids try to make her understand but she listens to none. She says that when God has snatched away her husband then everything else is nothing but a myth. She had come here for a change but even now, she keeps on crying. I have tried to explain to her so many times that what has happened was destiny; we cannot do anything about it. Be patient and care for the children God has given to you. God has given her so much wealth that she can easily sustain her life and fulfill the needs of her children. One's soul must be pure. What is the need of torturing this body? But she never listens to me. Now only you can try to make her understand. She might listen to you."

Amrit looked as if he was unaffected but inside him, he felt an excruciating pain ignited by Purnima's condition. He felt as if a violent earthquake had jarred the plinth on which he had built all his life's hopes. Today he realized that what he considered as a fact all through his life was nothing but a mirage, a dream.

His love and passion were destroyed by Purnima's self-control and ascetic nature. A new fact had been established in his life that if our heart can worship a stone statue as God then it can also worship a person as God. Purnima was still worshipping the loathsome man whom she had married.

Amrit said silently, "How can selfish people like us give advice to an ascetic? Our duty is to bow our heads in front of her and not to make them understand anything."

Purnima raised her veil slightly and said, "Your son still remembers you and often asks about you."

A Secret

I

Vimal Prakash entered Sevashram after cleaning the dirt off his hair and shoes. He goes for a morning walk daily and takes a round of Sevashram on his return. He was the ancillary and the director of this ashram.

That morning, the work at Sevashram had already started. The lady teachers were busy teaching the girls, the gardener was watering the plants and the students of class one were running on the green grass. Vimal took great care of the health and welfare of the girls.

He kept looking at the students playing with amusement for a while and then returned to his office. The clerk had placed the mail on his table. He went through the letters one by one and put them aside after a cursory glance at them. Suddenly he looked worried and disappointed. He had given an advertisement in the newspaper for donations but there had been no response. How would the institution continue to function? Are people so selfish? He had dedicated his body and soul for Sevashram. Whatever money he had, was already spent on its development. What did people expect from him? Does he still not deserve their trust and kindness?

Thinking about these, he got up and returned home. How would he face this difficult situation? Sevashram had a debt of twelve thousand rupees from last six months. By the end of the year, it would reach approximately twenty thousand. If he increased the school fee by one rupee then the income would increase by five hundred rupees and if he increased the hostel fee by two rupees, then the income would increase by another five hundred rupees. In this manner, he could earn twelve thousand rupees yearly, although he would have to compromise his ideology to provide excellent education to poor girls at a minimal fee. He hoped to find some teachers who would be ready work at a low salary. Were there not even ten to twenty educated and kind women in this whole country? He had advertised for the post of teachers in newspapers many times but nobody had responded. He had no other option but to increase the fees.

At this moment, a horse cart stopped outside his house and a woman got off from it and walked into the courtyard. Vimal got out of his room, welcomed her and brought her inside the house and made her sit on a chair. The lady was not the most beautiful but she looked well-educated and well-mannered. She had an average height, a slim figure and was very pleasant looking. She was simply dressed but elegance was evident in her simplicity. This was not an unusual event for Vimal. Since the time he had started Sevashram, ladies of reputed households came to his house to meet him.

After taking a seat, she said, "First, I must tell you my name. It is Manjula. A few days ago, I saw your notice in the Leader and have come to meet you regarding the same. I wanted to meet you since many days but could not get an opportunity. And I also did not want to come forcefully and waste your precious time. The sacrifice and dedication with which you are serving the little girls has left a deep impact on me and created so much respect for you that if I express it, you may take it as flattery. I had always wanted to do something like this and serve the society. But I have never been able to do that. Now it seems possible to follow my desire to serve the society and do it now with your help and support."

Viman was a silent servitor. He felt uncomfortable whenever anyone praised him. He never praised anybody in their presence, he always praised them in their absence. This was the reason that many people considered him heartless. But whenever he spoke ill about someone, he would always do it on their face. He expected the same from others as well.

He replied softly, "It is very kind of you and you are always welcome. But you must be aware of the poor financial condition of Sevashram."

"I have not come here for money."

"I had realized that earlier but I thought it would be better to make things clear. Do you live in this town?"

Manjula Devi belonged to Lucknow. She had done her schooling from Jalandhar's Girls School. She was fluent in English and was an expert in managing the household. But most importantly, she had a desire to serve. It would be splendid if such a woman would be able to take the responsibilities of Sevashram.

But Vimal had a doubt. He asked her, "Will your husband live with you?"

It was a simple question but it seemed to be repulsive for Manjula. She replied, "No, he will continue to live in Lucknow. He works in a bank and gets a very good salary."

The answer further complicated the matter. Vimal thought that if a man gets a good salary, then why his wife wished to live in Kashi leaving him in another city.

But he could only say, "All right!"

Manjula guessed his thoughts and said, "You must be thinking that such an occurrence is uncommon but what is the meaning of marriage according to you? Is it that a woman should forever hide behind her husband?"

Vimal replied passionately, "No, never."

"If I can reduce my needs to a zero then why should I be a burden to anyone?"

"Right!"

"My husband's and my thoughts differ due to various reasons. I think that devotion and worship are the truths of human life. He considers these things to be very petty, he does not even believe in God. I consider the Hindu culture as the best while he can only find faults in it. How can I live with such a man?"

Vimal himself did not believe such devotion and worship but he could not understand why any woman would leave her husband for such a petty reason. He knew many such women whose husbands turned to atheists but still did not abandon their husbands. He asked her, "I hope your husband won't have any objection on this matter."

Manjula said with pride, "I don't care about his objections. If men are free individuals, then so are women."

Then she said in a soft tone, "You may say that we are living separately since three years. We live in the same house but do not speak to each other. Whenever he fell sick, I nursed him back to health. If a crisis befell him, I sympathized with him and encouraged him. But even if I die today, he won't feel any grief. Rather, he would be happy that he would not have to pay for my subsistence..."

Her voice choked with emotion. She kept staring at the floor silently. Then she realized that Vimal might consider her a weak woman who has revealed her deep secrets of life and her sorrows in front of everyone. It was extremely important to clear his apprehension. So she told him that she had never told anyone about her personal problems. She had not even discussed these things with her mother. Vimal was the first person to whom she confided her secret because she thought that he was a good person and would understand the helplessness of a woman.

Vimal felt embarrassed and said, "It is your kindness to have such great thoughts about me."

Hearing her secrets, he felt reverence in his heart for Manjula. It had been a long time since he met a woman who had the courage to fulfill her convictions. He often rebels against the unfairness of society. Sevashram was a result of such a mental rebellion. He was confident that Manjula would be able to handle the responsibility of Sevashram with full dedication. She was prepared for it.

II

Manjula's life was full of self-sacrifices. She thought that the body was only a means of accomplishing the desires of the soul. There was no glory in the world that could give her peace. She was not interested in Mr. Mehra, because he was only interested in leading a luxurious life like many others and often ignored rules of the society and religion just to fulfill his selfish needs. If he had any consideration for her, he would have tried to understand her feelings and respected them or at least would have tried to sort out the differences of opinions that had arisen amongst them. If he had, she would have been happy but that great man had no sympathy for his wife; he always stood as a barrier in her way and made her feel extremely uneasy. He frustrated her to such an extent that her mind could no longer follow a suitable path and deviated in different directions. If only she was able to give this lack of interest a form of art, she would have felt content. She wanted to follow the path of her dreams and fulfill the unfulfilled desires in her life. But she neither had that talent nor creativity and therefore, she felt uneasy at home like a bird trapped in a cage. But now she had no more desires, she wanted to be free. She wanted to experience the happiness felt when one attains freedom. She was not just a branch that lived as a burden on a tree. She had a separate identity, a separate workspace.

But she felt that her dream and thoughts had no place in this practical world. They were wrong according to the societal norms. In Sevashram, to receive donations from guests, one had to flatter them but her self-respect never gave her permission to do so. To read the invitation letters that glorified them go to their house and invite them to visit Sevashram, or to receive them at the railway station, these were the things that she never liked to do. But she had to manage Sevashram, ignoring her inner feelings and she did it well. She was not satisfied with her work and therefore she found no joy and excitement in it. She had left her home because she did not want to compromise with her heart or soul but in reality, these compromises took a wilder form. Bitterness filled her heart and the desire to serve the humanity started vanishing.

Vimal, on the other hand, was the exact opposite. He never looked tired. He was always happy and full of zeal. He was always ready to serve as the situation demanded. If any student or teacher of Sevashram fell ill, he would be ready to nurse them. He was so full of dedication that his zeal never faltered. He had no doubts or misgivings. He had chosen a path and was ready to follow it. He had full faith that his chosen path will make him reach his goal. If he meets someone on his way, he befriends him or her. The one, who carries a refection with him, enjoys sharing and eating it with his friends. He had to bear a lot of problems, he had to flatter others to receive donations, bear insults, accept the advice of unworthy people, beg them for grants, but he did not repent. He was never disheartened and never felt bad. He had such zeal that he never gave up even after facing so many hardships and rejections. Teachers at the school would complain to him about simple matters. Sometimes they would get angry and wish to leave the job. For instance, when the washerwoman did not clean their clothes well, or the watchmen rebuked their dogs, or the sweeper did not clean their rooms properly, or the milkman mixed water with the milk. On such petty matters, the teachers start screaming and crying. And Vimal would try to pacify them and beg them to remain calm like a servitor. He would listen to their complaints and laugh off the matter. As a result, the teachers considered him more like a friend than the director of Sevashram.

But Manjula always maintained her distance from Vimal. She neither complained to him nor did she ask for his advice in any matter. Perhaps she realized that the work, which she had considered to be below her principles, was actually a much higher form of humanity, but she could still not forgo her principles. But despite her pride, she was attracted towards Vimal's pure and selfless nature. Based on her personal experience, she had created some notions in her heart regarding ordinary individuals. But Vimal's principles were much higher than that. He never thought of self-benefit. Arrogance had never even touched him. His sacrifice was limitless. According to Manjula, a man must possess these qualities to become ideal. But when she realized that Vimal was so near to this ideal image, it also made her realize she was still very far from becoming an ideal. The importance of the ideal was that it was something unachievable. If it were achieved, then how would it remain an ideal? Manjula wanted to raise her idea of the ideal human being so that Vimal could still not become the ideal person but as her affection towards him started to increase, she tried to control her feelings somehow and finally, she found a solution.

Manjula had realized that Vimal was not happy with her style of working. Then why didn't he complain about it and demand an explanation from her? She had observed that Vimal was attracted towards her, then why was his behavior so repentant? Does it prove that he is deceitful and cowardly? He spoke to everyone with affection and pleasure then why did he avoid her? Why does he talk to her superficially? Where was the pleasant manner of their first meeting? Does he want to show that he no longer cares for her or was he angry at her for not flattering the rich for donations? But she would never compromise on her self-respect. She would serve but would also keep her principles alive.

One morning, Manjula was walking in the garden when Vimal came to her and said, "We will be celebrating the annual function of Sevashram soon, so now we should start preparations for it."

Manjula asked in an indifferent tone, "This celebration happens every year?"

Vimal said, "Yes, every year, but we are planning to have a grand celebration this time."

"I will try my best to do what I can, but you know that I don't have much experience in this field."

"The success of this event totally depends on you."

"On me?"

"Yes, if you wish then Sevashram would reach great heights in no time."

"I think you have made a mistake in judging my capabilities."

Vimal said in a confident tone, "It will soon become clear whether I am right or wrong."

For the first time, Vimal had encouraged Manjula in any matter.

Since the day he had handed over the management of Sevashram to her, he had never ordered her to do anything with regard to the school. He never had the courage to demand anything from her. Every time they met, they discussed only general topics. Maybe he thought that the sacrifices she had already made were more than enough and he could not burden her with more responsibilities, or it could be possible that he was waiting for her to get comfortable at Sevashram and would then demand service. Today when he ordered her with respect and courtesy, Manjula felt a surge of renewed energy. She had never felt so attached to Sevashram before. All her complaints against Vimal disappeared and she got busy with the preparation of the annual function. She was now surprised at her own detachment with the school. She was busy the whole week, day and night, in welcoming and taking care of the guests. She did not even find time to eat. All the guests came by different trains. She was responsible to receive them and bring them to Sevashram. Sometimes she even had to go to the station at midnight to receive the guests. She had to take care of preparations and also prepare her thanksgiving speech. Finally, all her efforts were rewarded, as the annual function became a great success. Also, with the success of the function came donations in the form of thousands of rupees. But the day all the guests left, Manjula welcomed a new guest who did not allow her to raise her head for three days. She had never suffered from such high fever before. In three days, it seemed that she had been suffering for several years.

Vimal had also been busy in those days. Initially, he had been busy arranging for the *pandal*[1] and the feast for guests. After the annual function was over, he was busy returning the things to their respective owners. He did not get time to thank Manjula even though he was informed that she was suffering from fever. He assumed that she must be tired due to excessive work and ignored the news. But when he heard on the fourth day that she was still suffering from fever, he rushed to her side and asked her guiltily, "How are you feeling now? Why didn't you call me?"

---

1. *Pandal*: A large tent used for social or commercial functions.

Suddenly Manjula felt much better. Her headache also seemed to have decreased. She said, "Why are you standing? Please sit, otherwise, I will have to get up."

Vimal looked at her as if he wanted to take all her pain and then replied politely, "No, no, you keep resting, I will sit down. I am the one to be blamed. It is due to my negligence that you are suffering. I had asked you to do all the work. Please forgive me. I delegated the work that I should have done myself. I was not aware of your condition. Let me go and call the doctor."

He was about to leave when Manjula said, "There is no need to call the doctor. I am feeling much better. I will be able to sit up by tomorrow."

She wanted to say many things but she sealed her lips. She did not know what she would say in this condition. Till now Vimal had maintained his distance and considered her a Goddess. He remained far from her not because he did not want to come close to her but because he simply thinks that coming close to the Goddess might be taken as an offence and disrespect. Vimal did not know how truthful and great a man he was. Therefore, Manjula wanted him to remember her forever.

She said with a smile, "Yes, why not because you are a human being while I am a wooden toy."

"No, you are a Goddess."

"No, I am just an ordinary woman."

"Whatever you have accomplished in this short span of time was unattainable for me."

"Have you ever thought about the reason behind it? It was not the victory of a woman but rather her defeat. If I were a man with all my faults then I could not have achieved even one-fourth of what I have achieved, so it is not my victory. It is the victory of femininity. Beauty is just skin deep, it is not the truth. It is all a facade and fraud, to hide one's weaknesses."

Vimal said, "What are you saying, Manjula Devi? Beauty is the greatest truth of this world. Our scholars and ascetics have not given it its due respect, it is an injustice."

Manjula looked beautiful as she was glowing with pride. She had difficulty accepting that beauty had no value. Through her dedication and devotion, she was trying to overcome the falsehood. But the praise of her beauty coming from Vimal made her extremely happy. She controlled her excitement and replied, "Please forgive me, Vimal Babu, but you are wrong. It is nothing new for you to praise beauty. Men have always praised beauty. Some of our scholars and ascetics may not have believed in beauty but men have always appreciated it. They have not even bothered about their religion when it comes to beauty and even though the scholars and ascetics have not given value to beauty, they have praised it in their hearts. Whenever beauty tested their patience, they failed and beauty emerged as victorious. Thus, the truth shall remain the same. Beauty is just a matter of external attraction. It has no value in the eyes of the learned. At least I do not wish to hear any praises of beauty from you because I feel that you are like God and I respect you with all my heart."

Vimal was silent and thoughtful and continuously kept looking down at the floor. Suddenly he stood up and left the room like a criminal.

Manjula sat satisfied.

III

From that day suddenly Vimal lost all his zeal and energy for his work. It seemed that he had no courage to face anybody now. He felt that the secret had been revealed and everybody was laughing at him. He rarely came to Sevashram now and even when he came, he did not speak to any teacher. It seemed that he was trying to avoid everyone. He did not give Manjula an opportunity to talk to him and finally, when Manjula went to his house, he lied and told her that he was not at home and stayed hidden in the house.

Manjula was unable to understand his state of mind. There

was no doubt that Vimal had attracted her with his simplicity and good manners. She was aware that Vimal also liked her, and a little encouragement he would have admitted his deepest feelings in front of her. The life that he had led until then had no signs of love in it. He was very engrossed in his work and duty.

She could not have a moral or religious relationship with a man who did not love her and believe in her. She considers herself as a free individual. She wanted to have a relationship with Vimal but also wanted her self-respect to remain intact. Further, she also did not want to create any problems for Vimal because his life was sacred and pure. She just wanted to talk to him as a friend and discuss with him all the matters of her life. She had thought that she would make him drink a little bit of medicine and make him healthy. She considered him a lamp and wanted to enjoy its light because she knew that if she touched it then it would burn her. But now she realized that her medicine had created another disease for him. She wanted to be close to Vimal. He had a very unique quality, whenever he worked towards the achievement of an objective, he gave his hundred percent, but whenever he diverted his mind from a matter he never looked back. Manjula felt insulted by Vimal's behavior and bitterness filled her heart.

Finally, one day she found Vimal. She knew that he went for a walk near the river every day. Therefore, she went there and handed over her resignation to him.

Vimal was dumbfounded. He stared at the ground and said, "Why?"

"Because I don't feel that I am suitable for this work."

"But Sevashram is running very well."

"But I do not want to stay here."

"Have I made a mistake?"

"Just ask your heart."

Vimal could rightly guess the meaning of this, way beyond the imagination of Manjula. He grew pale as if the blood had stopped flowing through his veins. He had no answer. It was a decision that could not be appealed.

He said in a hurtful tone, "As you wish."

Manjula was saddened by his reply and said, "So, should I leave?"

"As you wish"

And he walked away as if he wanted to free himself from the problem as soon as possible. Manjula kept looking at him, with her eyes full of tears as if she was watching a boat sink.

IV

Vimal again busied himself in the workings of Sevashram. Everybody was informed that Manjula Devi's husband was unwell and therefore, she had to leave. A hardworking man does not have time to cry over his bygone love. Vimal got busy with the development of Sevashram to achieve his goal. Sometimes he did remember Manjula in his solitude and feel ashamed of his behavior. He had learnt a lesson for a lifetime. He had misbehaved with a faithful and devoted lady.

Three years had passed. The summer season had begun. Vimal had gone to visit Mussoorie for a vacation and was staying at a hotel. One day he was standing near the bus stop listening to a band playing music when he suddenly saw Manjula sitting on a nearby bench. She was looking beautiful in a colorful *sari* and lots of jewellery. She was with a young man wearing a coat and pant. They were chatting pleasantly. Their faces were shining brightly and both were deeply in love with each other. Several questions arose in Vimal's mind: Who is this young man? He could not be her husband. Or it might be possible that it could be him. The couple might have sorted their problems and reconciled. He could not muster the courage to face Manjula.

The next day, Vimal went to watch an English play at the theatre. During the interval, he came out and again saw Manjula in the café. She was wearing a western dress and was accompanied by the same young man. Today Vimal could not control his curiosity; before he could change his mind, he was standing in front of Manjula.

Manjula was surprised to see Vimal, but she steadied herself and said with a smile, "Hello Vimal Babu, what are you doing here?"

And then she introduced Vimal to the young man, "He is a learned man, the director of Sevashram in Kashi and he is Mr. Khanna, my friend, who has recently returned from England."

Both the men shook hands. And then Manjula said to Vimal, "Sevashram is running very well. I had read its annual reports in the newspaper. Where are you staying here?"

Vimal told her the name of the hotel.

The play had begun again. Mr. Khanna said, "The play has started. Let's go inside."

Manjula replied, "You go inside, I want to talk to Mr. Vimal."

Mr. Khanna looked at Vimal with jealous eyes and went inside haughtily. Manjula and Vimal came out into the garden and sat on the fresh grass. Vimal's heart was filled with pride.

Manjula asked in a serious tone, "I don't think you would have remembered me. Many a time I thought of writing to you but could not do that out of hesitation. I hope you were happy?"

Vimal felt bad. She was so happy and smiling and now she became so serious upon seeing him. He replied in a rude tone, "Yes, I have been very happy. And I think you are happy as well?"

Manjula sadly replied, "I have no happiness in my life, Mr. Vimal. My husband died last year. His debts were more than his income. I was continuously dealing with these difficulties. My health deteriorated. The doctors advised me to go to a hill station and since then I have been residing here."

"You did not even write a letter to me."

"You already have so many responsibilities to take care of. I didn't want to trouble you with my problems."

"At least as a friend you should have informed me."

Manjula said, "It is not your duty to indulge in such petty matters. God has made you for sacrifice and service. That is your work. I know that you have sympathy for me and I value your sympathy immensely.

If one, who has never received any love and sympathy turns towards these attributes then he can be pardoned. You can understand the sacrifice I have made by letting them go, but I considered it my duty. I can tolerate everything but I won't let you come down from the divine position that you hold in my mind. You are a learned man, you know that happiness cannot be continuous. I understand that you too are a human and have your desires but you have reached this level of dedication only after defeating them. So save yourself from these vices. Only spirituality can help you in this field. By practicing it, you will make your life successful and your soul pure."

Vimal had understood her relationship with Mr. Khanna, but still, he felt a true motivation in her advice. The lustful woman appeared like a true Goddess in his eyes. Vimal said in a humble tone, "I am grateful to you for the respect that you have shown for me. Tell me, what can I do for you?"

Manjula was now ready to leave. She said, "Your sympathy is enough for me."

At that time, Mr. Khanna was seen coming out of the theatre.

Repentance

I

It had become a matter of pride for officers to come late to the office. The superior the officer, the later he comes to the office, and the earliest he leaves. But the peon has to stay for twenty-four hours. He cannot even think of taking leave. When the head clerk of the Bareilly District Board, Babu Madarilal came to the office at eleven o' clock, it was as if the office had woken up from its slumber. The peon ran towards him, the lower clerk went inside his office and lifted the curtains, and the sweeper set out the files on his table.

Madarilal found a letter on his table. After reading the letter, he stood motionless for a few minutes. He has encountered several shocks in his life, but he had never felt so helpless before. The letter stated that the government had appointed Subodh Chandra for the post of the Board Secretary. The issue with the appointment was Madarilal's hatred for Subodh Chandra. Subodh Chandra was his high school classmate and Madarilal had tried his best to outrun him but was unable to do so. This was the same Subodh Chandra who was appointed as his officer.

Over the past few years, there had been no news of Subodh. The last time he heard of him was that he had joined the army. Madarilal had thought that he must have been killed during his service; but today, it was as if he was reborn and was coming to haunt him as the Secretary. Madarilal would have to work under him. It was better to die than face to such an insult. Subodh would certainly remember everything that had happened during school and college. Madarilal had once tried to get Subodh expelled from school and college, had raised false allegations against him, and defamed him. Is it possible that Subodh might have forgotten all about that? No, never. The moment he arrived, he would take his revenge. Madarilal could not think of a way to save his own life.

It seemed like Madarilal's and Subodh Chandra's stars were always against each other. Both had got enrolled in the same school on the same day and from that day onwards envy, jealousy and hatred pervaded between them and were still prevalent even after twenty years. Subodh's only fault was that he was better than Madarilal in almost all aspects -behaviour, good looks, character, and intelligence. Madarilal couldn't ever forgive him. Subodh had always been a thorn in Madarilal's heart for the past twenty years. While Subodh took the degree and went home, Madarilal failed. When he took up a job in this office, Madarilal got calm. When he came to know that Subodh was joining the army, he was happy. But what bad luck! Seeing the letter, he felt as if old wounds have reopened again. Now, Madarilal's fate was in Subodh's hands. How unjust God is! How cruel is fate!

When he calmed down a bit, Madarilal read out the news to all the clerks and said, "Now please be careful. Subodh Chandra is not a person who easily forgives faults."

One clerk asked, "Is he very strict?"

Madarilal smiled and said, "You will come to know in three to four days. Why should I complain about somebody else? I am just warning you beforehand. He is competent but extremely short-tempered and proud. He will digest thousands but won't let anybody take even a single paisa. Only God can save us from such a man! I am thinking of taking leave and going back home. You are not the servants of the government from now on, but instead, the Secretary's servants. You will have to go to his house twice. Someone will teach his son, someone will run errands for him in the market and someone will read out the newspaper to him. And the peons may not be seen in the office at all."

After manipulating the staffs against Subodh Chandra, Madarilal was satisfied.

II

After a week, Subodh Chandra got off the train to find all the employees of the office at the station. They had come to welcome him. He saw Madarilal and immediately hugged him and said, "Wonderful to see you, brother! How did you come here? I am meeting you after ages."

Madarilal said, "I am the Head Clerk in the District Board office. Are you fine?"

Subodh said, "Don't ask about me. I don't even remember where all I've been traveling, Basra, France, Greece. It is good that you are in this office. I had no idea how the work would be done as I am totally new. But wherever I go, my luck is with me. At Basra, all the officers were very happy. All were impressed in France too. In two years time, I made over twenty-five thousand rupees but I spent it all. After returning, I worked at the operations office. Now, I came here, and I found you." Then, looking at the clerks, he asked, "Who are they?"

Madarilal's heart was bleeding. He thought, "Subodh made twenty-five thousand rupees! And here I am tired of writing with a pen and I have not been able to save five hundred rupees."

Coming out of his thoughts, he replied, "They are the employees of the Board. They have come to welcome you."

Subodh shook hands with each one of them and said, "You people took out your precious time and have come here to welcome me, I am extremely grateful. I hope I won't have any complaints against you. Consider me not as your officer, but as your brother. Please work in such a way that the name of the Board shines and makes me happy. Your Head Clerk Sahib is an old childhood friend of mine."

One talkative clerk said, "We are your servants. We will keep you as happy as we can; but we are human and if there is some mistake, please forgive us."

Subodh said humbly, "This has been my principle wherever I go. Both you and I are serving a third person. Then what officer and what clerks? I will behave with you as a friend. Yes, we will do our duties sincerely."

When the employees took their leave and walked away, they started talking amongst themselves, "The man seems to be good."

"By what the Head Clerk had told us, it seemed as if he would finish all of us."

"Initially, everyone talks sweet."

III

It had been a month since Subodh's arrival. All the employees were very happy with his behavior. He was so cheerful and humble that anybody who met him became his friend for life. Even when he was angry, he never insulted anyone. But when you're in someone's bad books, even your good qualities look worse. Madarilal started disturbed by this. He was always busy scheming some plot or the other against Subodh. He tried to instigate the employees initially, but could not succeed. He tried to instigate the members of the Board but failed. He tried to influence the contractors but was not successful. He spoke to Subodh as if they were true friends but always waited for an opportunity to stab him in the back. Subodh had all the qualities, except the quality of recognizing the true nature of men. He considered Madarilal as his friend.

One day, when Madarilal went to the Secretary's office, he found the chair empty. On his table, he saw currency notes worth five thousand rupees kept in a bundle. This was to be used for the purchase of several wooden things which were being made for the *madrasas* of the Board. The contractor had been called to collect the money. The Secretary had given the cheque that day itself and had withdrawn the money from the bank. Madarilal peeped into the verandah, there was no sign of Subodh anywhere. His intentions changed. The wrath of greed mixed with that of jealousy. With trembling hands, he picked up the bundle and put it in his coat pocket. He came out of the room quickly and called out to the peon, "Is Babuji inside?" The peon came and said, "No. He just left. He was talking to someone in the court."

Madarilal came back to the office and told one clerk, "Go and show this message to Secretary Sahib."

The clerk went with the message. He came back after some time and said, "Secretary Sahib is not in his office. I have kept the file on his table."

Madarilal was irritated. He said, "Where does he go, leaving his office? Someday, he will suffer because of it."

The clerk said, "Who goes inside his office other than the office staff?"

Madarilal said in a grave tone, "So can we trust all of our staff members? They are not Gods. No one can say when temptation overpowers a person and someone comes in with a bad intention. That is merely human nature. You should go and close both the doors of his office."

The clerk said, "The peon is sitting at the door itself."

Madarilal said, "You do what I am telling you. Is the peon some sage? What will you do if the peon takes something? Nowadays, people can bail themselves out by paying just three hundred rupees. Here, every file is worth lakhs of rupees."

Saying this, Madarilal went and closed the door. When his heart was calm, he took out the notes and hid them between some papers in an almirah. Then he came back and started working.

Subodh Chandra came back after about an hour. The doors of his office were closed. He came to the office and said smiling, "Who closed the office, brother? Am I suspended?"

Madarilal stood up and said, "*Sahib*, please forgive me. I request you to kindly close doors whenever you leave your office, even if it is for a minute. There are many government files scattered on your table, and you never know when someone enters your office and an important paper goes missing. I had come to visit you an hour back. As you were not in your office, I closed the door."

Subodh Chandra thanked Madarilal. He went inside his cabin and started smoking a cigar. He was not aware that the currency notes on the table were missing.

Suddenly, the contractor came inside and saluted. Subodh got up from the chair and said, "You are late. I was waiting for you. I got the money collected at ten o'clock. Do you have the receipt?"

The contractor said, "Yes Sir, I have got the receipt."

Subodh said, "Then take the money. I am not happy with your work. You have used wood of poor quality and your work lacks finishing. If I come across such substandard work again, I would remove your name from the list of contractors."

Saying this, Subodh looked at the table and found the bundle of notes missing. He searched all the papers, under the files and everywhere in the office, but the bundle was nowhere to be seen. Subodh grew anxious, "Where did the money go? I had kept it on the table!" He searched the files again. His heart started beating faster. He calmed himself down and started analyzing the incidents of the past hour. He recapped the events systematically, "The peon came and gave the money to me, I remember that very well. I kept the notes on this table, without even counting them. Then the lawyer came, who is an old friend. I went out to talk to him. He brought some betel, and that is why I got late. I clearly remember that when I left my office, the bundle was on the table. Then where is the bundle? I did not keep it in any box, almirah or trunk. Then where did it go? Perhaps, somebody must have seen the notes in the office and kept it safely to give it to me later. I'm sure that's the case. There's no need to panic."

He came to the office and asked Madarilal, "Did you take the money from my table and keep it somewhere?"

Madarilal pretended to be surprised and said, "Was there any money on your table? I have not noticed. Pandit Sohanlal had gone to your office with a file and could not find you there. When I came to know that you had gone to speak to somebody, I closed the door. Can you not find the money?"

Subodh widened his eyes and said, "*Sahib*, there were five thousand rupees. I had just got the cheque encashed."

Madarilal beat his head and said, "Five thousand rupees! Oh God! Did you search the table well?"

"I have been searching for the last fifteen minutes."

"Did you ask the peon who all had come there?"

"Please come. You also search for it. I am lost."

The entire office started searching the Secretary's room. The table, almirah and trunks were searched. Registers were searched but there was no sign of the notes. At this moment, Subodh realized that someone has stolen the money. He took a deep sigh and sat on the chair. His face was pale.

Madarilal said sympathetically, "It is a catastrophe, what else? Till date, such a crisis had never occurred. It has been ten years since I have been working here, and not a single thing has ever been stolen. I wanted to warn you on the first day itself that you should be careful while handling money, but it did not strike me back then. I am sure someone has stolen the money. It is the peon's fault. Why did he allow anybody to enter the office at all? Even if he swears a thousand times that nobody came from outside, I won't believe. Only Pandit Sohanlal had come here with a file, and he kept the file from the door itself."

Sohanlal explained, "I did not even enter, *Sahib*! I swear by my young son, I did not step inside."

Madarilal said, "Why are you swearing? Who is asking you to do that? (Whispering in Subodh's ears) If there is some money in your bank, withdraw and give it to the contractor. Or else, it would be embarrassing. Whatever loss had to happen has happened. Why should you be defamed for it?"

Subodh said pitifully, "There is hardly two to four hundred rupees in the bank, brother. If I had enough money in the bank, there won't have been a problem. I don't even have enough money for my coffin."

Later that night, Subodh Chandra committed suicide. It was difficult for him to arrange so much money. He was so depressed that he couldn't find any other way to escape except death.

IV

Next morning, the peon went to Madarilal's house and called him. Madarilal could not sleep the whole night. He came out terrified. Seeing him, the peon said, "Sir! There has been a calamity! Secretary Sahib slit his throat yesterday."

Madarilal's eyes popped out, his face broadened and his whole body trembled as if he had just touched a live wire.

"Slit his throat?"

"Yes. It was found out in the morning. Police have come. You have been called."

"Is his body there?"

"Yes. It is going for postmortem."

"Are there lots of people?"

"All the big officers have come. Sir, no one has mustered enough courage to look at the dead body. Secretary Sahib was such a good person! Everybody is crying. He has two small children and a daughter of marriageable age. Madam is somehow being controlled, but she runs to the body again and again. There is nobody who is not consoling and wiping their tears. He had been here for a short span of time but had mingled so well with everybody. He never bothered about money. He had a heart of gold."

Madarilal felt dizzy. If he had not held on to the door, he would have fallen. He asked, "Is his wife crying?"

"Don't ask, Sir. Her tears continue to fall like the leaves of the autumn and have swelled her eyes."

"How many sons did you say?"

"He had two sons and a daughter."

"Yes. I have seen the boys. Is the girl grown-up?"

"Yes, she is of marriageable age. She also has been continuously crying. They are in a very bad state."

"There must have been some discussion about the money, I guess."

"Yes. Everybody says that it is the work of someone at the office. The police inspector wanted to arrest Sohanlal, but perhaps he will consult you before that. Secretary Sahib has left a letter saying that he does not suspect anybody."

"Has the Secretary Sahib left some letter behind?"

"Yes. It seems that before slitting his throat, he realized that the office staff would be held in suspicion. So he wrote a letter addressed to the collector saying that no one was responsible for his death."

"Has he written anything about me in the letter? Would you know?"

"Sir, how will I know? But everybody was saying that he has praised you a lot."

Madarilal's heart churned. Two big tears flowed down his eyes. He wiped the tears and said, "We had studied together, Nandoo! We were together for ten years. We used to be together all the time. We were like brothers. What has he written about me in the letter? But how would you know?"

"You are going there. So read it yourself."

"Has the coffin been arranged?"

"No, sir. I told you that the postmortem would be done now. Please come quickly before someone else comes to call you."

"Has everybody come from our office?"

"Yes, everyone from this colony is also present."

"Has the police questioned anybody about me?"

"No. They have not."

When Madarilal reached Subodh Chandra's house, he felt as if everybody was looking at him with suspicion. The police inspector called him and said, "You also give your statement. I have noted down the statements of other people."

Madarilal gave his statement so carefully that even the police officers were surprised. All the doubts in their minds vanished.

Just then, Subodh's son came crying to Madarilal and said, "Please come. Mother is calling you." Madarilal knew both of them. Madarilal came here almost daily, but he had never gone to Subodh's house. Subodh's wife was behind a veil in front of Madarilal. Hearing this invitation, his heart started beating, "I hope she does not doubt me. I hope Subodh had not said anything to her about me."

Hesitatingly, he went inside and was shocked to see the widow crying. Seeing him, another round of tears started flowing down her cheeks. The daughter came and fell at his feet. The boys also came running to him. Seeing their deep pain and anguish, Madarilal could not look at them. His conscience started pricking him. He had stabbed these people who had so much trust and faith in him! Because of him, the whole family was ruined. What will happen to these helpless people? Who would get the daughter married? Who would look after the children? Madarilal felt so guilty that he could not utter a single word of consolation. He felt that his face had been blackened and that he had been tremendously reduced in stature. When he stole the money, he had no idea that the repercussions would be so adverse. He had never intended to ruin their lives.

The widow said, "Brother, he has left us in the lurch. If I knew that he had decided to take such a drastic step, I would have offered whatever I had. He kept on telling me that he'll find some way to repay it. He wanted to approach some moneylender through you. I can't express how much he trusted you."

These words kept stabbing Madarilal's heart. He suddenly felt suffocated as if something was stuck in his throat.

Rameshwari said again, "When he went to sleep he was smiling. He drank milk like any other day; he kissed the children, played the harmonium for some time and then gargled before lying down. He did nothing suspicious. Seeing me worried, he said, 'You are unnecessarily getting worried. Babu Madarilal is my old friend. When will he be of some use? We have played together. He knows everybody in this town. He would arrange some money very easily.' I don't know when this thought came to his mind. I was in such deep slumber that I couldn't even notice anything. How could I know that he would commit suicide?"

Madarilal felt as if the whole world was floating in front of his eyes. He tried, but could not stop his tears.

Rameshwari wiped her tears and said, "Brother, what was destined to happen, has happened. But you must find the culprit who is responsible for all this! I'm sure it is someone from the office. Your friend was a good man. He kept on telling me that he did not doubt anybody, but surely it is the work of an insider. I only request you and ask for this one thing, that the sinner should not be allowed to go free. The police might be bribed to let him go. But if they saw you, they will not dare to do that. Now, who is there other than you? To whom should we tell our woes? It was fate to have the dead body in this state."

Madarilal felt for a moment that he should tell her everything. He wanted to tell them clearly; I am that cruel man, the sinner, and the pathetic man. He wanted to fall at the widow's feet and say, please slit my throat with that knife. But he could not open his mouth. He felt suddenly dizzy and fell unconscious.

V

By afternoon, the post mortem was over. The body was taken towards the river. The whole office and thousands of people were gathered. The cremation rites were to be performed by the sons, but since they were very young, the widow was getting ready to perform the rites when Madarilal went to her and said, "Let me do those rites. If you sit for those rites, who will look after the children? Subodh was my brother. I could not do anything for him in my life, so let me do something for him after his death. After all, I also had some rights over him."

Rameshwari cried and said, "God has given you a very kind heart, brother. Otherwise, who bothers after somebody's death? Other people from the office stood for hours with their hands tied behind and couldn't even care to give some false consolation."

Madarilal completed the last rites. He sat for thirteen days and completed all rites. On the thirteenth day, Brahmins were given lunch, beggars were given alms, friends were given a feast and Madarilal bore all the expenses. Rameshwari said that he had done more than enough. "Now I will not allow you to spend more. What can a friend do more than this", but Madarilal did not listen. His fame spread in the entire town. Friends should be like him.

On the sixteenth day, the widow told Madarilal, "Brother, we will remain indebted to you for all the help and support that you have given us. If you had not helped us, I don't know what would have happened. There was no help from anyone else. Now let us go back to our house. There would be fewer expenses in the village and I can also do some farming. Somehow these days of difficulty shall also pass."

Madarilal asked, "How much land is there in the village?"

Rameshwari answered, "What land? There is a small temporary house and ten to twelve *bighas*[1] of land. We were about to start to make a house with a permanent structure, but the money was not enough. It is incomplete now. Ten thousand rupees have been spent and the roof is yet to be built."

Madarilal asked, "Is there some money in the bank, or will you depend on farming only?"

The widow replied, "There are no savings at all, brother. Money never stayed in his hands. I would depend on farming."

Madarilal said, "Will there be enough crops to pay off the interest and to survive?"

Rameshwari said, "I've no option left, brother. We have to somehow survive. I'm glad I'm not alone in this. If I had no children, life would have been difficult to survive."

Madarilal asked, "And the daughter is also to be married?"

Widow said, "I am not worried about her marriage. There will be many farmers who would be willing to marry her, without any dowry."

Madarilal thought for a moment and said, "If I give you some advice, would you listen to me?"

1. *Bighas*: A measure of land area varying locally from 1/3 to 1 acre.

Rameshwari said, "Brother, if I won't listen to your advice, then whose advice would I listen to? Who else is there?"

Madarilal suggested, "Then I request you to come to my house instead of going to your village. Your children will live the same way as my children. You won't have any problem. And if God blesses us, your daughter would also get married to a good family."

The widow's eyes were wet. She said, "But brother, think..."

Madarilal interrupted her and said, "I would neither think about anything nor would I listen to anything either. Is it not possible for families of two brothers stay together under the same roof? I considered Subodh as my brother and will always think of him as my brother."

No matter how much she opposed, Madarilal insisted. Madarilal took Subodh's family with him and has been looking after them for the last ten years. Both the sons are now studying in college and the daughter has been married into a very good family. Madarilal and his wife serve Rameshwari with all their body and soul. Subconsciously, Madarilal is serving his penance through his service.

A Writer

I

Praveen Babu prepared a cup of tea with the remains of tea leaves, which had already been drained and strained to make tea twenty times before. It has been months now since he had been taking unsweetened tea without milk as his breakfast. Well, this is not the most important thing in his life right now. After having his tea, he went inside the house to ask for some money from his wife. Finding her asleep, covered with an old and tattered blanket, he did not feel like waking her up. He thought that perhaps she was unable to sleep last night due to the weather, so he let her sleep and returned without waking her up.

After drinking his tea, he took his inkpot and pen and engrossed himself in writing his book. He thought that he would create the greatest composition of the century and this publication would take him out of the anonymous world and would bring him fame and prosperity.

Half an hour later, his wife came out rubbing her eyes and asked, "Did you have your tea?"

Praveen said with a smile, "Yes, it was very nice."

"From where did you get the milk and sugar?"

"Since the past few days, I have stopped consuming milk and sugar. Nowadays, I prefer black tea. It becomes tasteless after adding milk and sugar to it. Even the doctors advise us to drink black tea. You know, in Europe, they never add milk to the tea."

"I don't understand how you like that kind of tea. Why didn't you wake me up? I had some money."

After finishing his argument with his wife, Praveen Babu started writing again. He had acquired this habit during his youth and it had stayed with him over the past twenty years. Due to this, his body had grown lean, his health was deteriorating and he looked way past his years, but the habit was incurable. From sunrise until sunset, his devotion to literature was undefeatable. He was detached from the whole world and offered all his attention and love to literature. But one should not completely ignore one aspect for the sake of another, like, total devotion to Goddess *Saraswati*[1] shouldn't lead to complete disregard to Goddess *Laxmi*[2]. If one pursued his passions without planning any prospective income, one would surely land up in a pitfall. But he had just one heart. How could he please both the Goddesses at the same time and receive their blessings simultaneously? The anger of Goddess *Laxmi* was not only evident in his lack of financial prospects but also reflected in the fact that all the editors and publisher of books were unhappy with him. He felt as if the whole world was against him. His lack of money had badly affected his confidence and self-respect. He started to doubt his literary capabilities and talent and failed to decipher the depth of his literary compositions. He felt as if he was wasting his precious human life and this feeling was heart-rending. He could no more derive satisfaction from believing that even though the world had not appreciated his talents, his life was not so worthless as opinions did not matter. Opinions have no power to define or destroy his literary competence. His requirement for a basic living was so limited to such an extent that he was quite near to becoming an ascetic. The only consolation was his better half, who was totally unaffected by these hardships that they had to face. Sumitra was happy even under such circumstances. Whereas Praveenji had several complaints against the world, Sumitra was a strong woman, never cried over her fate and always tried to protect him from any misfortune.

Sumitra picked up her cup of tea and said, "Why don't you go for a walk? You know it very well that there is no use of working all day and night when you get nothing in return. Why do you unnecessarily put your life at stake?"

---

1. *Saraswati*: The Hindu Goddess of Knowledge.
2. *Laxmi*: The Hindu Goddess of Wealth and Prosperity.

Without lifting up his head, Praveen replied, "At least I feel satisfied while I'm writing. I feel like I'm doing something. Whenever I go for a walk, I feel like I am wasting my time."

"Well, many well-educated people go to take a walk every day, and how many of them do you think are wasting their time?"

"Most of the people in this category are those who know that going for walks won't incur any difference to their income. You will mostly find government employees and wealthy people going out for walks. They have a fixed income, are well-established and hold a good reputation in the society. I am like a mere laborer of a mill. Have you ever seen labor going for a walk? Those who have plenty of food and lead a lavish lifestyle can afford to tame such interests. But those who face the difficulty to make their two ends meet, cannot afford to go on walks. For me, life is a burden and I don't want to bear this burden for my entire life."

Sumitra went inside with eyes brimming with tears. She believed in her heart that one day her husband's talent would definitely be recognized, even without the blessings of Goddess *Laxmi*. But Praveen Babu was losing his patience and going moving towards a depressing phase as he was unable to see even a single ray of hope.

II

One day, Praveen Babu was invited to a party, hosted by a person of great repute. His happiness knew no bounds and he started imagining about the big day - how would he be welcomed by the Raja Sahib to his party, how would he thank him for inviting him, what would be the topics of discussion, and how many guests would he be introduced to. He kept thinking and weaving imaginary conversations about such things. He had also composed a poem for this event where he drew a comparison between life to a beautiful garden. Today, he decided to keep aside all his notions of truth because he wanted to avoid hurting the emotions of such an eminent person.

He had already started his preparations since afternoon. He shaved, took his bath, and oiled his head. Now, the only concern he had was his clothes. He had an old coat, but he had bought that a long time ago and it was already old and tattered. The condition of his old coat matched his present state. Even though its condition was too delicate to wear it again, he still brushed and cleaned it, and decided to wear it to the party.

Sumitra said, "Why did you accept the invitation? You should have informed him that you are unwell. It is even worse to go in such horrible clothes."

Praveen answered philosophically, "The ones who are gifted with the power of judgment, judge a man by his character and not by his clothes as they only look for quality and character. Raja Sahib must have seen something in me, and that's why invited me to the party. I am not a landlord, contractor or a grantee, but just an ordinary writer. The value of a writer is judged by his writings. So, I don't see any reason to be ashamed of my condition."

Sumitra took pity on his simplicity and said, "You have been so engrossed in your idealistic world that you have detached yourself from the real world. I am telling you, everyone would be checking out each other's clothes at the party. Simplicity is a good thing but that doesn't mean that you would go like a gauche person."

Praveen Babu contemplated his wife's advice and replied, "I think I should go there after sunset."

"I don't think that you should go there at all."

"How do I make you understand, every human being has the need to be respected and looked up to. There is a necessity of gratifying such a need as it restores the lost self-respect and the fire of confidence that seems to have dwindled in me. We all are a part of this huge universe that is filled with such emotions. Even an atom is encapsulated in the characteristics of the universe. That is the reason why, we feel a natural pull towards respect, self-improvement and knowledge. I don't consider such a need to be harmful."

Sumitra did not want to prolong the argument, so she said, "All right, do as you please, I won't argue with you. But do make some arrangements for tomorrow because I have only one *anna* left with me. I have borrowed money from several moneylenders and have not been able to return their money. Now I won't be able to borrow any further."

Praveen replied after a moment, "I might get some money for the columns I had written in two magazines. Maybe they would process the payment tomorrow. Otherwise, we would fast. My duty is to work hard with all my heart and soul. If despite my hard work, we are left without food then I won't consider it as my fault. Ultimately, we might die of starvation. There are many people out there, who die of poverty, but the world does not stop and goes on as usual. So don't be afraid of death, we shall face life as it comes. I am a believer of Kabir's verses and his followers. Even on the sad account of someone's death, they take a dead body singing and dancing. I would try to make every possible effort to enhance the quality of my writings. When the whole world is lost in their dreams, I write with my pen. People enjoy themselves, have fun and meet each other but for me all of this is useless. I don't remember laughing for months. I don't even celebrate Holi these days. Even when fever inflicts upon me, I would still continue to write my compositions. When you were suffering from fever, I couldn't spare time to even go and call the doctor. If the society does not respect my dedication, then I won't force them. They would be at loss. The work of a lamp is to burn, whether its flame spreads light or it is hidden by some object is not its concern.

Every single friend or relative has helped me financially. I often feel ashamed to face these people. But still, I am satisfied that they do not consider me malicious. Even when they fail to help me, they at least sympathize with me. And today a man of well-repute has honored me by inviting me to his house. That is enough for my happiness."

He lifted his head in pride and said, "No, I won't go after sunset. My poverty has crossed the limit of dishonor. It is a waste to hide it. I will go right now. One who has invited such a famous person shouldn't be considered a commoner. Raja Sahib is a prominent man who holds great reverence in the whole country. If people still consider me an inferior then that would mean that they themselves are inferior."

III

It was evening. Praveen Babu put on his old coat with a crude cap and rotten shoes. His demeanor looked much like a thief. Due to his ill-shape and figure, Praveen Babu's style lacked dignity. Even the stoutness and health of a person represents the prestige that he holds. But such stoutness if often found missing in a writer. The work of a lamp is to burn. A lamp filled with oil is the lamp which has not yet burnt properly. But Praveen Babu's pride was evident in his every step.

Normally, he would stealthily pass the street to avoid the shopkeepers from whom he had borrowed money and was unable to pay them back. But today he passed by without any hesitation. Today he was ready to reply to their questions. But it was evening and shops were lined with customers. Nobody noticed him.

Praveen Babu took rounds in the market but was not satisfied as nobody called him and asked for payment. He took another round in the market but still, nobody addressed him. Perplexed, he went to Hafiz's shop. Hafiz was a cloth merchant. Long back, he had bought an umbrella from him but was not able to pay the price yet. When he saw Praveen, he said, "Praveen Babu, you have still not paid the money of the umbrella. If I get hundreds of such customers then I would be ruined. It had been so long."

Praveen replied, "I have not forgotten Hafiz, I had been busy. The workload was so much that I did not get any time to come here. I do not have the money right now but thanks to well-wishers like you, people are appreciating my stories. I am on my way to meet Raja Sahib, who stays at the bungalow near the corner of the street. There is a feast today at his house. These days, I'm loaded with such invitations."

Hafiz was impressed and said, "Oh you are going to meet Raja Sahib today. After all, you are a great poet, only noblemen can understand your poetry. I am a simple man but do not forget about me. Whenever you get time, do recommend my shop to him. He must be earning at least three lakhs rupees per year."

For Praveen, three lakhs was a worthless amount. He replied, "Only three lakhs! You are insulting him! He must be earning at least ten lakhs every year. He owns so many buildings, shops, money deposits and most importantly, he is favored by Lord Bahadur."

Hafiz said politely, "This shop belongs to you, Praveen Babu. Please come inside and have a betel leaf. If you need anything, please tell me. We know each other so well. Our relations are so cordial."

Praveen replied while chewing the betel leaf, "I am getting late now. I will come next time."

Now Praveen went to Manohardas's shop. He was surprised to see him. He thought that Praveen Babu was out of town. Seeing Praveen Babu in the shop, he thought that he had come to repay the loan and said, "Where have you been Praveen Babu? I sent my servant to your house many times but he couldn't find you."

On a different day, he would have been half dead with fear but today he stood like a soldier with armor that could not be broken. He replied , "Once I return from Raja Sahib's house I will come and talk to you. Right now I am getting late." Manohardas had sold clothes to Raja Sahib worth thousands of rupees but had still not received the payment for the same. He said, "Please have a betel leaf, Praveen Babu. Raja Sahib will meet you rarely but I am here for you all the time. Holi is approaching. Please have some clothes if you need them. If you get an opportunity, then please remind Raja Sahib's cashier about me. I need the money and they have not paid the bills for the last two years. Please ask him to clear the bills as soon as possible."

Praveen said, "All right, but I must leave now otherwise I will be late. He wants to meet me so it is my duty not to be late. I need only respect and not wealth. If somebody respects me, I would do anything for him. But if somebody shows pride then I will not care for him at all."

IV

When Praveen Babu reached Raja Sahib's bungalow the lamps had already been lighted. The cars of several noblemen were parked outside the gate. The gatekeepers were standing at the gate in their uniforms. A gentleman was standing at the gate to receive the guests. When Praveen Babu reached the gate, he asked him hesitatingly, "Do you have an invitation card?"

Praveen Babu had the invitation card in his pocket. But he felt angry at such discrimination. Why was he supposed to show the invitation card and not the others? He replied, "No, I don't have the card with me. I won't support such discrimination. Only when you ask others to show their invitation cards, will I show mine. I feel insulted by such discrimination. Please inform Raja Sahib that Praveen Babu had come and he left."

"No, no, please come in. I failed to recognize you. I am so sorry. You are the gem of the gathering today. God has given you such great expressive strength."

This gentleman had never met Praveen Babu earlier. But whatever he said could be said by anyone, about a writer. And no writer can deny this fact.

Praveen Babu entered the house and found that the courtyard was beautifully lit and decorated. There was a fountain in the center of the courtyard embellished with an attractive statue. It seemed that a rainbow was flowing out of the fountain. Round-tables and chairs were set around the courtyard, with a beautiful vase on every table.

Raja Sahib welcomed Praveen and said, "You are most welcome. I read your article in the Hans magazine. I was very impressed by your writings. I was pleasantly surprised to find out that we had a gem like you in our midst."

Then he introduced him to other people and addressed the audience and said, "You all must have heard about Praveen Babu. He is amongst us tonight. Such is his command on the language, such expressions, such imagination, such clarity, such flow. Excellent! I feel that my soul sways to his words."

A gentleman, dressed in an English suit, looked at Praveen Babu as if he had come out of a zoo and said, "Have you read any British poets like Byron, Shelley, Keats etc.?"

Praveen Babu replied harshly, "Yes, I have read a few of their compositions."

"If you could translate those poetries in Hindi, then Hindi literature would be elevated further."

Praveen Babu never considered him inferior to these great poets. They were English poets and their works were in accordance with their language and culture. Therefore, Praveen Babu did not consider it a matter of great honor to translate their poetry into Hindi. He replied, "We are not so inferior that we need to translate their poetries to enrich our literature. I feel that at least in this matter, India can teach the West a few different things."

This was a preposterous comment. The gentleman thought that Praveen was a mad man.

Raja Sahib looked at Praveen Babu in a manner that seemed to quieten him and stop him from replying so rudely. And then he tried to cover up and said, "I think English literature has no match in the whole world."

The gentleman arrogantly said to Praveen Babu, "Our poets have not yet been able to understand the meaning of poetry. They are still stuck at poetries that depict sadness and dejection."

Praveen replied strongly, "I think you have not read any recent poem or maybe you have simply gone through them without actually comprehending it."

Raja Sahib wanted Praveen to keep quiet and he said, "Praveen Babu, he is Mr. Pranjpeye, he is a famous writer, and his articles are always published in English magazines."

Now it seemed unbearable for Praveen Babu to see that a person who appreciated English language and poetry was given so much importance whereas India's national language was under-appreciated. But he could not do anything about it.

Another man joined the group. Raja Sahib welcomed him and said , "Please come Mr. Chadda, how are you?"

They both shook hands and then the doctor looked at Praveen with curiosity, "Who is he?"

Raja Sahib introduced him and said, "He is Praveen Babu. He is a good poet and writer of Hindi language."

The doctor said in a different tone, "Oh you are a poet!" And then he went his way.

Then another gentleman came towards them. He was a famous barrister. Raja Sahib again introduced him to Praveen Babu and he also said in a similar manner, "Oh you are a poet!" and then went his way. This sequence happened several times.

These comments made him feel that he was an obvious misfit in this society. He had been so happy when he got the invitation but had never expected that he would be insulted in such a manner. Now, he realized that he would have been much happier at his home which seemed like a heavenly place where he craved to return to. He rebuked himself, "This is the punishment for your greed to get respect. Now you know how much respect you deserve. You are treated as nobody amidst such eminent personalities. Why would they respect you? They will respect the lawyers and doctors. You are an ordinary writer whose mere work is to write. The world does not require people like you for its functioning."

Suddenly, a commotion signaled the arrival of the Chief Guest. He was the main reason Raja Sahib threw the party as the former had been given the post of Chief Justice in the High Court today. Raja Sahib shook hands with him, came to Praveen Babu, and said, "You must have written a poem for today?"

Praveen replied, "No, I have not prepared any poem for today."

"What? Oh! You have made a grave mistake, but please write a poem quickly. I don't want a full page, just a few lines would suffice. A poem must be recited on such occasions."

"I cannot write a poem at such short notice."

"Then it was a waste to introduce you to so many people."

"Yes, absolutely"

"All right brother, recite any old poem of any poet. Who would know anything here?"

"Sorry, but I cannot do such a thing," saying this Praveen Babu returned back to his home. When he reached there, there was a satisfied look on his face.

Sumitra asked with a smile, "How come you returned so early?"

"I was no longer needed there."

"But you are looking very happy. You must have felt honored."

"Yes, but not in accordance with my expectations."

"But you are so happy!"

"Because I have learnt a lesson for life. I am like a lamp and a lamp is bound to burn. Today I had forgotten this universal truth. But God did not let me wander away from my path for long. My house is my heaven. My work is my only salvation."

The Spell

I

It was evening. Doctor Chaddha was getting ready to play golf. The vehicle was at the door when he saw two people bringing someone. Behind them was an old man who was walking with a stick. They stopped in front of the dispensary. The old man slowly came to the door and glanced through the curtains. One was afraid to step onto such a clean floor. Doctor Sahib was standing in front of the table and he did not have the courage to say anything.

Doctor Sahib shouted from inside, "Who is it? What do you want?"

The old man said with folded hands, "Master, I am a very poor man. My son has been ill for many days."

Doctor Sahib lit a cigar and then said, "Come tomorrow morning; I don't see patients at this time."

The old man went down on his knees and said, "My child will die. For four days, he has not opened his eyes."

Doctor Chaddha looked at his watch. There were only ten minutes left. He removed the golf stick from the wall and said, "Come tomorrow morning; this is the time for me to play a game."

The old man removed his turban, kept it at the door and said, "Master, just look at him once. Just a glance! The boy will die. He is the only one left of all my sons. We will both die crying, master. May you prosper!"

Such stubborn villagers came there regularly. Doctor Sahib was familiar with such behavior. Whatsoever others may say, they would stick to what they said. They would not listen to anybody. He lifted the curtains, came outside and started walking towards his vehicle. The old man ran after him saying, "Lord! It will be a thing of great kindness. Please have mercy on me! I am very helpless. There is nobody else in this world, Babuji!"

But Doctor Sahib did not even turn back to look at him. He sat in the vehicle and said, "Come tomorrow."

The vehicle left. The old man stood there for a long time, motionless like a statue. There are people in this world, who keep their enjoyment above somebody's life. He could not believe that the cultured society was so cruel and hard. He was a creature of the old generation, who were always ready to extinguish a fire, give a shoulder to a dead body, repair somebody's roof and make peace in a fight. Till the time the vehicle could be seen, he stood there looking at it. Perhaps he had some hope that the doctor would return. Then he told the men to lift the boy and went back from where they had come. He had come to Doctor Chaddha after facing disappointment everywhere. He had heard a lot about him. But from here, he was not going to any other place. He just accepted his fate.

II

Many years passed by. Doctor Chaddha earned a lot of money and fame. But the uncommon thing was that he also maintained his fitness level. It was due to his disciplined lifestyle that even at fifty years of age, his energy and enthusiasm would make the youngsters feel ashamed. Every action of his was in accordance with a schedule, and he never budged from it. A lot of people follow rules to maintain their health when they become unhealthy. Doctor Chaddha understood the secrets of control and service. His children were also like him. He had only two children, a son and a daughter. There was no third child and therefore, Mrs Chaddha looked quite young. The girl was married, and the boy was in college. He was the hope of the parents. He was an epitome of humility and good behavior, cheerful and kind. He was also the pride of his school and the bright spark of the youth wing. His face exuded brightness. Today was his twentieth birthday.

It was dusk. Chairs were laid out on the green grass. The rich and well-to-do people of the city were on one side, and the college students were on the other side. They were having a hearty meal. The lights were shining bright. Every single item of entertainment was present. There was a small skit that was to be enacted, written by Kailashnath himself. He was the main lead as well. At this time, he was wearing a silk dress, without any cap or shoe, and was looking after his friends. Amidst the crowd, someone would call, "Kailash, please come here," someone else would call from the other side, "Kailash, will you stay there only?" Everybody teased him and played pranks on him. He did not have a minute to breathe. Suddenly a girl came near him and said, "Kailash, where are your snakes? Please show me."

Kailash shook her hands and said, "Mrinalini, please forgive me now. I will show you tomorrow."

Mrinalini said, "No, you will have to show them to me now. I won't listen to you today. You give the same excuse every day."

Mrinalini and Kailash were classmates and were in love with each other. Kailash liked to keep snakes, play with them and make them dance. He had all kinds of snakes. He would test their behavior and character. A few days back, he had given a talk on snakes and had even shown how they danced. Even the learned men of biology were surprised to hear his talk. He had learned all his techniques from an old snake charmer. He had also collected herbal medicines used against snakebites. If he came to know about a herb somewhere, he would immediately try to collect it. He would even spend thousands of rupees on them. Mrinalini had come to his house many times but had never asked him to show the snakes to her. It was unclear whether Mrinalini had a genuine interest in snakes or it was her attempt to increase her proximity with Kailash. But in any case, her wish was not apt for the occasion. There was a crowd present there, and it was possible that on seeing them the snakes would get alarmed. She did not even think about the consequences that may result by teasing the snakes at that particular occasion.

PREMCHAND

Kailash said, "No. But I will certainly show them to you tomorrow. I won't be able to show them properly now. There will not be any space in the room."

One person said, "Why don't you show them to her instead of creating a big ruckus over a small thing? Miss Govind, you should not give in. Let us see how he does not show."

Another said, "Miss Govind is so simple and straightforward, and that is why you say that your life is on offer for her."

Mrinalini saw that they were trying to have fun and said, "You don't have to take my side, as I can speak for myself. I don't want to see the snakes now that is all."

Their friends laughed at this. One of them said, "You want to, but someone should show it as well. Is it not so?"

Kailash looked at Mrinalini's face and realized that she was feeling bad. As soon as dinner was over and the songs started, he took Mrinalini and his other friends near the snakes and started playing the musical instrument of the snake charmers. Then he opened each cage and started releasing the snakes one by one. What a sight it was! It seemed as if those creatures understood every word and every feeling. He picked up one, put one around his neck, and wrapped another around his hands. Mrinalini kept on telling him not to put them around his neck and to show them from a distance. She just wanted to see them dance a bit. She was scared of seeing so many snakes around Kailash's neck. She repented on insisting Kailash show the snakes. But Kailash did not listen. Why would he let go of a chance to flaunt his skills in front of his beloved? One friend teased, "You must have broken all its teeth!"

Kailash laughed and said, "Breaking teeth is the work of snake charmers. None of them has their teeth removed. If you say, then I shall show you! Saying this, he caught a black snake and said, 'I don't have a bigger and more poisonous snake than this one. If it bites somebody, a man will die in seconds. No escape at all.' Shall I show its teeth?"

Mrinalini caught his hand and said, "No, Kailash. Leave it for God's sake. I beg of you."

On this, another friend said, "I can't believe it. But if you say so, I trust you."

Kailash caught the neck of the snake and said, "No Sahib, you look at it with your own eyes. If you break their teeth and then do these tricks, then what is the charm? Snakes are very intelligent. If they trust a man, then they will not bite him."

When Mrinalini saw that Kailash was adamant, she said with a view to avoid it, "All right, let us go now. See, the songs have already started. I also have to sing a song today." Saying this, she caught hold of Kailash's shoulders and indicated to him to leave and left the room; but Kailash wanted to silence the critics. He caught hold of the snake's mouth and pressed it hard. He pressed it so hard that its face went red, and all the nerves of its body went tight. The snake had never seen him behaving like this. It was unable to understand as to what he wanted from it. Perhaps, it felt that he was going to kill him, and so it got ready for self-defense.

Kailash pressed its neck harder and opened its mouth and then showing its poisonous teeth, said, "Any person who has got any doubts, may come and see. Do you believe me now?" His friends came closer, saw the teeth and were surprised. Where was the scope for doubt when the evidence was shown in person? After clearing the doubts of his friends, Kailash loosened his grip and wanted to put the snake down; but he had already agitated the snake. As soon as Kailash loosened his grip, it bit his hand and then ran away. Blood was dripping from Kailash's fingers. He pressed his finger hard and ran towards his room. There, in the drawer of the table, he had a herb, which, when applied as a paste, would remove even the most dangerous of poisons.

There was commotion among his friends. The news reached outside. Doctor Sahib ran to the place. The finger was tied up and the herb was given for making into a paste. Doctor Sahib did not trust the herb. He wanted to make a cut above the finger, but Kailash had complete trust on the herb. Mrinalini was sitting at the piano.

Hearing the news, she ran up to him and started wiping the blood off his fingers. The herb was made into a paste; but in that one-minute, Kailash's eyes started flapping, and his face started turning yellow. His mother kept his head on her lap and switched the table fan on.

Doctor Sahib asked him, "Kailash, How are you?"

Kailash slowly lifted his hands. But he could not speak. Mrinalini said, "Will the herb not work?" Doctor Sahib caught his head and said, "What can I say? I agreed to what he said. Now there will be no use of cutting and letting the blood flow also."

That was the state for half an hour. Kailash's state was getting worse with every passing moment. His eyes had gone pale, limbs had gone cold, the face had lost its shine, the pulse was not to be found and all signs of death were imminent. There was a commotion in the house. Mrinalini started beating her head, and his mother was also in a bad state. Doctor Chaddha was held back by friends; otherwise, he would have cut his own throat.

One of them said, "If we get somebody who knows the *mantra*[1], we might be able to save him even now."

One Muslim gentleman supported him, "Even dead bodies have risen from the grave. Such miracles could happen."

Doctor Chaddha said, "I shouldn't have agreed with him. If I had cut it, this state would not have arisen. I kept telling him, son, don't rear snakes but who would listen to me? Please call some miracle man. He can take everything I have, and I will keep everything at his feet. I will walk out of the house without anything, but my Kailash, my dear Kailash should live. For God's sake, please call someone."

Amongst the crowd, someone knew a man who could drive away ghosts and poison. He ran to him and brought him there; but seeing Kailash's state, he did not have the courage to try out the mantra. He said, "Now what can be done? Whatever was meant to happen has already happened."

Why you say that whatever was to happen has happened. The parents had not seen the support of their son. Mrinalini's love had not

---

1. *Mantra*: Magic verses.

blossomed. Did the wishes of their hearts get fulfilled? Instead, what was not supposed to happen have happened.

It was the same green park, the same moonlight, the same group of friends. But instead of laughter, there were only tears and cries of sorrow.

III

Many miles away from the city, an old man and woman were sitting in front of the fire and spending the night. The old man was drinking coconut water and coughing in-between. The old woman kept her head between her knees and was gazing into the fire. A bottle of kerosene was kept on the sill. There was no cot or bedding in the house. In the same cell, there was a cooking place too. The old woman used to collect twigs and leaves throughout the day. The old man used to make ropes and sold them in the market. That was their only means of livelihood. Nobody ever saw them laughing or crying. All their time was spent in their efforts to stay alive. Death was at their door, and there was no time to laugh or to cry. The old woman asked, "There are no raw materials for the rope tomorrow, what will you do?"

"I will go to Jhagadu Sahu and get some material on loan."

"We have not given his money, then why would he give it on loan?"

"If he won't, then let it be. The grass is there. Can't I cut grass worth even two *annas*?"

Suddenly, a man came to the door and knocked, "Bhagat, are you asleep? Please open the door."

Bhagat got up and opened the door. A man came inside and said, "Did you hear? Doctor Chaddha's son has been bitten by a snake."

Bhagat was surprised and said, "Chaddha Babu's son? Is it the same Chaddha Babu, who stays in the cantonment?"

"Yes. There is a commotion in the city. If you want, you can go."

The old man shook his heads with a hard expression and said, "I will never go. My enemy will go there. It is the same Chaddha. I had taken my son to him. He was going for a game at that time. I fell at his feet and begged him to have a look at him, but he did not even talk to me. God was listening. Now he will know how one feels when one loses a son. Has he got many sons?"

"No. He was the only son. I heard that everyone say that he cannot escape death."

"God is very just. At that time, tears had come out of my eyes but he did not have any mercy. Even if I was at their door, I would not go."

"So you won't go? Whatever I heard, I told you."

"The boy would be dead. You go. I would sleep peacefully tonight. (To the old woman) Bring me some tobacco. I would have a smoke. Now the Lala will come to know! All his aristocracy will vanish, and what can he do to us? By a son's death, no kingdom is lost! Where six children had died, another one was nothing but dust. But your kingdom would be empty. You had collected all this wealth for him. Now, what would you do with it? I would go to see him once. But I'll go only after some time."

The man left. Bhagat closed the door and started smoking.

The old woman said, "Who would go so late in this cold?"

"Even if it was afternoon, I would not have gone. Even if a vehicle was sent for me, I would not have gone. I have not forgotten. Munna's face is still floating in front of my eyes. This cruel man had not even looked at him once. Did I not know that he won't survive? I knew it very well. Chaddha was not God that he would have looked at him once and there would have been showers of elixir. No, it was merely a race of the mind. There would have been some consolation at least. That is why I had gone to him. Now I will again go some day and ask him, 'Why Sahib, tell me, how are you?' I don't care if the world says that I am bad. There is vanity only among the lower class people. The upper class does not have any flaws. They are Gods."

It was the first time that Bhagat had heard such news and had not gone. In 80 years, there was never an instance when he would hear news about snakes and not go to help the victim. He never thought if it was hot, raining, flooded river or whatever. He would start off immediately, unselfishly and without any interest. Getting a return of his service never crossed his mind. This was not such work. Who can give the price for life? This was holy work. Hundreds of helpless people were granted the boon of life with the mantra. But he did not step out that day. He was going to sleep after hearing the news.

The old woman said, "There is tobacco near the fire. I had to pay two and a half paise for that too. She was not giving it at all."

Saying this, the old woman lay down. The old man blew off the lamp and stood for some time. Then he sat down. In the end, he lay down as well. But the news remained in his heart like a big burden. He felt as if something within him was missing as if he was drenched with water or his feet were stuck in slush, as if someone was sitting in his heart and exhorting him to leave. The old woman started snoring within minutes. The old man kept talking and then fell asleep but woke up at the slightest of noise. Then he got up, took his stick and opened the door slowly.

The old woman asked, "Where are you going?"

"Nowhere. I was just seeing how dark it is."

"It is very dark. Go to sleep."

"I cannot sleep."

"How will you sleep? Your heart is in Chaddha's house."

"What good has Chaddha done to me, for me to go there? I won't go, even if he comes here and falls at my feet."

"But you cannot sleep because of that, right?"

"No, dear. I am not crazy to sow flowers for someone who has sown only thorns for me."

The old woman went to sleep. Bhagat locked the door and came back and sat down. His heart was like those listeners who went to hear a speech but heard only the sound of the band. Though their eyes were on the speaker, their ears were towards the band. The sound of the band kept reverberating in the ears. But due to shame, they won't get up. The thought of revenge was like the religious speaker, but his thoughts were inclined towards the young man who was dying and the delay of every minute may prove to be critical for him.

He again opened the door slowly so that the old woman would not wake up. He came outside. At that time, the village guard was on his rounds, and asked him, "How come you got up, Bhagat? It is very cold today. Are you going somewhere?" Bhagat replied, "Where will I go? I was just seeing how dark it is. What time is it?"

The guard said, "It must be one o' clock. I was coming from the police station and I saw a huge crowd outside Doctor Chaddha's house. You must have heard about his son. Some creature has bitten him. If you go, he might be saved. I have heard that he is willing to pay ten thousand rupees."

Bhagat said, "I will not go, even if it is a matter of ten lakhs. What would I do with all that money? If I die tomorrow, then who would be there to enjoy it after me?"

The guard went away and Bhagat started walking ahead. Bhagat's state was like that of a drunkard who put his foot somewhere and moved somewhere else, who said something and something else came out of his mouth. There was revenge in his heart, but his work was beyond the control of the mind. One who has never used a sword, cannot use it even when he wants to. His hands tremble, and he finds it impossible to lift it up at all.

Bhagat was moving forward with the support of his stick. His conscience was stopping him, but his subconscious mind was pushing him ahead. The servant was ruling over the master.

When he reached halfway, Bhagat stopped. Anger won over his goodness. I came this far just like that. Why should I take all the pains in this cold? Why did I not go to sleep in peace? If sleep was not coming, let it be so. I could have sung two or three devotional songs. I came this far unnecessarily. Why should I care whether Chaddha's son lives or dies? What has he done for me that I should die for him? There are thousands who die in this world and thousands who live. How am I concerned with all that?

But the subconscious mind took on a different shape made him think, "He was not going there to treat him, instead, he was going there to see what the people were doing. He wanted to see how Doctor Sahib would be beating his own chest and crying. He would see if the rich also cry like the poor, or whether they control their emotions. They are learned men and must be able to control their emotions." He encouraged this state of mind and moved forward.

Then he saw two men coming that way. They were talking amongst themselves, "Chaddha Babu's house is destroyed. He was the only son." Bhagat heard these voices. His speed increased. His feet did not move due to fatigue. But his upper body was moving so fast, that he almost stumbled and fell. He continued to walk like this for ten minutes and then he saw the house of Doctor Sahib. The lights were on, but there was complete silence. Am I too late? He started running. In his entire life, he had never run so fast. He was running as if death was pursuing him.

IV

It was two in the night. All the guests had left. Only the stars in the sky were crying. The people were waiting for the morning so that they could offer the dead body to Mother Ganges.

Suddenly, Bhagat reached the door and called out. Doctor Sahib thought that some patient had come. Some other day, he would have rejected him outright, but he came out that day. He saw an old man standing, his waist was bent, even his eyelids had white hair. He was trembling even with the support of a walking stick. He said humbly, "What is it, brother? Today we are in deep trouble and can't do much. Please come some other day. I may not see any patient for a month."

Bhagat said, "I have heard about it, Babuji. That is why I have come. Where is brother? Please show me. God is great, and he can even get a dead man back to life. Who knows? He might be so kind."

Chaddha said in a sad voice, "Please see, but it has been three to four hours. Whatever was to happen has already happened. Many people have tried their best and left."

Doctor Sahib had no hope. But he felt pity for the old man. He took him inside. Bhagat looked at the dead body for a minute. Then he smiled and said, "It is not too late even now. God willing, brother will recover in half an hour. You are a pessimist. Please tell the servants to get some water."

The servants started bathing Kailash with the water. The water in the pipe was over. The servants were less in number. So the guests started filling water from the well and gave it to the servants. Mrinalini was also helping. Bhagat was smiling and reading out his magic verses, as though victory was at the doorstep. When he finished the verses once, he made Kailash smell the herbs. This way, many pots of water were poured over Kailash and Bhagat kept reciting the verses again and again. At the end, when the sun opened its eyes with its first rays, the red eyes of Kailash also opened. In a minute, he turned over and asked for water to drink. Doctor Chaddha ran across and hugged Narayani. Narayani fell at Bhagat's feet and Mrinalini, with her eyes full of tears, asked Kailash, "How are you feeling now?"

In a minute, the news spread. Friends started coming to congratulate. Doctor Sahib was praising Bhagat in front of everybody with great humility and concern. Everybody wanted to see Bhagat, but when they went inside, there was no sign of Bhagat. The servants said, "He was sitting here and smoking just now. We offered him tobacco, but he did not take it. He took out his own tobacco and filled it."

Everyone started searching Bhagat but Bhagat was rushing home so as to reach before the old woman wakes up.

Narayani said, "I thought of giving him a huge amount for his service."

Chaddha confessed, "I did not recognize him during the night, but I recognized him when it was dawn. Once, he had brought a patient to me. I remember that I was going to play golf and had refused to see the patient. I can't express how bad I feel about that incident today. I would search him out and beg for his forgiveness. I know that he won't take anything. His goodness has shown me a principle which I shall forever abide for the rest of my life."

Blame

I

It was morning and Munnu, the sweeper, was busy cleaning *Munshi* Shyamkishore's courtyard and the *gusalkhana*[1]. After completing his work, he came to the door and shouted, "Madam, I have cleaned the whole place. Will I get something to eat today?"

Devi Rani came up to the door and said, "Not even ten days have passed since I paid your salary. And you started asking again?"

Munnu asked, "What can I do, Madam? The money I earn is insufficient. I am a single man. How can I manage both work and my household?"

Devi asked, "Then why don't you get married?"

Munnu replied, "They ask for money, Madam! There is hardly anything left after my expenses. From where shall I get the money?"

Devi asked, "You are still young and I'm sure you can manage. But how long will you live alone?" Munnu said, "With your blessings, something good will definitely happen. Will you help me?"

Devi said, "Yes, first you need to start looking for a suitable bride. And then I will do whatever I can."

Munnu said, "You have a wonderful nature, you are so caring. In other houses, the Madams do not even listen to us. Allah has not only given you great beauty but also a very kind heart. Allah only knows that just by looking at all, all my hunger, thirst and pain would vanish. I have seen many ladies who live in the big bungalows but they are not beautiful as you are."

Devi said, "You liar! I am not that beautiful."

Munnu said, "Now how do I explain to you? I have seen a lot of

---

1. *Gusalkhana*: Bathroom/Toilet.

ladies; but most have only fair skin and nothing else. Where is the beauty that you possess?"

Devi asked, "Will one rupee be enough for you?"

Munnu replied, "Please give me two rupees."

Devi said, "All right! Take it and leave."

Munnu said, "I am leaving, Madam! If you won't get angry, shall I ask you something?"

Devi said, "Ask quickly, as I need to go and light the fire to prepare food."

Munnu said, "Then you go, Madam. I will ask later."

Devi insisted, "No, no. You can ask me. What is it? It is not that urgent."

Munnu asked, "Do you have any relatives staying at Dalmandi?"

Devi replied, "No, there is nobody there."

Munnu said, "Then there must be some friend. I often see Babu Sahib getting down at a bungalow there."

Devi enquired, "But Dalmandi is the area of prostitutes, is it not?"

Munnu said, "Yes, Madam. There are lots of them. But Babu Sahib[2] looks like a simple man. Does he come home late?"

Devi said, "No, he comes back before evening and never goes anywhere after that. Yes, sometimes he goes to the library."

Munnu said, "Yes that must be it. If you get the chance, then do caution him not to go there at night. No matter how pure a man's heart is people may still suspect him."

At that time, Babu Shyamkishore arrived. Munnu saluted him, took the bucket and left the place.

Shyamkishore asked, "What was Munnu doing here?"

Devi replied, "Nothing. He was just telling me his sad story. He was asking for food. So I gave him two rupees. He talks so much."

Shyamkishore said, "Even you are extremely talkative. If you don't find anybody to speak to, then let it be the sweeper. I don't know how you manage to talk to that idiot!"

---

2. *Sahib:* Sir.

Devi said, "What can I do, if he starts talking himself? He is a poor man. When he tells me about his problems, how can I turn my back on him?"

Babu Sahib took out a garland of flowers and put it around her neck but there was no sign of happiness on her face. She looked at him from the corner of her eyes and said, "Nowadays, you go to Dalmandi quite often?"

Shyamkishore asked, "Who? Me?"

Devi said, "Yes, you. You make the excuse of going to the library, and instead you end up having fun there."

Shyamkishore exerted, "An absolute lie. Who told you all this rubbish? Munnu?"

Devi said, "Munnu did not tell me anything. But I keep getting all the news about you."

Shyamkishore said, "You don't keep track of my activities, do you? Suspicion is a great folly; if you get into this habit it may become catastrophic for both of us. Why will I go to Dalmandi? Is there anyone better than you? I am the slave of your beautiful eyes. Even if an angel comes in front of me, I will not notice her. Where is Sharda today?"

Devi replied, "She went to play with other kids."

Shyamkishore warned her, "Don't send her on the road to play, there are so many vehicles. Who knows what may happen. Today only, there was an incident at Ardali Market. Three boys died in an accident."

Devi exclaimed, "Three boys! It is catastrophic. Whose vehicle was it?"

Shyamkishore said, "That is still unknown. Oh God! This flower garland looks beautiful on you."

Devi said, "Don't lie."

II

After three days, Munnu said to Devi, "Madam, my engagement has been fixed. I have great trust in you and I am going ahead."

Devi asked, "Did you see the girl? How is she?"

Munnu said, "No Madam, I have not seen the girl. It would be as destined. At least now I will get food, otherwise, I had to cook on my own. She has a straightforward nature. In our caste, women are very fretful. You won't get one good woman even in a crowd of hundred."

Devi asked, "You don't say anything to your women?"

Munnu replied, "What can we say, madam? We are afraid of them as they may complain to our boss and get us dismissed. The Babus always have their eyes on the servants."

Devi said (laughing), "You liar! Are the wives of the Babus worse than the sweeper women?"

Munnu said, "Don't ask me such questions, Madam. But I have not met anyone other than you, who I can praise. I am a man who belongs to the lower caste, Madam. But if my wife were like the Babu's wives, even I wouldn't feel like speaking with her. I have not seen any lady who is as beautiful as you."

Devi said, "You liar, where did you learn to flatter so much?"

Munnu clarified, "It is not false praise, Madam. I am telling the truth. You were standing at the window one day when Raja *Mian*[3] saw you. He is the owner of a big shoe shop. Allah has given him a good heart, along with the wealth that he possesses. The moment he saw you, he lowered his eyes. Today, while talking to me, he started praising you and I said, 'Allah has also given her a heart as beautiful as her beauty.'"

Devi asked, "Is he that tall and dusky young man?"

Munnu replied, "Yes, Madam, he is the one. He told me that he wanted to get another glimpse of you. I scolded him that how dare he spoke to me about you like that! He won't be able to succeed with me."

---

3. *Mian*: A way of addressing Muslim men.

Devi said, "You did a good thing. May his eyes be gorged out! Whenever he passes by, his eyes are always on the window. Tell him not look here even by mistake!"

Munnu said, "I have already told him. With your permission, I will leave now. Is there anything else to be cleaned? It is time for the Babu Sahib to come home. If he sees me here, he will say, 'What nonsense is he talking again?'"

Devi said, "Take these *rotis*. Today, you will be saved from the effort of cooking."

Munnu said, "May Allah keep you healthy! I wish to stay at this door itself and eat whatever crumbs come my way. Truthfully, the moment I see you, my hunger and thirst disappear."

Munnu was leaving when Babu Shyamkishore was on his way inside and his last words reached his ears. As soon as Munnu left, Babu Sahib told Devi, "I told you not to talk to Munnu, but you do not listen to me. These servants gossip and spread the news everywhere. You should not talk to them. What was he saying about his hunger and thirst vanishing?"

Devi said, "I don't know. What hunger and thirst? There was no such talk."

Shyam said, "How is that possible? I heard it very clearly."

Devi replied, "I do not remember. He must have said something. I do not listen to everything that he says."

Shyam asked, "Then does he talks to the walls? I saw a man has just passed by looking at this window. He is a Muslim from the same neighborhood. He has a shoe shop. Why do you keep standing near the window?"

Devi replied, "There is a bamboo shade."

Shyam said, "Even if you stand behind the shade, any man can see you clearly."

Devi said, "I did not know that. Now I will not open that window again."

Shyam said, "But what is the use? Don't let Munnu come inside."

Devi asked, "But then who will clean the courtyard?"

Shyam said, "Then let him come, but don't talk to him. Today a new theatre group has come to town, let us go and watch it. I have heard that the actors are very good."

Sharda came running in with a box of sweets. Devi asked her, "Who gave you these sweets?"

Sharda said, "Raja Bhaiya gave them to me."

Shyam asked, "Who is this Raja Bhaiya?"

Sharda said, "He is the one, who just passed by."

Shyam asked, "Is he that tall and dusky man?"

Sharda replied, "Yes, he is the one. Can I go to their house every day?"

Devi asked, "Did you go to his house?"

Sharda said, "He only lifted me up and took me to his house."

Shyam said, "Stop playing on the road downstairs. Someday, you will come under a vehicle. Don't you see how many vehicles pass by?"

Sharda said, "Raja Bhaiya was saying that he would take me for a ride in his car."

Shyam asked, "What do you do sitting here all day, can't you keep an eye on the girl?"

Devi said, "I can't lock her in a cage."

Shyam said, "You have a sharp tongue. Why don't you admit that you don't get time to look after her because you keep talking all the time?"

Devi said, "Whom do I talk to? I don't even have a woman neighbour here."

Shyam exclaimed, "Munnu is there!"

Devi said (biting her lips), "Is Munnu, my relative, that I will sit and talk to him? He is a poor man and keeps telling me about his grief. What do I say to him? I can't scold him."

Shyam said, "Anyway, prepare the food. The play will start at nine. It is already seven."

Devi said, "You go and watch it. I will not come."

Shyam said, "You were the one who kept telling me for months that you wanted to watch that play. Now, what happened? Have you taken a vow that you will oppose whatever I say?"

Devi said, "I don't know why you think that. I do everything after asking you. If I come with you, then more money will be spent and then you will say that the expenses have increased. That is why I said that I will not go. If you want me to come, I will definitely go. Who does not like to watch a play?"

III

At nine o' clock, Shyamkishore, Sharda and Devi left for the theatre in a *tanga*[4]. They had gone some distance when another *tanga* started following them. Raja was sitting in it. And next to him was Munnu. Devi lowered her head on seeing them. She was surprised to see that Munnu had such close relations with Raja that Raja would take him in his *tanga*. Sharda saw Raja and said immediately, "Babuji, see, Raja Bhaiya is coming. (Clapping) Raja Bhaiya, we are going to watch the play."

Raja smiled and Babu Sahib became angry. He thought, "This man is following us. The two of them are working together in this plan. Otherwise, why would Raja bring Munnu along?" To set them off their pursuit, he told the *tanga* driver, "Drive the *tanga* fast, we are getting late." The *tanga* started moving ahead faster. Raja also increased the speed of his *tanga*. When Babu Sahib asked the driver to slow down, Raja also slowed down. Irritated, he said, "You take the *tanga* to the cantonment. We will not go to the theatre." The *tanga* driver looked at him in amusement and turned the *tanga*. Raja also turned his *tanga*. Babu Sahib was now so angry that he was about to challenge Raja; but he was afraid that if it led to a fight, a lot of people would assemble unnecessarily and things would get serious.

---

4. *Tanga:* A horse cart.

He controlled himself. He was getting irritated that since he chose to watch the theatre that day. But who knew that these two devils would follow them. Babu Sahib decided, "I will dismiss Munnu tomorrow itself." After some distance, Raja's *tanga* turned in a different direction and his anger slowly subsided. But now there was no time to go to the theatre. From the cantonment, they returned home.

Devi asked angrily, "We gave two rupees to the *tanga* just like that."

Shyamkishore looked at her with blood-red eyes full of anger and said, "Talk to Munnu more often and enjoy watching Raja from the window. I don't understand what you are up to!"

Devi asked, "Aren't you ashamed to say such things? You are insulting me for no reason. The result of this will not be good. I don't consider any other man to be close to even the sand under your feet then what is the status of that sweeper? Do you think I am so low?"

Shyamkishore replied, "No, I do not consider you so, but you are foolish. You should not have talked to him at all. Now you know that he is a rogue, or do you still have any doubt?"

Devi said, "I will dismiss him tomorrow itself."

Munshiji went to work the next day but his heart was still turbulent. How could he know what Devi did behind his back. He knew that Devi was a devoted wife. But he also knew that beautiful women loved to show off their beauty. Devi must be getting ready at the moment and standing next to the window. And the young men in the colony must be looking at her and getting a lot of ideas. He felt that it was beyond his control to stop this business. The young men were good at seduction. God forbid if the bad glances of these men fall on the brides and daughters of any house! How to get rid of them?

After a great deal of contemplation, he decided to leave the house. There was no other solution that he could think off. He told Devi, "If you agree, we will leave this house. Staying amidst these rogues, there is always the danger of losing one's respect." Devi said, "As you wish!"

Shyam said, "You tell me the way out."

Devi asked, "What can I tell you? A way out of what? I don't see any need to leave the house. Not one or two, even if there are one or two lakhs, so what? Does anyone leave one's house because of some barking dogs?"

Shyam said, "Sometimes, the dogs bite too."

Devi did not reply. She was afraid that it would raise her husband's suspicion even more. He was suspicious by nature and would have taken some different meaning of her reply.

Shyam Babu left the house three days after the incident.

IV

A week had passed since they came to the new house. One day, Munnu came limping with a stick and a bandage around his head and called out. Devi recognized his voice but did not scold him. She opened the door. She wanted to hear the news about the old house.

Munnu came inside and said, "Madam, after you left that house, I have not gone there at all. I feel like crying whenever I see it. I wish that I could also come to this colony. I roam around like a madman and I don't feel like doing anything. I always keep thinking about you. Who will treat me the way you did? This house is very small."

Devi said, "We had to leave that house because of you."

Munnu asked, "Fie on me! What mistake did I commit, Madam?"

Devi said, "You were the one who was sitting with Raja and following us. Any man would be suspicious of such a man!"

Munnu said, "Madam, don't ask me about that night. Raja Mian wanted to go and meet a lawyer. He stays in the cantonment. He asked me to accompany him. His apprentice had gone somewhere. Out of respect for you, we did not overtake. And you say that it was our mistake. There is no nicer man than him in the entire colony. He prays five times a day and keeps all fasts. He has a wife and children at home. He would never dare to misbehave with anyone!"

Devi said, "Anyway, it must be true. Why have you tied the band around your head?"

Munnu said, "Don't ask me about it, Madam! If I hear anyone say anything bad about you, I get very angry. The sweet shop owner at the door started saying, 'Babuji has to give me some money.' I said, 'He is not the kind of person who will not pay your money.' And we started arguing and a fight started. I was washing the gutter in front of the shop. He came and pushed me inside. I was unprepared and fell on the road. But I also abused him to such an extent that he will remember it for the rest of his life. Now the wound is improving."

Devi exclaimed, "Ram! Ram! You picked a fight with him. It was a simple matter. You should have said, 'If he owes you money, go and ask for it.' We are in the same city. We have not run away to another country."

Munnu said, "Madam, I can't hear anyone speak ill about you. He must be the owner in his house, how am I concerned with it?"

Devi asked, "Has someone come to that house as yet?"

Munnu said, "Lots of people came to see the house. But where you have stayed, how can someone else stay? We instigated those people to leave. Raja Mian has given up food and water since the day you left. He remembers your daughter and keeps crying. But why would you remember us poor people?"

Devi asked, "Why would I not? Am I not human? Even animals don't eat for one or two days after leaving their old habitat. Take this money! You must be hungry. Go to the market and buy yourself something to eat."

Munnu said, "By your blessings, there is no dearth of food. People see the heart of a man, Madam. What is the need for money? I ate whatever you gave me. Your nature is such that without a whip a man can become your slave. Now I will leave, madam. Babuji must be coming. He will say, 'The devil has come here also.'"

Devi said, "There is still a lot of time before he comes home."

Munnu said, "Oh! I forgot to tell you something. Raja Mian had given these toys for your daughter. In our conversation, I forgot all about it. Where is she?"

Devi said, "She has not yet returned from the *Madarsa*. But there was no need to send so many toys. What has Raja done? Even if he wanted to send something, he should have sent toys worth two or four *annas*. That 'Madam' toy alone will be worth at least three or four rupees. In totality, these toys would be worth thirty to thirty-five rupees."

Munnu said, "I don't know, Madam. I have never bought any toys. Even if it is worth thirty or thirty-five rupees, what is it to him? From his shop alone, he earns a daily profit of fifty rupees."

Devi said, "No, you return all these. What will she do with so many toys? I will just keep this 'Madam' toy."

Munnu said, "Madam, Raja Mian will be very unhappy. He will not leave me alive. He is very sentimental, madam! If his wife leaves for her house for two or four days, he gets very perturbed."

Sharda came back from school at that moment and seeing the toys, grabbed all of them. Devi scolded her and said, "What are you doing? You take one toy, what will you do with all of them?"

Sharda said, "I will take all of them. I will keep the Madam in the toy car and take her for a ride. The dog will run after them. I will prepare food for the toys in these utensils. Where have they come from, Madam? Tell me."

Devi replied, "They have not come from anywhere. I had asked to bring them for just seeing. You may take any one of them."

Sharda asked, "From where did you get these Munnu? Tell me."

Munnu said, "Your Raja Bhaiya has sent them for you."

Sharda exclaimed, "Raja Bhaiya has sent them! Oh! (Dancing) Raja Bhaiya is a nice man. Tomorrow, I will show it to all my friends. Nobody has such toys."

Devi said, "Munnu, you leave now. And tell Raja Bhaiya not to send any more toys."

After Munnu had left, Devi told Sharda, "Bring them here, Sharda, I will put the toys away. If your Babuji sees them, he will get irritated and ask us why we took the toys from Raja Bhaiya? He will break all of them and throw them away. Don't even discuss these toys with him by mistake."

Sharda said, "Yes, *Amma*. Babuji will break them."

Devi said, "Don't tell him that Raja Bhaiya had sent these toys. Otherwise, Babuji will hit Raja Bhaiya and will pull your ears too. He will say, this girl keeps begging for toys from everyone."

Sharda said, "Yes, *Amma*. Babuji will break them."

By then Shyamkishore came back from the office. He was angry and said as soon as he entered, "That scoundrel Munnu has started coming to this colony also. I saw him today. Did he come here too?"

Devi said hesitatingly, "Yes, he did come here."

Shyamkishore said, "And you let him in? Didn't I tell you not to let him enter the house again?"

Devi said, "He came and started knocking at the door, what was I supposed to do?"

Shyamkishore said, "I am sure that you did not tell him not to come here again."

Devi replied, "I do not remember. And why will he come again?"

Shyamkishore said, "For the same reason that he came today. You are hell-bent on ruining my reputation."

Devi said angrily, "Don't talk like that, do you understand? Are you not ashamed to say such things? You have already said such things before. Today, you are again repeating the same thing. If I hear this for the third time, the result will not be good, I warn you. Do you think I am a prostitute?"

Shyamkishore said, "I do not want him to come to my house."

Devi said, "Then why don't you tell him? Did I stop you?"

Shyamkishore said, "Why can't you tell him?"

Devi asked, "Are you ashamed to tell him?"

Shyamkishore said, "It is pointless for me to tell him. Even if I do tell him, he will keep coming unless you don't ask him to stop."

Devi bit her lips and said, "What is the harm if he keeps coming? Sweepers go to all houses."

Shyamkishore said, "If I see Munnu here again, it won't be good for you."

Saying this, Shyamkishore went down, and Devi stood motionless. Her heart was hurt by this accusation and distrust. She started crying profusely. The biggest hurt was caused by the fact that her husband considered her so lowly and shameless. "He is suspecting me of things that even a prostitute will not do."

V

As soon as Shyamkishore had entered the house, Sharda had run away with the toys fearing that Babuji might break them. She went downstairs and started thinking of a place to hide them. She was lost in these thoughts when a friend of hers came into the courtyard. Sharda wanted to show off her toys. She could not overcome this temptation. She thought, "Babuji went upstairs, and he will not come down so soon. Till then, I can show the toys to her." She called out to her friend and both of them got so engrossed in inspecting the new toys, that they did not realize that Babu Shyamkishore had come downstairs.

Shyamkishore, on seeing the toys, came to Sharda and asked, "From where did you get these toys?"

Sharda was scared. She started trembling out of fear. And not a word came out of her mouth.

Shyamkishore shouted again and asked, "Why don't you speak? Who gave you these toys?"

Sharda started crying. Shyamkishore cajoled her and said, "Don't cry. I am only asking you where did you get these beautiful toys from?"

When he assured her three or four times, Sharda gained some courage and blurted out the entire story. Catastrophe! It would have been far better had Sharda kept quiet. Her silence would also have been fine. Devi would have made some excuse and gotten out of the situation. But who can avert the inevitable? Shyamkishore was extremely angry. Leaving the toys, he went upstairs and shaking Devi by her shoulders, asked her, "Do you want to stay in this house or not? Tell me clearly."

Devi was still crying. Hearing this hurtful question, her tears vanished. Fearing a bigger catastrophe, she forgot the earlier problem. It was like a patient running away from his bed, on seeing a killer's sword. She looked at Shyamkishore with fear in her eyes but did not utter a word. Every cell of her body was silently asking, "What is the meaning of this question?"

Shyamkishore said again, "Whatever your wish is, tell me clearly. If you are tired of living with me, then you are free to leave. I do not wish to keep you here by force. You do not have to lie to me or cheat on me. I am ready to bid farewell happily. If you have decided something in your heart, then I have also decided something. You cannot stay in this house anymore. You don't deserve to live here."

Devi said in a stable tone, "What has happened to you nowadays? Why do you keep spitting venom all the time? If you are tired of me, give me some poison. Why do you kill me by setting me on fire? Talking to the sweeper was not such a big crime. When he came and called out, I went and opened the door. If I knew that it would become such a big issue, then I would have scolded him for sure."

Shyamkishore said, "I wish I could pull your tongue out. Talking to them, communicating by sign language and now gifts have also started coming. What is left now?"

Devi asked, "Why are you being so heartless? You will not get anything by taking the life of a helpless woman."

Shyamkishore said, "Am I lying?"

Devi replied, "Yes, you are lying."

Shyamkishore asked, "Where did these toys come from?"

Devi's heart almost stopped beating. She understood that the stars were against her now. All the bad things were happening together. She thought, "Why did I take them instead of returning them then and there?" She made up an excuse and said, "How could I stop the child? I kept saying not to take them, but she did not listen to me, what could I do? Yes, if I knew that these toys would become such a big problem in my life, I would have forcefully taken them and thrown them away."

Shyamkishore asked, "What other things have come with them? It will be better if you bring them out right now."

Devi replied, "Whatever has come, will be in this house only. Why don't you search it yourself? It is not such a big house that will take two or three days to search for it?"

Shyamkishore said, "I do not have so much time. It will be better for you to bring out whatever has come; bring them now. It is not possible that he has sent toys for your daughter and did not send you any gift. Even if you promise on the river Ganges, I will not believe it."

Devi said, "Then why don't you search for it in the house?"

Shyamkishore clenched his fist and said, "I told you, I don't have that kind of time. You bring all the things here, otherwise, I will strangle you to death."

Devi said, "Kill me if you want to; but how can I show you the things that have not come?"

Shyamkishore was very angry, and he pushed Devi so hard that she fell on the floor.

He put his hands on her neck and said, "Shall I kill you? Will you not show me the other things?"

Devi said, "Fulfill whatever your wishes are!"

Shyamkishore shouted, "I will drink your blood. What do you think of me?"

Devi said, "If your heart's thirst is fulfilled by that, then drink it."

Shyamkishore asked, "Will you again talk to that sweeper? If I see that Munnu or that pimp at the door, I will cut off his head."

Saying this, Babuji left Devi and walked out of the house. Devi remained in that state for a long time. There was no love for her husband at that time in her heart. She wanted to take revenge. At this moment, if she had heard that someone had beaten Shyamkishore in the market, she would have felt happy. After getting hit for many days, this wind broke the wall of love and it fell down, and there was nothing left to save the heart. Today, there was only a thin thread of hesitation and worldly shame that could break at any moment.

VI

When Shyamkishore left, Sharda also went out with her toys. Babuji did not say anything after seeing the toys. So what was there to fear now! Why should she not show the toys to her friend?

Across the road, there was a sweet shop. The sweet shop owner's daughter was standing at the door. Sharda started towards her in order to show her the toys. To reach her friend's house she had to cross a road that was full of traffic. Sharda was lost in her own thoughts, unaware of the dangers. With childlike exuberance, she ran across with the toys. Little did she know that death was also running towards her to play the game of life and death? She saw a vehicle coming from one side. From the other side, a carriage was coming. Sharda wanted to run across quickly. The vehicle honked; Sharda speeded up thinking that she would cross over, but who can prevent destiny? The vehicle crushed Sharda and sped away. On the road, she remained as a mangled piece of flesh. The toys remained intact. Not even one of them had broken. The toys remained but the one who played with them had gone. Who is mortal amongst the two, who will decide?

People ran from all sides. Oh! This is Babuji's daughter, who stays upstairs. Who will lift up the body? One of them leapt up the stairs and shouted at the door, "Babuji! Was your daughter playing on the road? Please come down."

Devi looked down from the terrace and saw Sharda's mangled body lying on the road. She shrieked and ran downstairs. She reached the road and lifted the body on her lap. Her legs were trembling. She was stunned by this strike of lightning. She could not even cry.

Many people in the colony started asking, "Where has Babuji gone? How do we call him?"

What could Devi say? She was silent. Taking the dead body in her lap, drenched with her daughter's blood in the process, she looked up at the sky, as if asking God, "Have you written all the pain in my destiny?"

It was getting dark, but there was no news of Babuji. Nobody knew where he had gone. Slowly, the clock showed that it was nine o' clock. But Babuji had not returned. He was never out for so long. Why did he choose to vanish today itself? It was ten o' clock by then. Now Devi started crying. She was more upset at her helplessness than at her daughter's death. How would she cremate her? Who would go with her? Would anyone be ready to go so late in the night? If nobody came forward, she would have to go alone. Would the body remain here throughout the night?

As the silence was increasing, Devi was growing more and more afraid. She regretted not taking the body in the evening itself.

It was eleven in the night. Suddenly someone opened the door. Devi stood up. She thought Babuji had come. Her heart was full and she came out crying. However, it was not Babuji. It was the policemen, who had come to investigate the incident The incident had occurred at five o'clock. The investigation was held at eleven. After all, the officer-in-charge was also a human being; he also went out in the evenings.

The investigation went on for about an hour. Devi saw that there was no point in being hesitant. Whatever questions were asked, she replied nonchalantly. She did not hesitate at all. The officer-in-charge was surprised.

When he was about to leave after recording the statement, Devi said, "Will you be able to find out about the vehicle?"

The policeman replied, "Now, it is doubtful whether we will be able to find it."

Devi asked, "Then he will get no punishment?"

The policeman replied, "We are helpless. Nobody knows the number."

Devi asked, "Can't the government do something about it? Will the children of the poor continue to be crushed like this?"

The policeman said, "What can be done about this? We can't stop the vehicles from plying."

Devi said, "At least the policemen should ensure that no vehicles speed in the city. But why would you do that? Your officers sit in these vehicles. If you stop these vehicles, then how will you continue to serve?"

The officer was ashamed. When they reached the road, one of the policemen said, "She has great beauty."

Officer said, "She made me speechless. What beauty she has! But I did not even look at her. I did not have the courage."

Babu Shyamkishore came back drunk after twelve in the night. He had received the news on the way itself. He entered the house crying. Devi had decided, "Whatever happens, I will scold him today." But when she saw him crying, all her anger disappeared. She also started crying. Both of them kept crying for a long time. This accident brought them closer than ever. They felt as if they had developed love like the old days.

In the morning, when the people returned after the cremation, Shyamkishore looked at Devi lovingly and said, "How will you spend your time alone?"

Devi asked, "Can't you take leave for five or ten days?"

Shyamkishore said, "That is what I was also thinking. I will take fifteen days leave."

Shyam Babu went to the office to take leave. Even in this sad state, Devi's heart was happy like never before in the past few months. By losing her daughter, she had regained the love and trust of her husband.

But destiny had its own plans. It smiled and said, "Oh! Unlucky woman! Don't be happy. There is still another last catastrophe to strike your life, and you can't even imagine what that could be."

VII

The next day, Shyamkishore was at home when Munnu came and saluted. Shyamkishore asked in a very harsh tone, "What is it? Why do you come here so often?"

Munnu said in a very pathetic tone, "Babu Sahib, anyone who hears about yesterday, will be filled with sadness. I am, after all, your slave. So what if I am no longer your servant? I have eaten your salt. How can I forget that? Sometimes, I come to ask whether everything is all right. Since I heard about yesterday's incident, I am in such pain that I cannot express it in words. She was such a sweet girl that on seeing her, I forgot all my worries. The moment she saw me, she would come running and shout 'Munnu, Munnu'. When we outsiders are feeling this way, I can understand what must be going through your mind."

Shyam Babu became a little soft and said, "What can man do in front of Allah's wish? My house is now filled with darkness. Now I don't feel like staying here."

Munnu said, "Madam must be in a more distraught state."

Shyam said, "She would be. I used to feed her in the evening and morning. But she was with her throughout the day. I will forget in the midst of work. How will she forget? She will cry over it for her entire life."

Hearing her husband talk to Munnu, Devi looked out at the courtyard. Seeing Munnu, her eyes became moist. She said, "Munnu, I have been destroyed!"

Munnu consoled her, "Madam, control yourself. What is the use of crying now? Seeing this darkness, I feel like calling Allah a devil sometimes. The dishonest ones continue to thrive and even Allah is afraid of them. All bad things befall the simple and straightforward."

Munnu kept expressing his condolences to Devi. Shyam Babu was also supporting him. When he left, he said, "The man does not seem to be a bad person."

Devi said, "He is a loving man. If he had not felt sad, then why would he come?"

VIII

Fifteen days passed by. Babu Sahib started going to the office again. Munnu did not come again in between. Till now, Devi's day was spent talking to her husband. But now when he went to the office, she remembered Sharda. Thus, her entire days were spent crying. Two or three women of the lower caste staying in the colony came to her sometimes. But Devi could never talk to them. Showing false sympathy, they wanted to get something out of her.

One day, Munnu came around four o' clock. He stood in the courtyard and said, "Madam, it is me Munnu. Please come down."

Devi asked from the top only, "What is it? Tell me." Munnu, "Please come."

Devi came down and Munnu said, "Raja Mian is standing outside; he wants to express his condolences to you."

Devi said, "You go and tell him, it is all Allah's wish."

Raja was standing at the door. He heard her very clearly. He said from there, "Allah knows, from the time I have heard this news, my heart was broken. I had gone to Delhi. I have come back today. If it had happened in my presence, what else could I have done? But I would not have left the vehicle owner scot-free, even if it was the king's vehicle. I would have searched the whole city. Babu Sahib kept quiet, but that is not done. Will someone drive a vehicle and take someone's life? The cruel man killed the sweet girl. Now, who will call me Raja

Bhaiya? I swear I had brought so many toys for her from Delhi. How would I know that this catastrophe has happened here? Munnu, take this holy thread and give it to madam. She should tie it in her hair. Allah willing, she will be saved from all dangers. She would be having bad dreams, she would not be getting proper sleep and her heart must be always troubled. All those problems will disappear after tying this thread. I have got it from a very learned holy man."

Munnu and Raja did not go from the door till they saw Babu Sahib coming their way. Shyamkishore saw them leaving. He went upstairs and asked in a serious tone, "Why did Raja come here?"

Devi said, "He had come to express his condolences. He has come from Delhi today. Hearing the news, he came here."

Shyamkishore said, "Men express condolences to men or women?"

Devi replied, "You were not here, so he expressed it to me and went away."

Shyamkishore said, "That means if any man comes to meet me, he can meet you if I am not there. There is no problem in that, is it not?"

Devi said, "Am I going to meet all of them?"

Shyamkishore asked, "Then is Raja my brother-in-law?"

Devi said, "You become agitated at the smallest of things".

Shyamkishore said, "This is a small thing. A woman from a good family talking to a pimp, is it a small thing? It is not a small thing that if I strangle you to death, I will not be committing a sin; I can see that you have gone back to your old ways. You have not learnt even after getting such a big punishment. Now, do you want to take my life?"

Devi was stunned into silence. On the one hand, was the shock of losing her daughter; and on top of that, these abuses and accusations! She felt dizzy. She sat down and started crying. "Death is far better than this life!" That was all she said.

Babu Sahib shouted and said, "That will surely happen. Don't worry. Don't worry, that will happen. If you wish to die, I also do not expect you to remain immortal. The sooner you die the better it will be. At least the family reputation will not be ruined."

Devi said crying, "Why are you doing this injustice to a helpless woman? Don't you feel any compassion?"

Shyamkishore said, "I tell you, don't say another word!"

Devi retorted, "Why should I not? Will you close my mouth?"

Shyamkishore said, "You are talking again? I will get up and break your head."

Devi said, "Will you break my head? Is it?"

Shyamkishore replied, "Then call your well-wishers. Let me see who they are."

Saying this, Babu Sahib got up agitated, and slapped Devi many times and kicked her. But she did not cry or shout or utter a single word. She kept looking at her husband with empty eyes as if to decide whether he was a human being or something else.

When Shyamkishore had hit her and pulled away, Devi said, "If your heart is not contented, then you can hit me some more. Perhaps you will not get another chance."

Shyamkishore replied, "I will cut your head off. What do you think of yourself?"

Saying this, he went down, opened the door in a push, threw it shut and went away somewhere.

Now Devi started crying.

It was ten in the night, but Shyamkishore did not return. Due to all the crying, Devi's eyes had swollen because of crying. In her anger, all the sweet memories faded away. Devi started feeling as if Shyamkishore had actually never loved her. Yes, for some days he had been very loving and compassionate but it was all falsehood. It was only to enjoy her youth that he had expressed his love. It was all fraud. She could not remember when he had actually loved her. Now she did not have her youth, looks, or novelty. Then why would he not torture her? She thought, "Nothing! Now his heart has turned away from me and that is why he starts shouting at me for every little thing. He wants to accuse me of something or the other and get rid of me. If that is the case then why should I stay here to cook for him and to hear his abuses? When there is no love, then there is no point in my staying here." In her own house, there may not be much but there won't be this insult. If that is his wish, then so be it. I will consider that I have become a widow.

As the night progressed, Devi was more and more terrified. She was afraid as to whether he will return and start hitting her again. He had left seething with anger. Oh my destiny! Now I have become so low that I am having affairs with sweepers and shoemakers! Why is this man not ashamed to say such things? I don't understand how can he even think of such things! He is a bad man and he is selfish. One should behave lowly with such people. I suffered so long due to my own fault.. Where there is no respect, no love, and no trust, there is no reason to stay. I have not sold myself to him that he will do anything to me, beat me and cut me and I will keep suffering in silence. If there were wives like Sita, there were also husbands like Ram.

Devi started having genuine doubts as to whether Shyamkishore would actually kill her when he came back. She had read a lot of such news in the newspapers. There had been such incidents in the city also. She was suddenly afraid. She felt that her life was in danger.

Devi packed some of her clothes in a bundle and started thinking, "How do I get out from here? And where do I go?" If she knew where Munnu was at that moment, he would have been of great help. "Will he not take me to my house?" she thought. She just wanted to reach her house somehow. Then even if her husband kept crying, she would not come back. He would also regret. Why should she leave the money? So that he enjoys it on his own? I have raised the money by saving it with great difficulty. He does not have any savings. If she wanted to spend, then there would have been nothing left. She kept the savings.

Devi went down and closed the main door. Then she opened the trunk and took out all her jewellery and money and packed it in the bundle. All of it was in currency notes, therefore, it was not that heavy.

Suddenly someone pushed at the door violently. Devi was afraid. She glanced from the top and saw that it was Shyam Babu. She could not muster the courage to go and open the door. Then Babu Sahib started pushing the door violently as if to break it open. To try to open the door in anger was enough indication of his state of mind. Devi did not have the courage to go into the lion's mouth.

In the end, Shyamkishore shouted and said, "Open the door! I will kill you otherwise. Open the door!"

Devi lost whatever little courage she had. Shyamkishore was drunk. In his senses, he might have felt a little kindness, but he had come back drunk. She thought, "I will not open the door, you will have to break it to reach me. If you cannot enter the house, how will you hit me? I have recognised you now."

Shyamkishore kept shouting for some fifteen to twenty minutes and then went off muttering something. Some neighbours also shouted back at him. "Despite being an educated man, you come home after midnight! After all, it is sleeping time. If she does not wake up, what can be done? Go and sleep at some friend's house. Come in the morning."

As soon as Shyamkishore left, Devi took the bundle and came down. For some time, she put her ears to the door and confirmed that Shyamkishore had indeed left. When she was sure, she opened the door slowly and walked out. She did not have any anger or sadness. She just had one wish and that was to run away. There was no man she could trust or who could be of any use to her at this time of adversity. Only Munnu. Now all her hopes were pinned on finding him. Only after meeting him, she would decide where and how to go. Now she did not wish to go to her house. She was afraid that she would not be safe even there. On not finding her here, he would certainly go to her house and bring her back forcefully. She was willing to suffer everything, but she did not want to see Shyamkishore again. Love, when insulted, becomes hatred.

At a small distance was the crossroad, and *tangas* were standing there. Devi took one of them and asked him to go to the station.

IX

Devi spent the night at the station. In the morning, she hired a *tanga*. Staying behind the veil she reached the crossroad. The shops had not yet opened, but she enquired Raja Mian's address. A boy was sweeping at his shop. Devi called him and said, "Go and tell Raja Mian that Sharda's mother has come to meet him. Tell him to come soon."

In ten minutes, Raja and Munnu came there.

Devi said with wet eyes, "After you both left, I had to leave my house. Your coming to my house yesterday was a catastrophe. Whatever happened, I will tell you later. Please get me a house somewhere. The house should be such that Babu Sahib should not come to know about it. Otherwise, he will not leave me alive."

Raja looked at Munnu as if to say, "See, how good our plan was!" He told Devi, "You don't worry. I will get you a house that even Babu Sahib will not be able to find. You will not have any trouble there. To tell you the truth, Babu Sahib never really deserved you."

Munnu said, "You are fit to be a queen. I used to tell madam that Babuji had the habit of going to Dalmandi, but she never believed me. Tonight only, I saw him coming from Gulaabjaan's den. He was completely drunk."

Devi said, "Lie. He does not have that habit. He is short tempered, and in his anger, he does lose his senses. But he is not bad that way."

Munnu replied, "Madam does not believe me; so what can I do? All right, I will show you someday, and then you will believe me."

Raja said, "You show her later. Right now, you take her to my house. Take her upstairs. Till then, let me go and search for a house for her."

Devi asked, "Will there be any woman in your house?"

Raja replied, "There is nobody, except an old woman. There will be no problem for you. I will go and look for a house."

Devi said, "Come back from Babu Sahib's side. Just see if he has returned."

Raja replied, "I am now agitated at Babu Sahib. If I see him, I might fight with him. A man who does not respect a beauty like you is not a man."

Munnu said, "You are right, brother. I don't understand how anyone can scold someone like her! I have been serving for so long, I have not been told anything!"

Raja went in search of the house, and the *tanga* went towards Raja's house.

Devi's mind suddenly developed some doubts, "Are these two really bad people? But how shall I find out?" It was true that Devi had left her husband forever. But in the short span of time, she was regretting it! How will she stay alone and do what? She could not understand anything. Her heart said, "Why not return home? God willing, he may not have come back as yet." She told Munnu, "Run home and find out if Babu Sahib has returned."

Munnu said, "You go and sit in peace. I will then go and find out."

Devi replied, "I will not go inside."

Munnu said, "I swear in the name of Allah, the house is empty. You doubt us. We are those people who are willing to do anything on your command."

Devi got down and went inside. The bird, on being caught, flapped its wings; but because the feet were caught, could not fly away. And the hunter kept it in his bag. Will that unlucky woman be able to fly ever again? Will it have the good fortune to sit on the branches and chirp?

X

Shyamkishore returned home in the morning, his heart was now peaceful. He was doubtful as to whether Devi would be home or not. He saw the door open and his heart stopped. Open doors in the morning are not a good omen. He stood at the door for a moment and listened. He did not hear any sound. He went into the courtyard, and there was no sound there too. Upstairs also, all was silent. The house was biting him. Shyamkishore grew alert and started looking around. No money in the trunk. The jewellery box was also empty. No doubt was now left in his mind! When someone goes to have a dip in the Ganges, they don't take the money from the house. He knew where she had gone. If he went immediately, perhaps she can be brought back, but what will the world say?

Shyamkishore sat on the cot and started analysing the incident with a cool mind. There was no doubt about the fact that Raja and Munnu had influenced her. After all, what could Babuji have done? He had left the old house and had tried to explain things to Devi. What else could he do beyond that? Was it wrong to hit her? Even if you consider it incorrect for a moment, was it right for Devi to leave the house and go away like this? Any other woman, in whose heart poison is not already injected, would have left like this after being hit by her husband? Certainly, Devi's mind was polluted.

Babu Sahib thought again, "After sometime, the maid will come. She will not find Devi here and start asking questions. What will I say? The news will spread in the entire colony. Oh God! What will I do?" There was no regret or kindness in Shyamkishore's heart at this moment. If he could get Devi somehow, he would not have had the slightest hesitation in killing her. Her leaving the house, even if there was no other reason other than impulse, was not forgivable in his eyes. Anger sometimes leads to insensitivity. Shyamkishore started hating the world. When one's own wife cheats him, what can he expect from others? When the woman for whom he would live and die for, to see her happy he was willing to give his own life, when she could not be his, what to expect from others? What did he not do to keep this woman happy? Fought with his own family, severed all relations with his brothers, so much so that they don't wish to see his face ever again. There was no wish of hers that he had left unfulfilled. When she had even a minor headache, he would get worried. Throughout the night, he would look after her. That woman had cheated him today. On hearing lies from a thug, she has gone away after leaving him in shame.

To blame the thug is like trying to make the heart understand. How can someone be influenced, if the heart is clear and blemish free? When this woman has cheated on him, it must be considered that there is no love and trust in this world. Emotions are merely the imagination of some emotional creatures. What can you get by living in such a world other than sadness and bad thoughts? Oh cruel woman! You are free from today. Now there will be nobody to hold your hand. You have done this cruel thing to the person whom you always called your love! I wish I could drag you to the court and get you punished but what is the use? God will punish you for your misdeeds.

Shyamkishore came downstairs silently, he did not say anything to anybody, and did not hear anything and leaving the door open, walked towards the banks of the Ganges.

About the Author

Regarded as one of the celebrated writers of Indian literature, Munshi Premchand is also referred as the '*Upanyas Samrat*'. A teacher by profession, he has written over three hundred short stories, numerous essays, letters, plays and translations. His myriad range of works realistically portrays the unpolished and blunt edges of Indian life and highlights various social and national issues like corruption, child widowhood, exploitation of rural peasantry and several other aspects of the early twentieth century Indian society. Filled with artful expressiveness, his works aim to break through superstitions and social evils and strive to raise social awareness among the rural and upper-middle class of the society. Reverberating with patriotic overtones and illustrating the 'Indianness' of rural life, his writings is a creative blend of rationalism and emotion. Premchand's writings reflect a sharpness of perception, which aims to stir our emotions and put our thoughts in motion. An author of remarkable works of art, Premchand appeals more to the heart than to the mind. As stated by the Marxist writer Namwar Singh, "Premchand is the one writer we have in whose works the immortal saga of our struggle for independence has been narrated in all its fullness." From all his works, the novels *Sevasadan, Rangbhumi, Karmabhumi* and *Godaan* are considered among his greatest works in Hindi.